DANGEROUS PARADISE

K.J. GILLENWATER

Dangerous Paradise

ISBN Print: 979-8-9944436-0-6

ISBN eBook: 979-8-9876112-9-6

Cover by Miblart

DAY ONE

1

Pascal Dubois squinted against the Caribbean sun, scanning the water and counting heads. Eleven snorkelers bobbed in the swells around the excursion boat, their bright masks and snorkels breaking the surface as they rested between dives. Still missing: the American woman with the underwater camera and the quiet man with the high-end dive watch. Both had ventured toward the deeper reef.

Twenty years as a dive master at Tesoro Bay—a private resort stop for the Meridian Cruise Line—had taught Pascal to keep an exact mental tally. Thirteen guests had boarded his boat that morning for the advanced snorkeling tour, all eager for more thrills than the usual beach break. They'd signed the waivers, passed the safety briefings, and proved they could swim. Just another routine trip—until the phone buzzed against his hip.

Pascal frowned. He carried his phone only for emergencies, and the cruise line knew better than to call during an excursion without good reason. He checked the screen. His manager's number. A ripple of unease passed through him.

"Fifteen more minutes, everyone!" he called to the group. "Then we head back for lunch."

He stepped toward the stern of the dive boat, away from the guests, and answered, "*Oui?*"

Rapid-fire French burst through the line. Urgent. Rushed. Pascal's easy smile vanished. He tightened his grip on the phone.

"How many?" he asked, slipping into English as the gravity of the situation took hold. "When?"

The answer chilled him.

"Get them back now," his manager said. "The ship's preparing for emergency departure. You have thirty min—"

The line went dead.

Pascal froze. His instinct was to run, but he had a duty to account for every last swimmer.

His gaze swept the nearest guests, then out toward the deeper water. No sign of the two stragglers. The woman had drifted near the coral garden the last time he'd seen her. The man had mentioned checking the drop-off to the west.

His hand hovered over the boat's horn—the universal recall signal. Three long blasts. Then wait.

His phone buzzed in his hand.

A group text had been sent to the whole of the Tesoro Bay staff: EVACUATE NOW.

"Everyone back to the boat!" He fired up the engine and cast off from the mooring buoy. "Emergency! We must return immediately!"

Nearby snorkelers hesitated, alarm rising as they caught the tone in his voice. Then they kicked toward the boat.

"What's going on?" asked a red-faced man as Pascal helped him aboard. "You said we had fifteen more minutes."

"The ship's leaving early—weather issues," Pascal lied, helping others up while scanning the horizon. If the two missing people didn't surface soon, he was leaving without them. His manager's voice had carried raw fear—reason enough to move.

Eleven of the thirteen climbed aboard.

Pascal searched the empty water. Counted to thirty. Then thirty more.

Nothing.

He turned the boat toward shore.

"Wait!" A middle-aged woman in blue swim shorts and a matching modest top shaded her eyes. "I think there's still someone out there." She pointed toward the reef flat.

He could've cursed. "I'll make a sweep," he said tightly. "Everyone sit, please."

The fear twisting in his gut made the lie effortless.

He steered the boat in a wide arc, angling closer to the shore with each pass. On the distant beach, maybe two hundred feet from the watersports dock, he spotted movement. Several dark figures moved with purpose.

Screw this. The stragglers were on their own.

Pascal throttled up and turned for Tesoro Bay.

"I have to take you back. Now." He didn't stop to explain further, brushing off their protests as he gunned the engine.

A bitter taste rose in his throat. But it was simple, brutal math.

Thirteen lives versus eleven.

As the boat surged toward shore, leaving two people behind, Pascal didn't look back. He had made his choice.

May God forgive him for it.

2

The sun beat down on Skylar Harris's shoulders as she adjusted her mask and slipped beneath the surface one more time. The underwater world opened around her in a blur of coral fans and darting tropical fish—so vivid and alive, it almost made her forget she was stuck on her brother's wedding cruise. Here, suspended in the quiet blue, she could finally breathe.

She raised her new waterproof camera toward a striking coral formation, focusing on a cluster of tiny yellow fish flitting in and out of its branches. Thirty seconds passed. Maybe a minute. She lost track.

This advanced snorkeling excursion had been the perfect escape from the wedding party's endless chatter about center-pieces and playlists. Her older brother, Ethan, had looked wounded when she chose to skip the all-girl mimosa brunch on Sunrise Beach with his bride-to-be, Kayla, but she needed a break from the matching robes and group selfies. Kayla would be fine without another bridesmaid, and Skylar had been dying to try the camera.

A strong kick to hold her buoyancy above the reef sent a sharp pain through her hip—a reminder she wasn't fully healed from her accident. Pascal, the dive master, had stressed not to touch the reef, but getting the right angle for her photo required more precision than she'd anticipated. She'd spent years rock climbing, where control and balance were paramount, which made the weakness now even more frustrating. A feeling she'd been battling for months during her recovery.

The ache sharpened. Time to head back. She wasn't ready for this kind of strain yet. Her physical therapist had been annoyingly right—she needed to take it slow.

When she surfaced, the silence hit her first.

No voices. No laughter. No hum of the boat's engine.

She spun in place, water spraying from her braid. Nothing but open sea to the west and a distant strip of beach to the east —a thin line of yellow with dark jungle behind it.

The boat was gone.

What the hell?

"Hello?" Her voice sounded small. Only the soft slap of waves answered her.

Then—a ripple. Thirty yards away, a head broke through the surface. A man with dark hair slicked to his skull, his mask fogged, his expression mirroring her own stunned disbelief.

Their eyes met.

"Where's the boat?" he asked.

"Gone," Skylar said, squinting against the glare. "Did you see what happened?"

He shook his head and swam toward her, his strokes strong and sure. She recognized him from the locker room—he'd been stowing his cell phone and wallet while Pascal ran through the safety briefing. The quiet guy with the fancy dive watch who didn't act like a tourist.

"I was out at the drop-off," he said, pushing his mask onto

his forehead when he reached her. His brown eyes were tight with concern. "You?"

"Photographing coral." She held up her camera strapped to her wrist. "I didn't hear a thing. No signal to return?"

"Not that I caught. Maybe we missed it?" He treaded water beside her, searching the coastline.

Tesoro Bay was a small peninsula of land, leased from the Saint Marielle government to provide a private stop for Meridian Cruise Line customers. It wasn't more than seven or eight miles in length from the southern security-monitored fence line to the untamed rocky point at its northern end.

"Could they have relocated?" he asked

She glanced toward shore. It looked a mile off, maybe more. The white buildings of the main tourist area gleamed in the sun, and she could just make out the cruise ship moored at the pier on the opposite side of the peninsula to the south. Ethan was probably drinking another beer by now with his grooms-men, oblivious his younger sister had been abandoned in the open ocean with a stranger.

"They wouldn't leave without a headcount," she said. "That's—"

"Completely against safety rules," he finished.

"Something must've happened."

"Right before I dove last time," he said, "Pascal looked...rat-tled. Whatever it was, it must've been serious."

"And he still left without checking for everyone?" Anger flared through her. "That's more than unprofessional. It's dangerous."

"Agreed." His voice was calm but clipped.

They fell into silence, both treading water. Anxiety stirred in her gut. She pushed it down. Panic didn't solve problems.

"I'm Skylar Harris," she said finally, snugging the camera

strap around her wrist. "Since it looks as if we're about to swim for our lives together."

"Noah Reed." He gave a short nod. "Though let's not be dramatic yet. You're a strong swimmer?"

Skylar raised an eyebrow. "I can handle myself." She shifted slightly, trying not to overuse her right leg as they drifted in the water. The ache had settled into a throb, dull but constant.

"Good to know."

"You?"

"I swim a few times a week to deal with work stress. We should be fine, assuming no surprises."

Skylar studied him more closely. The expensive gear had thrown her off at first, but now she saw the lean muscle in his shoulders and arms built from habit, not vanity.

"There's a current," she said, feeling it tug at her side. "We'll need to angle southeast or we'll drift."

Noah nodded. "About thirty-five minutes to shore, based on the drag. Let's switch leads every ten minutes. Conserve energy."

"Works for me." She readjusted her mask while burying the worry about her injury and whether she was up to the strain. No time to worry about that now. She had no choice. "I'll start. Follow me. If you see anything in the water—"

"I'll tug on your fin," he said.

Skylar nodded once, then struck out for shore.

The reef that had shimmered with wonder earlier now felt colder. Emptier. She focused on her breathing, slow and even, and kept her pace steady. Any twinge in her hip, she ignored. Noah swam behind her, his presence reassuring—a stranger turned lifeline.

She didn't expect to fail, but just in case, it was good to have him around.

Surfacing every few minutes, she checked their progress and adjusted course. It was hard to measure as the beach never seemed to get closer. She bit back a curse and then recentered herself.

Focus on the task. One stroke at a time.

Ten minutes passed. Noah grabbed her fin. Shift change.

Skylar eased back, gladly letting Noah glide forward. As she fell in behind him, the silence under the waves gave her too much space to think. Why would Pascal leave them behind? What emergency would justify abandoning two people in open water? Mechanical failure? Medical emergency? Storm warning?

But none of it added up. The sky was clear, the boat had seemed fine, and no crew would leave without a full count—*unless* they had no choice.

When it was her turn again, she reassessed the distance. They'd gained ground. She could make out buildings now, more toward the center of Tesoro Bay—the food stands, shopping kiosks, restrooms, and spa. A private club had been tucked away in the trees, but that was barely visible from their location. The main pier, however, had more definition; the cruise ship, more shape. They were close.

Noah surfaced beside her, pushing up his mask. "We're doing great. Another fifteen minutes."

Skylar nodded, then paused.

"Do you see that?" she asked, squinting toward the beach and the watersports dock where the dive boats, jet skis, and kayaks were tied.

Noah looked, shielding his eyes. "Yeah. Something's off."

Figures moved along the shoreline near the pickleball courts and a tiki bar. Not tourists. Not staff. Their clothes, identical faded orange shirts and pants, made her stomach drop. They moved together like a swarm of hornets ready to sting.

Where were the cruisers in bikinis and swim shorts

sunning in lounge chairs? The kids roaming the wet sand with pails and shovels on the hunt for seashells?

Cold spread through Skylar's body.

"Something's not right."

Noah's voice sharpened. "Let's pick up the pace. Whatever's going on, better to face it on land than floating here."

She nodded, took a breath, and kicked harder despite the sharp burn in her hip.

The pain was nothing compared to the dread clawing at her gut.

Deep down, she knew something was very wrong. Pascal leaving them stranded. The empty beach. The orange-clad figures.

They weren't swimming to safety.

They were swimming straight into danger.

3

Fifty yards from the beach, the world tilted sideways.

A sharp series of pops echoed across the water.

"Gunfire," Noah said quietly.

Skylar faltered mid-stroke. "Are you sure?"

"Positive," he said, without looking at her.

Her limbs dragged. Her injured leg had held up longer than she'd expected, but now every kick sent pain radiating through her hip. She shifted her stroke to relieve the strain, but the imbalance only made her body fight harder against the slow pull of the current.

The water wasn't cold, but the long swim had sapped her heat anyway. She remembered reading somewhere that you could get hypothermia even in tropical water. It had sounded like one of those survival myths. She wasn't dismissing it now.

The shoreline of Tesoro Bay was tantalizingly close. What had been a pristine private beach leased by Meridian Cruise Lines had turned chaotic. From a distance, it had looked deserted. Closer, the beach revealed itself as anything but—terrified families clutching children, retirees stumbling through the sand, sunburned tourists abandoning their belongings as they fled toward the pier. Bright orange figures surged after them, closing the gap with every stride.

"What's happening?" Fear tore through her insides. Where was her brother? His fiancée? "I thought Tesoro Bay had security. Is this some kind of protest?"

The word that sat just beneath her question—*terrorism*—didn't need to be spoken aloud. Saint Marielle was a struggling island nation plagued by political unrest, widespread poverty, and rising crime. Meridian had operated its private enclave for years without incident, but something had clearly changed—and not for the better.

Thank God Mom and Dad had to cancel.

Her father's deteriorating health had meant her parents had to bow out at the last minute. Who knew it would be a blessing they'd stayed home?

"I don't know." Noah's brow furrowed as he took in the scene.

He remained calm. Too calm. Like someone whose first instinct was to analyze, not react.

She turned her head to study him as they swam the final yards to shore.

"Do you ever get rattled?" she asked before she could stop herself.

He didn't answer, and for a moment she regretted asking.

Despite the pain and weakness, she gritted her teeth and forced her legs to keep kicking.

"We need a plan," she said. Her hot-pink bikini suddenly felt ridiculously conspicuous beneath her white rash guard. "The beach is too exposed. We swim straight in, we'd be sitting ducks."

Noah pointed to the left. "There's a rocky outcrop a couple of hundred feet down from the watersports dock, to the left of the dive shop. Less visible. Might give us a better entry."

She followed his gaze and nodded.

They veered off course, adjusting their strokes. The muscles in her bad leg had seized into a knot, every kick demanding more effort. Still, she kept going.

The sounds from shore grew louder and louder. Shouts, bursts of gunfire, the sharp pitch of human panic. Tesoro Bay had become unrecognizable from the idyllic vacation stop it had been earlier that day. The curated fantasy had dissolved.

The water grew shallow, and Skylar's fins scraped bottom. She tore them off, then the mask and snorkel, leaving everything in a pile at the water's edge. Her legs barely held her as she stumbled behind a low rock formation and sank to her knees. The camera hung heavy on her wrist—somehow she'd held onto it.

Noah followed, shedding his gear and crouching beside her. His eyes immediately went to the beach to the south.

"You all right?" he asked.

Skylar gave a tight nod, keeping her gaze low. Her leg throbbed as if it had a pulse of its own, and her lungs still hadn't caught up with her body's demand for air.

They stayed there for a long moment, crouched in silence and watching. Listening.

The breeze brought the sounds closer—more gunfire, shouted commands in a language she couldn't make out, the rhythmic churn of something mechanical. Maybe a boat engine or vehicle. Then a scream—shrill and cut short.

"What the hell is going on?" she whispered.

Noah's gaze remained fixed. "Looks like a raid. Or a coordinated attack."

Skylar stared at him. "This is Tesoro Bay. A tourist spot. Who would launch an attack here?"

"Could be anything. Political extremists. Drug cartels. Local insurgents."

The ship sat at the pier, almost peaceful from this far out. The illusion shattered when she spotted the passengers sprinting across the sand, bodies flinching at distant gunshots. She strained to see if the ramps were still down, if crew members were guiding people aboard. Nothing but chaos and too much distance to know for sure.

"We need to get back on board." Between them and the ship was an unknown number of armed men. "My brother...his fiancée. They might've been caught up in all of this." She hoped Ethan and his entire wedding party would already be safely aboard. They'd been closest to the pier at Sunrise Beach.

"At least the ship's still there," Noah said quietly, finally glancing at her. "But it won't wait forever."

Would they pull up the ramps and sail without her? Without Ethan knowing where she was?

No, not if Ethan had any say in it.

But what if he didn't?

She rose into a crouch to get a better view. Movement caught her eye—something fast and frantic.

A Meridian staffer burst from the trees, running hard to the shoreline.

Pascal!

Two figures in faded orange chased after him, one of them raising a rifle.

A single shot cracked across the beach.

Pascal stumbled, crumpled forward, and collapsed.

Skylar jerked instinctively to go to him, but Noah grabbed her wrist, his grip sharp.

"Don't," he said. "You can't help him."

She froze. She knew he was right, but it didn't stop the rush of heat and helplessness rising in her chest.

"We can't leave him there. I could—"

"No, you'd only make yourself a target."

On the sand, the two men caught up with the fallen dive master. One kicked him onto his back and rifled through his pockets. The other kept the weapon pointed at his chest.

Even at a distance, their posture made it clear they weren't checking for signs of life.

Finished with the body, they headed south along the beach, past the kayak rentals and toward the cluster of shops near the main pier. In seconds, they were out of sight.

"Those are prison uniforms," Noah said, his voice lower now.

Skylar swallowed. "A prison break? On Saint Marielle?"

He nodded. "Would explain Pascal leaving. If the port was overrun..."

Her gaze fell on the body. Red blood pooled in the sand. A hole was blown in his side. Her stomach rolled.

She turned away, pressing her hand against the rocks to steady herself. "I'm going to be sick," she whispered.

"We need to move." Noah shifted into a crouch, as if preparing to run. "We're too exposed here."

He looked back, and his expression changed.

"You don't look good. Are you okay?"

Skylar nodded, swallowing down the sick feeling in her stomach. Last April she'd clawed her way back from what should have been an unsurvivable fall in the Black Canyon. She could get through this, too. She pushed past the initial shock. Her hip ached and her legs felt like rubber, but she nodded. "I'll make it."

She scanned the beach. "There's a path behind the cabanas. Looks like some kind of maintenance access. Maybe we can make it there unseen and find a way to the pier?"

He followed her line of sight, then gave a quick nod. "Let's use it. Ready?"

Skylar took one more look at Pascal's body on the beach, avoiding the blood and sending up a silent apology for not helping. Then she nodded. "Ready."

Moving quickly, they skirted the edge of the shoreline.

The service path cut through hedges designed to hide Tesoro Bay logistics from guests. A hidden corridor for staff would be their best chance at avoiding notice while they figured out their best route to the ship.

Skylar looked at Noah.

He nodded once.

They sprinted across the open sand toward the hedgerow. Skylar's aqua shoes sank into the soft surface with every step. The twenty seconds it took to reach the hedge felt like an eternity—too exposed, too slow—but they made it without incident, ducking behind the thick wall of greenery with matching exhalations of relief.

"You're bleeding." Noah looked at her leg.

A thin ribbon of blood trailed from her knee, likely from the rocks when she'd hauled herself out of the water. "It's nothing." In comparison with the throbbing of her hip and thigh, the scrape was minor.

Noah studied her for a beat. He didn't press. "It's not deep," he said. "Still, we should rinse it, disinfect it, if we get the chance."

Skylar almost laughed. Her knee was the least of their problems. Somewhere north of the pristine tourist zone and deep in the jungle, a plume of smoke curled into the air. First the beach, now the interior.

They were momentarily safe, tucked in the shadow of the hidden infrastructure path—a narrow strip of sand and stone meant for maintenance staff, deliveries, and utility access. A place guests weren't meant to see.

Noah crouched beside her, one knee in the sand, his eyes flicking between gaps in the hedge and the buildings that made up the main 'street' on Tesoro Bay where cruise passengers shopped, drank, or had a snack.

"We have to reach the pier," he said quietly. "That ship is our way out of here."

"But we'd have to get past bad guys with guns first."

Neither of them spoke for a moment.

Skylar wiped a bit of grit from her brow and glanced sideways at Noah. His bare chest was streaked with sand, but he didn't seem to mind. If he was scared, it didn't show. She didn't know the first thing about him, but she was starting to be grateful he was here.

"You ever done anything like this before?"

His mouth twitched slightly at the corner. "Abandoned at sea and welcomed ashore with bullets? First time for everything."

She gave him a look. "You know what I mean."

Noah's gaze shifted back to the path ahead. "I've done some work in unstable places. Not like this exactly, but...close enough."

It wasn't much of an answer, but it was honest in its own way.

"And you?"

"I climb," she said. "Mountains. Rock faces. Ice when I can get to it."

He looked back at her then, properly, as if recalibrating something he'd assumed.

"I figured you for a runner. Or yoga."

Skylar almost smiled. "I'm insulted."

"Meant it as a compliment."

They lapsed into silence again, both listening.

Somewhere nearby, a voice barked an order. It was close enough to make Skylar flinch. A few seconds later, another shot cracked through the air. Farther off than before, but not far enough. She'd give anything to be walking up that gangway right now.

Noah edged carefully toward the corner of the hedge. "We're about two hundred yards from the pier," he said. "I'm worried about my team. They're probably back on the ship, but..."

Skylar's curiosity sharpened. "Your team?"

He hesitated for a second, as if debating how much to share. "I started a company. Reed Security Systems. We do IT security for high-risk clients—customer solutions, mostly corporate or government contracts."

A humorless smile flickered across his face. "This cruise was supposed to be a celebration. We just landed a big Homeland Security contract, and Vanessa—the current CEO—insisted the leadership team needed bonding time."

His voice tightened subtly on the last part. A flicker crossed his face, something between frustration and resignation.

Skylar caught it. "Vanessa," she echoed. "I take it she's more than just your CEO?"

Noah didn't answer immediately. His gaze remained fixed on the trees beyond the hedge. "We were involved. Once."

Skylar didn't push. Whatever history lived in that silence, this wasn't the time.

"So this is basically your worst-case scenario vacation," she said.

That earned a faint smile. "Yeah. You could say that."

She answered his earlier question. "My brother Ethan's getting married on the ship. Ceremony's the day after tomorrow."

"Bad timing."

"Yeah. His fiancée's family is...curated. Old money. The kind that thinks paying someone to peel your grapes in normal."

"And you don't exactly blend in with that crowd."

"Three days of being the awkward outsider among champagne-sipping, designer-draped perfection? I needed an escape." She gestured toward the watersports dock. "So I signed up for the snorkeling excursion. Lucky me."

"Life's full of surprises," Noah said, adjusting his position to keep an eye on the path ahead.

"You don't seem like a surprise kind of guy."

"I'm not. Most of my day is spent on server security protocols and digital audits. This is a little outside my comfort zone."

She smiled faintly. "You're doing all right."

He didn't respond.

"Any idea how to reach the ship?" she asked.

In the space between them and safety, several orange-clad figures prowled the edge of Seashell Beach—a family-friendly stretch with floating platforms, a water slide, and climbing features now eerily deserted. The men moved casually, rifling through abandoned beach bags and purses, more interested in looting than the panicked crowd fleeing toward the pier. But the paved walkway that connected Seashell Beach to the eastern pier was the main route back to the ship—and whether they realized it or not, they were slowly heading that way.

Beside her, Noah took in the same grim scene. "Still working on it," he said. "But we need to move soon. If things get worse, the captain's going to pull anchor. He won't have a choice."

The idea of the ship sailing away, with Ethan on board and no idea she was even alive, twisted in her gut.

"Then we don't sit here. We move."

Noah nodded once. "The direct path is too risky. We should

stick to the shoreline behind those guys, keep low, duck behind whatever we can. Once we're closer, we see what we're dealing with at the pier."

"And then?"

He gave her a sideways glance. "One problem at a time."

Skylar took a long breath, grounding herself the way she did before a difficult climb. Focus on the next move. Not the summit.

She pulled her braid tighter. "Alright," she said. "Let's go."

4

N oah Reed hadn't built a multimillion-dollar company by ignoring his instincts. And right now, every one of them was lit up like a server room alarm. Danger was coming fast.

"Stay low," he told Skylar, the athletic brunette who'd gone from stranger to survival partner in a single panicked hour. He hadn't expected to be running for his life with a woman in a bikini, but here they were. Vanessa would've had something snide to say about it, probably involving the company's PR department.

Vanessa. His ex—currently both the bane of his existence and the CEO of Reed Security Systems. He'd argued against this cruise the minute she proposed it, but she insisted the entire leadership team needed a break after landing the government contract. A morale boost, she'd called it. Now he only hoped the team had made it safely back to the ship. Vanessa included.

He pulled his focus back to the present. As they moved along the narrow crescent of Tesoro Bay, his eyes swept the beach—looking for orange jumpsuits, for anyone suspicious, for somewhere to duck if things went sideways. His brain wanted to treat this like a problem to solve, but the variables kept multiplying. No phone. No help. No Plan B.

Beside him, Skylar's hot-pink bathing suit stood out like a flare despite her long-sleeved rash guard. She moved with a climber's sure-footed grace, but he'd seen the way she winced with her right leg. She was pushing herself harder than she should, and it bothered him.

He pointed to a fringe of low palms lining the beach path. "Over there. We can see the pier without being out in the open."

Skylar nodded.

While they hid behind the fronds, Noah had a clear view of the disaster unfolding. Passengers had mobbed the pier, shoving, crying, clawing toward the gangway. The Meridian Voyager's crew was making final preparations. Ropes coiled tight. Cargo doors clanged shut. They were running out of time.

"They haven't left yet," Skylar whispered.

"But they will." The bustle of crew activity told the story. "Soon."

A commotion erupted at the small booth where crew members checked IDs before letting passengers onto the pier. Two Meridian security officers stood in tense conversation with a shaken crew member, his uniform torn and dirt-streaked. The man gestured wildly toward the trees that lined the inland edge of the resort.

"Let's get closer." Noah nodded in the direction of the security guys.

They circled wide along the beach's edge, the pandemonium providing all the distraction they needed. Most of the tourists were focused on reaching the ship, creating a one-way flow of people that allowed Noah and Skylar to move perpendicular to the crowd without drawing undue attention.

As they approached the security booth, fragments of the conversation cut through the noise.

"—they came in on rafts," the crew member said, his voice tight with disbelief. "Makeshift ones. Landed on that undeveloped stretch up north."

One of the security officers stiffened. "By the cliffs?"

"Exactly," the crewman said. "Resort security never gave that area a second thought. All rocks and bad current—they figured it was a natural barrier. Guess not."

"They moved fast—straight toward the staff maintenance path. As if they knew where they were going. They were armed, in prison orange. I got a good look."

Noah's stomach clenched. Meridian had set up an exclusive resort on a politically unstable island, trading steady tourism dollars for a promise of security. But it had always been a thin illusion. Today, it snapped.

"They used the ocean to go around," Skylar murmured beside him. "Avoided all the security."

Escaped prisoners were running loose. Noah didn't need to hear anything else. There wasn't time to unravel the larger implications. All that mattered now was getting aboard the ship. He studied the pier again, mapping out their route—how many people they'd have to push through, how close the crew were to pulling the ramp.

"We need to move," he said. "But smart. That crowd's one shove away from a stampede."

As if to underscore his words, an explosion ripped through the air behind them. He didn't see what blew, didn't want to know. The crowd surged as if the devil himself had appeared.

Screams rose as people shoved forward in blind panic. Crew members on the pier shouted for calm, but it was already spreading like a brushfire.

"We have to get out of here. Now." Noah fixed his eyes on the boarding ramp. They were going to make it. They had to.

Before they could move, the blare of the ship's horn cut through the chaos—three long blasts that split the air like cannon fire.

"They're leaving." Skylar's voice was barely audible; her face drained of color.

Not without both of us.

Noah didn't waste time replying. He grabbed her hand, and they sprinted toward the pier. Behind them, gunfire cracked like distant thunder, but he shoved his fear aside. One goal consumed him: to reach the ship.

When they hit the edge of the pier, they collided with the crowd. Dozens of cruisers pushed, clawed, and shouted to be let on. The crush was suffocating. A surge of bodies ripped Skylar's hand from his. He reached for her blindly, and his fingers found the camera strap at her wrist. He held tight—it was the only thing keeping them connected in the churn of panicked cruisers.

"Stay with me," he shouted, not sure she could hear him above the pandemonium.

The security checkpoint had all but disintegrated, officers doing little more than ushering people through as fast as possible. IDs and protocols had become meaningless. All that mattered was the gangway, and it was still down, for now.

Then, someone shoved into Skylar from the side. The camera strap snapped, and she stumbled, almost going down. Noah caught her, wrapping an arm around her waist to pull her upright. The camera skittered across the pier and disappeared under the stampede of feet.

"My camera," she said, looking back at the madness unfolding. It was probably in pieces by now.

He saw the disappointment cross her face, then vanish.

She didn't say another word about it.

"Almost there," he said. He barely knew her. But somewhere in the last hour, her survival had become personal.

They broke through the final tangle of bodies. The gangway loomed. Less than fifty feet away. He could see crew members poised to raise it. They still had time. Maybe.

But then he heard the metallic groan of hydraulics. The gangway was closing.

No.

Other passengers realized it too. A woman nearby collapsed to her knees, sobbing. A man in a striped shirt hurled his backpack into the sea.

The Meridian Voyager inched from the pier, the space between widening by the second. Its massive engines rumbled, a vibration Noah felt in his bones.

"Ethan!" Skylar's voice cracked on her brother's name—a desperate, hopeless shout into the crush of people.

Gunfire cracked again, closer this time. Screams rippled through the remaining crowd. Some bolted inland. Others dove straight into the ocean rather than face whatever was coming.

The ship moved slowly away, taking over three thousand souls with it. Skylar stood frozen, watching in stunned disbelief. Noah let her have the moment, but his mind was already pivoting.

The ship was gone. That escape plan was over.

Now it was survival.

He scanned the pier. A handful of stunned passengers still lingered. Three Meridian crew members huddled together, one barking uselessly into a radio. The security team had disappeared.

But it was the movement beyond the palms that caught his eye—men in orange emerging from the trees. Prison uniforms. At least five. Maybe more.

"Skylar," he said urgently. "Let's go."

She turned, her grief overtaken by fear as she followed his gaze. "Oh God."

"In the water," Noah ordered, already moving. "It's our only chance."

No time for argument. No time to explain. He grabbed her arm—and jumped.

5

N oah and Skylar hit the water hard. When they surfaced, he shook the salt from his eyes and pointed.

"Under the pier," he said.

They swam beneath the wooden structure and found a spot near the pilings where they could hold on and stay mostly submerged. They clung to the support beams, water lapping around their shoulders.

From their position, they could see that armed men had reached the pier and were rounding up the stragglers—cruise passengers too slow to escape or too exposed to hide. One prisoner stood out: massive, covered in prison tattoos, his half-lidded gaze swept the pier as if he owned it. He barked commands and gestured toward the resort buildings.

"They're taking hostages," Noah said under his breath. "They'll want leverage."

Skylar's voice was tight. "To bargain with the cruise line?"

"Maybe. Or local authorities. Could be they only want supplies and a way off this island."

"What do we do now?" she asked.

Noah didn't have an answer. Staying put would only work for so long. The tide was moving. Eventually, they'd have to come out of their hiding place. And when they did, they'd better have a plan.

He ran through the options: wait and hope for rescue? Risky. Signal someone? This private cruise stop was too remote. Try to steal a boat? Maybe. But if they were spotted, they'd be easy targets.

"We need information," he said. "And someplace we can hole up, at least for a little while."

"Where do we start?"

Before he could answer, a commotion drew his attention. One of the hostages made a run for it. A man in cargo shorts took off toward the snack bar.

He didn't make it far. A prisoner with a shaved head and goatee raised a rifle and fired.

The man dropped hard onto the sand.

Skylar's breath caught. Her hand dug into Noah's arm.

"They'll shoot anyone who runs," he said quietly. "We can't make the same mistake."

She nodded once. No hysteria. Whatever she was feeling, she wasn't letting it win. He respected that.

As the hostages were marched off toward the center of the resort, Noah thought past the next few minutes. The full leadership team must be on the ship—Vanessa included. He hadn't seen any of them at the pier. Odds were, they'd made it. How long would it take them to figure out he was missing?

And Skylar—she'd screamed her brother's name as the ship pulled away. Would he try to come back for her? Or even know what had happened to her?

"We wait until the beach is clear," he said. "Then we move and look for somewhere to hole up. Maintenance buildings, staff housing—places not worth checking unless they're thorough."

Skylar nodded. "And after that?"

He met her eyes, considered giving her something comforting. But she didn't strike him as the type who wanted empty promises.

"Then we survive. One hour at a time."

She took a steadying breath and gave a faint nod. "Okay."

Noah watched her for a beat. They were barely more than strangers, but he was already grateful she was the one he'd been stranded with.

Maybe there was more to her than he'd assumed. He tucked the thought away for later.

For now, they had more immediate concerns—namely, not ending up like the man face-down in the sand.

Skylar's arms burned from gripping the algae-slicked pier support as the waves slapped against her. The water, warm as a bath when they'd first jumped in, now seemed to be leeching the heat from her body. Beside her, Noah maintained his vigilance, scanning the beach through the gap between the water and the decking.

Twenty minutes had passed since they'd witnessed the horrific shooting of the tourist who tried to run. The image replayed in Skylar's mind—the casual way the gunman had raised his weapon and pulled the trigger. It was obvious he'd done it before. How many other escaped prisoners had murdered someone before today?

"I think it's clear," Noah whispered.

Skylar followed his gaze to confirm for herself. No more orange, no more gunshots, no more screaming.

"Where do we go?" she asked.

His brow furrowed. Skylar was beginning to recognize this expression—Noah processing information and analyzing options. His patterns were quickly becoming familiar.

"When we were on that hidden employee path, I saw a service road that runs behind the beach facilities," he said finally. "Looked as if it led to some maintenance buildings. It might have been overlooked in their initial sweep."

It was a solid suggestion. Skylar had noticed the service road and two employees in a golf cart on her way to the water-sports dock that morning for the snorkeling excursion. "Good thinking."

"We'll need to move quickly and stay low," he continued. "The open area between the pier and the palm trees is our biggest vulnerability."

Skylar nodded, preparing herself mentally. "On your signal."

He took one more careful look around, and then nodded. "Now."

They pushed away from the safety of the pier, swimming silently toward shore. As the water grew shallow, Skylar felt acutely aware of her bikini. The hot-pink color that had seemed fun and carefree on a vacation now felt like a target painted on her body.

They emerged onto the rocky shoreline. A wide concrete path stretched ahead—completely exposed. They sprinted for the trees and the service road west of Sunrise Beach. Hours ago, Skylar's brother and his wedding party had been there, sipping cocktails in the sun. Now it was just another route to stay alive.

Primal fear drove her forward. She'd faced danger before—flash floods, sudden lightning storms, even a bear encounter during a climbing trip in Montana—but nothing like this. Nothing with human malice behind it.

They ducked into the trees, and Skylar pressed herself against the rough bark of a palm, lungs burning. Beside her, Noah was breathing hard, his face flushed.

"You okay?" he asked.

She nodded. "Just need a second." Her hip throbbed from the exertion, but she swallowed it. She couldn't afford to slow them down. Without him by her side, she didn't know if she could make it on her own.

"This way," he whispered, leading her through a row of hibiscus bushes until they reached the narrow paved track of the service road.

Other than a golf cart crashing into a palm tree and left behind, there was no sign of an invasion.

As the road curved away from the eastern coastline, it led them to a cluster of utilitarian buildings surrounded by a chain-link fence. The plain concrete structures looked out of place against the lush tropical foliage—the practical reality behind Tesoro Bay's carefully crafted paradise.

"Maintenance compound," Noah whispered. "Should have supplies, and if we're lucky, some kind of communication equipment." Their phones were useless—locked in cubbies back at the dive hut, along with everything else they'd stored before the snorkeling trip.

Skylar noticed his gaze lingered on the cameras mounted near the entrance. The security systems designer was clearly in his element, analyzing the compound's vulnerabilities just as she would assess a rock face for climbing routes.

The compound spread out before them—a gravel yard ringed by low concrete buildings. Storage sheds. A garage. What looked like a small office with darkened windows. Everything still and quiet, a sharp contrast to the madness behind them.

"The gate's open." She nodded toward the entrance, where the chain-link hung ajar, its padlock cut or broken.

Noah frowned. "Someone's been here recently."

They moved through the gate and crossed the gravel lot, checking each building in turn. The first was nothing but landscaping supplies—mowers, rakes, hedge trimmers, and pallets of bagged fertilizer. The second offered more promise: a gutted golf cart, a workbench cluttered with tools, and a row of staff lockers along one wall. Skylar worked her way down the row. Locked. Empty. Locked. Then—finally—a few that weren't. She pulled out two Meridian polo shirts, work pants, several unopened water bottles. And tucked in the back of one, a small first-aid kit.

"Found some clothes." She handed him what looked like might fit him. "Better than running around in swimwear."

He accepted the polo and pants she offered with a grateful nod. Skylar turned her back as he changed, giving him privacy despite their dire circumstances. She took off her sandy rash guard and pulled the other polo over her damp bikini top, relishing the feel of dry fabric against her skin. Before pulling on the pants, she noticed her knee—scraped raw, grit embedded in the wound. It needed cleaning. Later. She stepped into the comically large pants and made them workable with some creative rolling and a belt from another locker. The pockets were useful—she stashed the first-aid kit and moved on.

"Running for your life really makes you reevaluate your wardrobe choices," she quipped as she turned around, trying to lighten the mood.

She was rewarded with a small smile that transformed his face, softening the worry lines around his eyes. It struck Skylar that under different circumstances—meeting on the cruise ship perhaps or out at a bar socializing with friends—she might have found Noah Reed intriguing. The thought was so incongruous with their current situation that she almost laughed.

"Any boots?" he asked hopefully.

Skylar shook her head. "No such luck."

Their aqua shoes would have to suffice.

The third building, which looked more like an office space with windows, proved more promising.

But as they approached the entrance, voices drifted from inside. Noah grabbed Skylar's arm and pulled her back against the wall.

"I know places," an accented voice said. "Trails in the jungle they won't find."

"Julia can barely walk," a man replied. "Where are we supposed to go?"

"—can't stay here much longer," a woman was saying. "They'll start searching the buildings soon."

Noah's face went pale. Then, in a whisper so quiet she barely caught it: "Vanessa?"

Before she could ask anything, the voices grew closer. Noah stepped around the corner into the doorway.

A woman's shocked gasp came from inside.

"Noah? Oh my God, you're alive!"

6

V*anessa.*

Skylar experienced a jolt of recognition as she followed Noah inside the third building. So this was the ex-girlfriend and business partner Noah had mentioned.

Standing near the doorway was a slender Asian woman in her early thirties, impeccably dressed in linen pants and a silk blouse that somehow looked freshly pressed. Around her neck she wore a multi-strand graduated pearl necklace with the distinctive lustre of natural pearls, not cultured. Her short black bob framed a face that managed to be both beautiful and intimidating at the same time.

Skylar tried to imagine Noah and Vanessa together, dating, and felt an unexpected stab of something she didn't want to examine too closely.

The woman rushed forward, throwing her arms around Noah in what appeared to be a rare display of emotion, judging by how quickly she composed herself afterward. Skylar watched the embrace longer than she should have, noting how naturally Vanessa fit against Noah's frame, how his hands settled automatically on her back as if muscle memory hadn't forgotten what used to be between them.

Behind Vanessa were a few more people: a middle-aged couple and a Hispanic man.

"I thought you'd be on the ship," Noah said. "Where's the rest of the team?"

Vanessa stepped back, her perfectly manicured hands lingering briefly on Noah's arms.

"I was in the spa when everything happened," she explained. "So were Mark and Julia." She gestured to the older couple. "Diego found us, got us to safety. We owe him our lives." Her expression darkened. "But it was already too late. The ship was leaving. They left us, Noah. Just left us."

"I'm not sure they had any choice when the shooting began," Noah said.

Skylar cleared her throat quietly, feeling like an intruder in a private moment. Both Noah and Vanessa turned toward her. The woman's gaze swept over Skylar as if she were cataloguing the competition.

"Who's this?" Vanessa asked, her tone sharpening slightly.

Skylar's face heated. Compared to sophisticated Vanessa, she probably looked disheveled and awkward in her oversized getup. More troubling was how much she suddenly cared about the comparison.

"This is Skylar," Noah said, stepping aside. "We were on the same snorkeling excursion. The guide abandoned us offshore when everything started."

Skylar extended her hand, determined to maintain basic civility despite the absurdity of formal introductions in their current situation. "Hi. Skylar Harris."

Vanessa took her hand briefly, her grip cool. "Vanessa Park. CEO at Reed Security Systems." Maybe Skylar would find out a little more about the relationship between these two. Noah had been a bit evasive when he'd mentioned her earlier.

"I run the practical side of the business while Noah handles the theoretical design work," Vanessa said, putting a slight emphasis on 'practical' that wasn't lost on Skylar. There was a hint of superiority in her tone, and something else—a subtle claim of ownership that made Skylar's jaw clench.

"Let me introduce you to everyone," Vanessa continued smoothly, gesturing toward the back of the room where the others had been waiting quietly. "Mark and Julia Thompson, whom I met at the spa this morning. And Diego—he works for the resort."

The middle-aged couple stepped forward first. Mark was of average height with graying hair and the soft build of a man who spent his days behind a desk, probably in accounting or middle management. His Hawaiian shirt was wrinkled and stained with sweat, and he kept one protective arm around his wife. Julia was petite with short blonde hair and laugh lines around her eyes, though she wasn't laughing now. She leaned heavily on Mark, her left ankle wrapped in what looked like a torn Meridian branded towel.

"Twisted it running from those animals," Julia explained, her voice shaky. "Mark practically carried me here." She had the slightly stunned look of someone whose carefully planned vacation had turned into a nightmare.

"We're from Phoenix," Mark added unnecessarily, as if normal social conventions still applied. "This was supposed to be our anniversary trip." His voice carried a bewildered tone.

The third person stepped forward—a man in his early thirties with sun-weathered skin and the lean build of someone who worked outdoors. He wore the khaki uniform of Tesoro Bay staff, though it was now dirty and torn. Unlike the others, he seemed alert rather than shell-shocked.

"Diego Morales," he said, his accent slight but noticeable. "I'm a scuba instructor here and know Tesoro Bay pretty well."

An awkward silence descended, the kind Skylar associated with uncomfortable dinner parties rather than life-or-death situations. Vanessa stood out from the others, having arrived looking perfectly put together. Even the most risk-taking of rock climbers usually had a gut-check moment when facing real danger. This woman seemed unnaturally composed.

"Have you seen anyone else?" Skylar asked. "Other tourists or staff?"

Vanessa's rigid posture straightened further. "A few. Most were rounded up by the creeps in orange. I think they're going to use them as hostages."

"How many guys in orange did you see?" Noah asked.

"At least a dozen," Diego replied grimly. "Maybe more. They came in fast, organized. Brought weapons with them—rifles, knives."

"The security guards at the pier said they got here on rafts from the main part of the island," said Noah. "Landed up on the north end."

Diego's eyebrows reached his hairline.

"We really need to get going," Vanessa said, moving to the window and peering through the blinds.

Skylar spoke up. "Shouldn't we decide where we're going first? We can't just rush out there without some kind of plan."

The look Vanessa turned on her could have flash-frozen the Caribbean. "And you think you're qualified to make a plan because...?"

After the accumulated stress of the day, the condescension in her tone triggered something in Skylar. She raised an eyebrow. "I have common sense."

"There's a communications station," Diego interrupted, sensing the tension. "Up on the ridge. Emergency facility with satellite equipment." He shook his head grimly. "Cell service went dead about two hours ago. Word is the prisoners torched the Wi-Fi tower near the main entrance. They didn't want anyone calling for help."

Noah's attention immediately focused. "How far is the station?"

"Few hours through the jungle," Diego replied. "Rough terrain, but it's our best shot."

Diego moved to a laminated map of Tesoro Bay hanging on the wall. "Here," he said, pointing to their current location north of Sunrise Beach. "We're at the bottom of the ridge system. The communications station is here—" His finger traced further north to a small building symbol near the peak of the highest ridge.

Noah joined him at the map. "What kind of equipment are we talking about?"

"Satellite uplink, backup power, emergency radio systems," Diego explained. "It's designed to stay operational during hurricanes."

Skylar moved closer to study the map, hyperaware of how Vanessa positioned herself on Noah's other side, flanking him. The layout was clearly marked with different colored zones and facility labels, trails winding through green areas marked as undeveloped jungle. She noticed a red dotted line along the southern edge marked "Perimeter Fence (Electrified)"—the resort's boundary with the rest of Saint Marielle.

"The route's not easy," Diego continued. "We'll have to skirt around here—" he pointed to an open area marked as the main plaza where all the shops and food kiosks were located, "—then pick up this old maintenance trail."

"Are you sure the prisoners won't see us?" Julia asked.

"Not if we time it right," Diego said. "They're focused on the beach area and the guest facilities. The maintenance trails are hidden—most tourists don't even know they exist."

Julia shifted uncomfortably next to her husband. "I don't know if I can make that kind of hike. My ankle..."

"We'll help you," Skylar said firmly. "All of us together."

Mark squeezed his wife's hand. "We can't stay here, honey. It's not safe."

Vanessa traced various routes on the map with her manicured nail. As if she were memorizing it.

Skylar found herself studying the other woman. Everything about Vanessa Park screamed competence and control, from her unwrinkled clothes to her steady voice. Even her hair remained perfectly in place, while Skylar's own tangled braid dripped seawater down her back. But there was something else. The way Noah watched Vanessa and angled toward her without seeming to realize it. They had a history—that much was obvious.

Skylar couldn't explain why, but something about the whole picture felt off.

"What about supplies?" Noah asked.

Skylar held up the first-aid kit for the group. "We found this and some water bottles in the lockers. Might be more if we keep looking."

"There's a vending machine in the break room," Diego said. "Protein bars, chips, drinks."

Vanessa took charge. "Clean it out. We'll need every bit of it for the hike—and whatever else we can scavenge."

They fanned out, gathering anything useful—water from a mini-fridge, a flashlight from a maintenance kit, even a small tarp that might provide shelter if needed. Bags were improvised from what the maintenance crew had left behind: a vinyl tool bag, a uniform laundry sack, a battered backpack with a faded resort logo. Skylar dug pain medication out of the first-aid kit for Julia, who dry-swallowed two pills without complaint.

"Hold up." Noah moved to the window, parting the blinds with one finger. "We've got company."

Skylar looked and her stomach clenched. It was the massive man from the pier with the tattoos crawling up his arms and neck. She'd watched him herd passengers like cattle.

"That's one of them," she breathed. "From the pier."

Mark joined them at the window. "Everyone stay calm," he said quietly. "We wait him out. Running now would be suicide." A canvas bag hung from his shoulder, revealing sandals, a paperback book, and a balled-up sweater inside.

Strange priorities, Skylar thought, when the rest of them were stuffing their bags with food and water. But she let it go. People did strange things under stress.

The prisoner circled the lot slowly, checked the garage bay, then moved on down the service road.

"Now," Diego whispered. "Back exit. Stay low."

Noah touched Skylar's arm as they gathered their things. "You good?" he asked quietly, his voice carrying genuine concern.

"Yep." She adjusted the faded tote bag she'd found in the break room across her midsection and tried not to favor her injured hip. The stiffness had gotten worse, and she didn't want Noah or Vanessa thinking she couldn't handle the difficult terrain ahead. Julia was enough of a problem with her ankle.

Something flickered in Noah's eyes—worry, perhaps. Had he noticed her limp?

"We need to move," Diego said, abandoning the plan they'd made. "Out the back. Now."

He opened a back door, checked outside, and motioned them forward. "Stay together. Follow my lead. And whatever you do, don't make any noise."

_____

7

One by one, the improvised group of strangers slipped out of the maintenance building, through a break in the chain-link fence, and into the wild tangle of the interior. As the jungle closed in, Noah's mind yanked him back to the Katanga province of the Democratic Republic of Congo—his first job after college, long before Reed Security Systems existed. He'd been hired to install a secure communications network at a remote cobalt mine, the kind of high-paying job no one wanted for all the right reasons.

Back then, he was young and chasing adventure. But what was meant to be a simple two-week upgrade turned into a nightmare when armed rebels attacked. The site went into lockdown, local workers scattered, and Noah spent sixteen hours hiding in a supply shed with nothing but a sat phone and a fire extinguisher.

It wasn't the danger that stuck with him—it was the waiting. The helplessness. The knowledge that no one was coming to help.

He never thought he'd be in that situation again. But as the trail wound on, something old and familiar kicked in—a hyper-awareness he hadn't felt in years. Vanessa and Skylar had no clue how badly things could go wrong in an instant.

"Stay single file," Diego whispered, barely audible. "Step where I step. Don't touch anything unless I do first."

They followed what appeared to be an animal trail, barely visible in the thick undergrowth. Diego pushed confidently ahead. Julia leaned hard on Mark as they fell behind.

Vanessa kept her composure, slipping into the same cool detachment she used to shut him out when they were dating. Even as the jungle took its toll on her linen pants and silk blouse, she didn't flinch, didn't ask for help. Classic Vanessa.

Noah ended up right behind Skylar. Despite her limp, she managed the rocky, overgrown path without complaint.

After about ten minutes, Diego froze, holding up his hand. Everyone stopped instantly. Diego crouched low to hide in the ferns. They all followed suit.

"Did you hear that?" Skylar whispered.

From somewhere behind them, voices drifted through the jungle—men calling to each other in a mixture of French and English.

"Voices," Vanessa said.

Maybe two hundred feet behind them, orange-clad figures moved between the trees.

"Prisoners?" Skylar asked.

"Has to be." Noah watched the shapes disappear behind massive tree trunks. He added to his running mental tally of the number of convicts he and Skylar had encountered. "But I don't think they saw us."

To be certain, they waited, listening. Nothing but the distant sounds of waves against the shore. A mosquito buzzed in Noah's ear, and he waved it away. Sweat dripped down his forehead and into his eyes. It stung. The heat and the bugs were beginning to make him irritable.

"We keep going," Diego said. "Stay low, follow the trail. We're almost at the base of the climb. The station's at the top."

They continued deeper into the jungle. Diego never slowed, never consulted the map he'd tucked in his pocket. He just moved—around boulders, under low-hanging limbs, through patches of undergrowth that looked impassable until he pushed through them. Although they'd only just met the guy, Noah had to trust he had their best interests in mind. What other choice did they have at this point?

Diego held up a fist, and everyone froze. Then Noah heard it too—voices, closer this time, filtering through the trees to their left. He found a gap in the leaves and saw them—the bald guy from the pier with the rifle, and the hulking figure covered in prison ink who'd been poking around the maintenance area. The big one moved like a predator, unhurried and sure.

Had he followed them somehow?

At that moment, Julia stumbled over a fallen branch, the crack echoing through the jungle.

The short prisoner called out, "*Tu as entendu ça?*"

Diego's head whipped around. "Move!" he hissed. "Now—go!"

They bolted into the undergrowth like startled deer, crashing through vines and ferns. Diego veered off the narrow trail, cutting into a denser section of jungle where everything grew wild and tangled.

Julia was struggling, barely able to keep up. Mark looped an arm under her shoulders and half-dragged her forward as they thrashed through the brush.

Behind them, the prisoners shouted again—closer now.

"We know you're out there! You think you can hide? We'll find you!"

A gunshot cracked through the air, but the voices started to fade as distance and foliage swallowed the fleeing group.

Noah kept moving, heart pounding, ears straining for any sign they were being followed. Eventually, the shouts behind them grew fainter, then stopped altogether.

Diego raised a hand at the base of a rocky hill. A steep path cut upward through the rocks, more goat track than trail, crumbling at the edges. This was it—the way up to the comms station.

"That was close," Noah said, letting out a breath.

"If those guys try to find us, the trail to the communications station is tricky to find. It's rarely used these days. They've been working on a more direct route on the other side of the mountain that can handle heavier equipment. It should be complete by next spring." Diego took a water bottle out of a string pack and gulped some down. "Everyone should hydrate. This is going to be rough."

They'd lost them. For now.

It wouldn't take long for those men to regroup, and when they came back, they'd be hunting—not stumbling around firing warning shots.

Noah kept that thought to himself.

The trail carved into the rock face wound upward into the hills that formed the spine of Tesoro Bay. What had once been a rudimentary service road for maintenance had deteriorated into a full-on mountain climb. With Skylar's climbing background, she naturally took the lead.

"Watch the loose rock here," she pointed out. "Test each step before you commit your weight."

Julia gave her husband a worried glance. The run through the jungle had only made things worse for her ankle. Neither she nor Mark was in the best of shape. Noah wondered if they'd be able to make it to the top.

They'd been climbing for nearly fifteen minutes, following switchbacks that zigzagged up increasingly steep grades. The path was barely wide enough for single file in places, with crumbling edges that revealed stomach-dropping falls to the jungle below.

Noah kept careful pace behind Skylar, trying not to look down at the dizzying drops that grew more treacherous with each turn. His palms were sweating, and he found himself wanting to hug as close to the rock face as possible.

Skylar had more guts than most men he knew. The more he saw her in action, the more impressive she became.

"There's a washout ahead," she said, pausing at a section where recent rains had carved away part of the trail, leaving a gap of loose scree and exposed roots hanging over a sheer drop. "We'll need to edge along the left side, then step across."

Noah's stomach clenched as he saw what she meant. The gap was maybe three feet wide, but below it was nothing but air and a fall that would definitely be fatal.

"I don't think I can do that," he said, his voice tighter than he intended.

"Heights aren't your thing?" Skylar asked, no judgment in her tone.

"Not really, no."

Vanessa muttered under her breath, then said more loudly, "Seriously? It's just a little step across."

"It's fine," Skylar said, shooting Vanessa a sharp look before turning back to Noah. "Heights affect everyone differently. Here's what we'll do—I'll go first, then I can guide you through it step by step."

She demonstrated, testing each handhold on the rock face before trusting it with her weight. Noah watched her movements, trying to focus on her technique rather than the drop below.

"Your turn," she said, reaching a hand toward him. "Don't look down, just focus on my voice. First, put your left hand on that gray rock about shoulder height."

Noah's hand shook slightly as he reached for the hold. "Like this?" A wave of humiliation ran through him. Skylar must think he was a wimp.

"Perfect. Now your right foot goes on that little ledge. Feel how solid it is?"

"Oh, God," Vanessa sighed. "We're going to be here all day."

Diego waited behind her, but Mark and Julia had only caught up to the group moments ago.

"We're doing fine," Skylar said firmly. "Noah, you're doing great. Now step across—I've got you."

Somehow, with Skylar's calm guidance and her outstretched hand, Noah made it across the gap. His heart was racing, but the solid ground under his feet felt like salvation. He'd never been more humbled.

"See? Not so bad." Skylar gave him an encouraging smile.

Vanessa crossed next with theatrical sighs and eye rolls. "Can we move a little faster? Some of us would like to reach the top before sunset."

Diego crossed without a word.

Noah caught sight of Mark's worried face as he prepped to help his injured and exhausted wife climb across using only one foot. Skylar skillfully stepped onto the last foothold to grab Julia and half-carried her to safety. It was as if Skylar had done it before. But when Julia leaned into her body for the final few feet, he noticed Skylar's features scrunch up in pain.

Mark crossed quickly on his own, his canvas bag slung across his chest, before taking up the position of 'crutch' under his wife's left arm to help her up the steep hill.

"Looks as if the trail levels out once we reach the ridgeline." Skylar gazed up-slope at the remaining climb. "Maybe another ten minutes."

"Honestly," Vanessa directed at Noah, "how did you survive in the corporate world with a phobia like that?"

"Vanessa," he said through gritted teeth, "not helping."

Skylar glanced back with something that might have been irritation. "Everyone has things that challenge them. The important thing is pushing through it when it matters."

Noah caught the subtle rebuke in her words and appreciated her defense. Thanks to Skylar's calm coaching, he'd conquered his worst fear and crossed terrain he never thought possible.

The trail leveled out as they neared the top, and Noah allowed himself a breath. The hardest stretch was done.

A month ago, public speaking had topped his list of fears. Now that seemed laughable. Had it really been only a few weeks since they'd gathered at their headquarters in New Jersey to celebrate, clinking glasses as if the future was guaranteed?

"To Reed Security Systems and the federal contract that's going to put us on the map!" Marcus Gutman, their corporate counsel who'd shepherded the Homeland Security contract through its final negotiating stages, raised his champagne flute high. The core team echoed the toast—Vanessa, Derek, Lisbeth, Raj, and the half-dozen others who'd made the impossible proposal deadline happen.

Noah smiled tightly, nodding in acknowledgment of their achievement while fighting the urge to shrink from the attention. He'd never been comfortable as the figurehead, preferring to lose himself in the elegant logic of system design rather than the messy business of interpersonal dynamics and schmoozing with federal contracting officers.

"Speech from our CEO!" Derek Vincenza, their CFO, set off a round of encouraging applause. "Noah, come on up here."

Noah suppressed a wince. Public speaking had never been his forte—another reason he'd been grateful when Vanessa, as Director of Marketing, had taken over client presentations. He cleared his throat awkwardly.

"I, uh—" he began, before Vanessa interjected.

"What our brilliant founder means to say," she said with a practiced smile, while stepping up to the front of the room, "is that this achievement represents Reed Security's evolution into a major player. Noah may have designed the original architecture, but together we've built something much bigger."

The team laughed appreciatively, but Noah caught something in her phrasing that made him uneasy. *We've* built something bigger. Not *he'd* built it with their help, but they'd built it despite him. He may not be the charismatic CEO many companies wanted, but this company was his baby, his idea. Without him, there would be no Reed Security Systems.

"To the team," he managed, raising his glass.

"To the team!" they echoed.

Later, as the group dispersed to head back to their respective offices, Vanessa cornered him by the windows that overlooked Chambers Street in the heart of Princeton. They were outgrowing their office, an older two-story brick building within walking distance of the university.

"You need to accept Reed Security has moved past its startup phase," she said in her matter-of-fact tone—the one that always grated on him. "This contract means we're playing in the big leagues now. We need leadership capable of handling the responsibility."

Noah bristled. "I founded this company, Vanessa. The technology, the vision, the core values—"

"Were perfect for getting us started," she interrupted. "But scalability requires different skills. You're brilliant with systems, Noah, but business is about more than the code and the hardware."

He stared at her, suddenly seeing their dynamic with new clarity. "You're talking about me as if I'm some kind of liability."

Vanessa's smile held no warmth now. "I'm talking about maximizing our potential. The board agrees that having a CEO who can actually function in corporate environments is essential for our next phase of growth."

The casual cruelty hit him like a physical blow. She must have spent months while they were dating positioning herself as his ally while systematically undermining his authority with the board. All those times she'd 'rescued' him from social situations, she'd been building a narrative he was unfit to lead the company he'd created. Was that the reason she'd dumped him? Part of some plan?

"The board you helped stack with your contacts," he said quietly.

"The board recognizes talent and leadership when they see it," Vanessa replied. "Don't take it personally, Noah. You'll still be CTO. You'll still get to play with your encryption protocols and system architectures. You just won't have to worry about all those messy business decisions you hate anyway."

Noah nodded slowly, understanding finally dawning. She hadn't joined Reed Security to help him build something meaningful—she'd seen an opportunity to take it over. Every conversation about his 'social awkwardness,' every time she'd stepped in to handle a presentation, had been calculated moves in a longer game. And he thought she was merely a devoted girlfriend wanting to see him succeed.

"Promise me you'll remember what this company was supposed to stand for," he said. "Protecting people's privacy, building systems that serve users instead of exploiting them."

Vanessa's cell phone rang, and she stared at the screen. "Of course," she said absently. "Though we may need to be more...flexible about some of those idealistic constraints if we want to compete at a higher level."

She walked out of the conference room chatting with a senior DHS official about the transition onto the contract.

And there it was. She didn't care about his vision or values —she cared about power and profit. The company he'd built to make the digital world safer was only another acquisition to her, another stepping stone in her climb up the corporate ladder.

"Don't I always take care of things?" Vanessa said to the person on the other end of the line, as Noah headed back to his office.

Yes, Noah thought bitterly. She always took care of things— especially when those things stood in her way.

"Noah? Did you hear me?"

He blinked. The memory dissolved. Skylar was beside him, concern etched on her face. He hadn't even noticed they'd stopped walking.

"Sorry," he mumbled. "Just thinking."

"Diego says we're almost there. He's doing a little recon to make sure we're in the clear." She studied his face. As she leaned against a boulder, Noah noticed how she'd shifted weight off her right leg. "Are you sure you're okay?"

"I should be asking you that," he said, gesturing toward her stance. "You're favoring that leg again."

Skylar's lips pressed together. "I'm fine."

"You've been limping for a while now," Noah pressed gently. "What happened? And don't say it's nothing—I've been watching you compensate all day."

For a moment, she looked as if she might deflect again, but something in his expression must've made her relent. "Old climbing accident. Broke my pelvis and leg pretty badly. It's mostly healed, but long hikes on uneven terrain..." She shrugged. "Sometimes it flares up."

A broken pelvis—damn, that was serious. An injury that could have killed her or left her permanently disabled. He tried to imagine what kind of fall could cause that level of damage, and the mental image made him feel sick. She'd survived something catastrophic and was out here hiking treacherous terrain as if it were nothing.

"You should have said something. We could've taken more rest stops."

"I don't need to be babied." Skylar arched a brow. "I've learned to work through it."

There was a whole history in that sentence. Noah recognized it—the voice of someone who'd had to justify her choices one too many times.

Before he could respond, Diego appeared up ahead on the trail.

"We made it," he said. "Just over this ridge."

Everyone climbed the final section together. When they crested the ridge, the view that greeted them was both promising and daunting.

8

Below them lay a small clearing carved into the mountainside. Two buildings sat near the edge of a dramatic cliff face that dropped hundreds of feet to the churning ocean below. The larger structure was concrete with a corrugated metal roof, solar panels, and a small satellite dish mounted on top. The smaller building looked more residential —a simple casita with multiple windows and two visible doors.

"The communications shack." Diego pointed to the larger building. "The other is emergency housing for maintenance crews during hurricane season."

Noah studied the concrete building with growing excitement. Solar panels, satellite dish—this looked promising.

"We had a bad hurricane last month," Diego said. "Damaged some of the older equipment up here—lightning fried one of the transformers, wind tore the cabling off the main tower. But the resort Wi-Fi was working fine until the prisoners took out the relay station. They wanted us cut off."

"Maybe I can bring it back online," Noah said, eager to see what he could salvage.

Mark shifted Julia's weight, his face flushed with exertion. "Please tell me we can rest soon. Julia needs to get off this ankle."

Diego nodded toward the smaller building. "Couple of bunk beds in the casita. Not fancy, but she can lie down and elevate that ankle properly."

Vanessa had been quiet during the last tough push to the top. Seemed as if all those Pilates workouts weren't as intense as she had insisted. Her silk blouse clung to her, armpits stained with sweat, and her hair hung limply around her red face.

Maybe she wasn't so bulletproof after all.

Skylar handed her an unopened bottle of water, and his ex drank greedily. They could all use some rest after the horrible events of the day.

"We need to let the authorities know what they're dealing with." Noah might be as tired as everyone else, but their purpose in coming up here was twofold: safety and contact with the outside world. "The captain of the Voyager only knows so much—and is he even aware yet how many passengers and employees are missing? If we're lucky, the antenna's still live. I'll check it out. Someone's got to explain what's happening here." He nodded toward Diego. "Go on without me. I'll find you when I'm done."

Vanessa fluffed up her hair and crumpled up her empty water bottle, flinging it into the rocks. "I'll help you, Noah."

He rubbed the back of his neck. "Okay."

What was she up to? She didn't know anything about fixing a comms array.

"I'll help get Julia settled in the casita." Skylar looked at Mark's exhausted wife with sympathy. "We can make a list of our supplies and figure out how to ration it all." Her inquisitive gaze lingered on Noah as Vanessa joined him for the trek down to the communications station.

The station itself was rudimentary—a concrete building with faded solar panels and satellite equipment that appeared to be a decade old. But from a communications perspective, the position was excellent—commanding views to the north, south and east with a clear line of sight to the maintenance facility they'd abandoned and the cruise pier far to the southeast.

The metal access door to the building was unlocked but dented, so it didn't close completely. Noah had to shove it open with his shoulder. It was hard to know whether the hurricane had caused the damage or something else. A musty smell filled his nostrils, and he turned on the single light in the space that must've been powered by the solar panels. The anemic light revealed equipment that made his fingers itch with anticipation —a wall-mounted radio base station, a dusty satellite uplink modem, a shortwave transceiver, two aging desktop towers stacked under a laminate counter, and a weather-beaten signal router blinking faintly in the corner. Finally, something in his wheelhouse.

"This is better than I expected." He was already cataloguing and assessing. For a remote resort, the setup was surprisingly functional.

But as he checked connections and power indicators, his initial excitement faded. "The solar's working or we wouldn't have any light, but all the transmission systems are offline."

"The hurricane?" Vanessa picked up the transceiver and turned it upside down, as if she could figure out what was wrong. Then she set it back down again, wiping her hands together to rid herself of the dust.

Noah frowned as he examined the setup more closely. "Looks like it. The storm must've knocked out some key components." He pointed to a few open slots and disconnected wires in the rack. "Without the signal converters and power amps, this is just expensive furniture."

"So we came all the way up here for nothing?" Vanessa crossed her arms.

"I didn't say that." Possibilities formed in his mind. He loved a good technical challenge. It was one of the reasons he was able to leave contract work behind and build his own company. "The hurricane took out the obvious components but left plenty behind. With the right parts, I could build a simple transmitter. Not full communications, but enough to send a distress signal." Against the far wall, half-hidden in shadow, shelving held spare parts and boxes of odds and ends. He went to investigate.

"I can help," Vanessa said, glancing around the dim interior. "Just tell me what you need me to do."

"Perfect." Whatever their past, having an extra set of hands would be helpful.

Noah spent the next couple of hours sorting through equipment, testing connections, and rebuilding what he could from the limited components on hand. Vanessa stayed nearby, handing him tools, holding a penlight, and keeping track of the parts they salvaged. She didn't say much, which suited him fine. By late afternoon, they'd almost cobbled together a workable solution—jury-rigging components, bypassing damaged boards, and coaxing life from outdated gear. A basic transmitter was now within reach after a few more tweaks.

But when his stomach growled, he noticed his concentration was starting to slip.

"We might actually pull this off," Noah said, studying a salvaged circuit board. "I should be able to get it back online." He blinked hard, trying to focus. "But not tonight. I'm running on fumes here—one wrong connection and I could set us back hours."

Back at the casita, Skylar helped Mark settle Julia on one of the narrow beds. The space was basic but functional—a couple of bunk beds on opposite walls in back, an old recliner near a small window by the main door, and a simple table with mismatched chairs in the center of the room. A rudimentary kitchen along the far wall held some canned food and basic supplies, though not much.

"Thank God," Julia breathed as Mark eased her onto the mattress. "I didn't think I was going to make it."

The older woman's face had gone pale with weariness and pain, and her ankle had blown up to twice the size it had been earlier in the day.

"You did great," Skylar assured her, though privately she'd been worried about Julia's condition during the last hour of the climb. The woman had pushed herself to the absolute limit.

"Do you think those men will find us up here?" Julia's whole body seemed to deflate against the mattress. "I really thought they were going to kill us."

Skylar patted her arm and then handed her a bottle of water. "Let's not think about it right now. It wasn't an easy climb, and it's going to be dark soon. We can talk when Noah and Vanessa come back, okay?"

Skylar wished she had something reassuring to say, but the same worry was eating at her. Armed men were combing the jungle below—men who'd already shown they had no problem pulling the trigger. Without rescue, staying hidden was only delaying the inevitable.

Mark, who had been doing a quick search of the place, handed some pain medication and an instant cold pack to his wife. "This should help with the swelling."

Julia smiled, and the stress around her eyes softened. "Thanks, honey."

Diego moved around the casita with familiarity, opening cabinets and drawers. "Water's good, propane's full. We've got canned food, some basic medical supplies. Should be comfortable for a few days."

Seemed strange to Skylar that a scuba instructor would have so much knowledge about this part of Tesoro Bay. Why would he ever have had a need to come up here prior to today? Wouldn't that be something the maintenance or security crew would be responsible for?

"How often do maintenance crews use this place?" she asked. Although the supplies looked fresh, the bed frame had a layer of dust on it as if no one had been here in months.

"Not often," Diego replied, not meeting her eyes. "Maybe once every few months. Emergency shelter mostly."

"You seem to know it well. As if you've been here before—recently."

He busied himself with stacking cans of chili on the small countertop. "Part of my job is to know all the facilities. Sometimes we have job overlap in a place this remote."

Skylar let it drop but filed away her concerns. Something about Diego's story didn't quite add up. But what did she know about running a place like this?

She moved to the south-facing window, studying the view toward the pier below as the light faded from the sky. From here, she could make out the distant main plaza and the dark gray concrete of the maintenance area where they'd met for the first time. Smoke rose from several locations, and even at this distance, the orange figures were visible moving between buildings, causing a wave of fear to run through her.

"Hard to believe that was paradise this morning," Mark said quietly, joining her.

"Your anniversary trip," Skylar remembered. "I'm sorry this happened."

Mark's expression was grim. "Twenty-five years of marriage, and this is how we celebrate. Julia keeps saying it's her fault we came here instead of going to Europe like we originally planned."

"It's nobody's fault." Skylar turned away from the window. "You couldn't have known this would happen."

But even as she said it, a sharp throb pulsed through her hip, stealing her breath. The ache was a brutal reminder—if they ran into those men again, she might not be fast enough. The thought twisted in her gut. They were trapped with armed fugitives and no clear way out.

9

Noah and Vanessa made their way back to the casita after his promising work on the transmitter. With a few more solid hours tomorrow when his head was clearer and his body well rested, they might actually send a signal out. As they crossed the open flat area between the two ridgetop structures, he could see lamplight flickering through the casita's windows.

"Do you trust those people?" Noah wasn't sure what to think of their new companions. Sure, Diego had been helpful in navigating them to a safer spot, but the only thing linking everyone together was happenstance.

"When everything fell apart, people were panicking," Vanessa said. "I'd just met Mark and Julia at the spa—we were all getting treatments. Gunfire, men in orange running around. We had no idea what was happening. Most of the workers fled. Diego found us and took us to the maintenance compound before any of those creeps saw us." As they neared the casita, she slowed her steps. "He didn't have to do that. If he hadn't come along when he did, who knows where we'd be right now." She shivered.

He wasn't sure if that was from the disturbing memory she had or from the early evening sea breeze.

"That's how I feel about Skylar," he said. "We were sort of thrown together out in the ocean. It could've gone wrong, but she's been solid since we met."

His ex nodded. She'd softened some since they'd made the climb—a brief glimpse of the woman he'd once been attracted to. Maybe she could act like a human every once in a while.

"I'm glad there are six of us now," she said. "A team. If things go down, we might have a fighting chance to make it out of here in one piece. Except for Julia—"

Vanessa didn't expand on that statement. But Noah knew what she meant. Julia was a worry, and Vanessa was the type who would sacrifice someone else to save herself. She'd done as much when she took control of his company—saw a vulnerability and took advantage.

"I'm hoping it doesn't come to that," Noah said as they reached the door. "All we need is to contact someone who can help us. Let them know where we are. Avoid the dangerous areas. Stay alive."

When they entered together, everyone looked up from their scattered spots around the room. Julia lay on the bottom bunk, her leg elevated on a stack of folded towels. Her face was pale, features pinched with pain. Her husband organized food stores on the small kitchen counter. Skylar sat at the table, sorting through medical supplies. Diego fussed with an old but serviceable portable stove while a few cans of chili dumped into a pot stood waiting.

Skylar looked up when the door opened and smiled. "Hope you have some good news for us."

She must've re-braided her hair, as all the messy loose strands had been slicked away.

"I think we can get it running again," he said. "Diego was

right. There was clearly some damage from the hurricane that hadn't been fixed." Noah pulled up a chair across from Sklyar. "My brain is pretty much toast right now, though. I couldn't think straight. With some rest and some food, I'm hoping we'll be sending a signal tomorrow."

"Good," said Julia, "because I don't like how exposed we are here."

The room went quiet.

Julia shifted uncomfortably, adjusting the ice pack on her ankle. "I need you all to promise me something." She looked around the room. "If those men show up and I can't move fast enough—don't wait for me. Just go."

"Nobody's leaving anyone behind," Skylar said firmly.

Noah slid his gaze to Vanessa, who only a few minutes ago had expressed her fears about Julia holding them back. Her face was blank, but he knew what was behind her dark eyes.

"Still, we're sitting here in the open, hoping no one comes looking." Julia's voice began to rise. Out of everyone in the room, Julia was the one Noah would think most likely to panic if she came face to face with one of those prisoners. "I'd sleep a lot better tonight if I knew someone was keeping watch."

Vanessa had taken a seat on the bottom bunk opposite Julia. "She's right. They gave up the chase in the jungle but threatened to track us down. We should take that seriously, no matter how hidden the trail was. We should act as if they're coming."

Diego coaxed a flame from the old propane stove and set the pot of chili on top. "I can't argue with that."

Mark leaned against the counter and crossed his arms. "Then let's get organized. Set up a night watch—two-person shifts, every few hours."

"I'll take a shift," Skylar said immediately.

Her willingness to volunteer didn't surprise Noah. She'd

been a force all day...he knew she was hurting, but she never complained once and kept up with him when it mattered.

"Me too," Noah added. "Skylar and I can pair up." That would probably tick off Vanessa, but he didn't care. He trusted the rock climber he'd just met more than he trusted his ex. Vanessa's actions had always been about what benefitted her the most.

The CEO glared at him from across the room. Not pleased with his choice. "I'll take first shift, say ten to one a.m. Mark, want to team up with me?"

"Sure."

Noah was surprised Vanessa didn't choose the younger and more-in-shape Diego as her partner.

"We can take the shift after you guys," Skylar said.

Since Julia was injured, Diego volunteered to take the four to seven a.m. shift by himself.

"Thanks," said Julia. "I'm grateful for everyone stepping up."

Mark came over and gave her a kiss on the head. "Babe, it was a good idea. We'll get through this. Don't worry. Before long we'll be back home worrying about the tile we want to put in for the pool."

Julia sheepishly looked at everyone. "My other anniversary gift was an in-ground pool. Don't I have the best hubby? He spoils me."

———

After their meager dinner, Noah lay on the top bunk across from Skylar and stared at the ceiling. He wanted to sleep, but his mind wouldn't turn off.

"That was pretty tricky how you ended up with a top bunk," Skylar whispered.

The darkness in the casita hid her expression.

Noah smiled to himself and then rolled over on his side to face her. "Nobody else would make a move. Someone had to be first."

"Poor Diego has to make do with the recliner."

"I'm fine," Diego said across the room. "It's actually more comfortable than it looks."

"Whoops," said Skylar. "You weren't supposed to hear us."

"Have you seen how small this room is?"

Julia groaned, and the bottom mattress beneath Noah creaked. "If you all don't mind, I'm exhausted. Can we try to sleep?"

"Sorry, Julia," said Skylar, giving Noah a grimace. "See you at I a.m."

He folded the stolen work shirt under his head as a makeshift pillow. "Gives us about two-and-a-half hours of sleep." He focused on the dive watch strapped to his wrist. The luminescent hands made it easy to read in the darkness.

Before he knew it, hands were shaking him awake. His eyes snapped open. "Your turn." It was Vanessa.

Noah sat up. "Wow, it feels like I just went to sleep."

"Here, take the flashlight. I'm beat." She gave no report of where they'd been or what they'd seen. Guess that meant all was quiet.

Noah took it and climbed down. Mark had already gotten into the bottom bunk beside his wife. Skylar was slipping into her aqua shoes that she'd left drying near the door.

"Ready?" she asked.

"Yeah."

The door creaked softly as they stepped out.

After a hot and sticky climb to the communications post, the cool night air was a welcome change. They moved in silence, skirting the casita's exterior. Noah angled the flashlight low, letting Skylar lead. It made the most sense to circle around the back of the casita, then follow the slope to the communications shack, check the older path they'd climbed from the jungle below, and then return to the casita from the other side. Diego had mentioned that the newer route up the mountain was located to the north and nearly completed. That could be an easier way for the guys in orange to reach them, if they were were going to make good on their threat.

A snap echoed from the underbrush. They froze.

Noah lifted the beam. Just a little green lizard darting through the ferns.

They continued on.

After a while, Skylar murmured, "You ever think we're just background characters in someone else's disaster movie?"

He smirked. "If this is a movie, I'd like a rewrite."

They reached the ridge overlooking the jungle they had come from earlier that day. Moonlight filtered through ragged clouds, washing the treetops in silvery light. Far below, the resort's lights still glowed—a strange illusion of normalcy. From this distance, Tesoro Bay looked exactly as it had that morning, before everything fell apart.

Skylar took a few steps closer to the edge, peering over the drop.

This woman had zero fear of heights as far as he could tell. Just watching her lean forward to look hundreds of feet down gave him a gut check.

"Seriously," he said, keeping a few feet back. "Do heights just not register for you?"

She glanced over her shoulder. "Only when I don't trust my footing."

"You didn't even blink on the trail up here. I was one wrong move from grabbing a defibrillator."

Skylar smirked, then looked back out at the view. "You handled it fine."

"Nope. I froze. You got me past it."

She shrugged. "Kind of my thing."

"Meaning?"

"I teach climbing. Back home."

He stepped a little closer, curiosity piqued. "At a gym?"

"Yeah. In Boulder." She glanced back again. "Of course."

He chuckled. "That tracks."

She gave the drop one last glance, then turned and rejoined him at a safer distance. "I take people out on real rock, too. Once they're ready. Eldorado Canyon, Shelf Road, Flatirons. There's a ledge in Eldorado where the whole canyon turns gold at sunset. Even you would forget to breathe."

"No, I'd definitely pass out."

She laughed. "Then we'll start with the gym."

He studied her in the moonlight. Oversized uniform, hair in a braid, no nonsense. She didn't brag. Just stated facts as if none of them were a big deal.

But they were. She was the kind of person who did hard things as if they were normal. Like helping a scared guy past a vertical drop without making him feel like an idiot.

"You ever climb outside the U.S.?" he asked.

"Not for fun," she said. "Only guiding. Couple of trips to Mexico. One to Costa Rica. Mostly corporate groups who want to feel adventurous without actually being in danger."

"And now here you are. Real danger."

She nodded. "Not the itinerary I signed up for."

They started walking the rest of their security route.

"I think I'm starting to get who you are," he said.

She raised an eyebrow. "And?"

"Remind me not to underestimate you."

She didn't answer, but he caught the flicker of something in her expression—something soft, then gone.

"I wish I'd gotten the transceiver working tonight, but it was a mess in there. Diego mentioned a hurricane taking everything out, but honestly it looked more like sabotage to me."

"Seriously?" The worry in Skylar's voice was unmistakable.

"It wasn't just a blown-down antenna and some wires shorting out. In fact, the solar-powered lights worked like a charm." He hadn't really taken the time to analyze what he'd seen when he and Vanessa had entered the shack, but now that he'd had time to reflect, something about the state of the place didn't seem right. "I was so focused on sending out a message and getting us some help, I didn't really think much about it. Until now..."

"If the escaped convicts showed up around noon and we've been up here since about four o'clock, when would they have had time to do that? Unless..."

Noah filled in the blanks for her. "Someone here at Tesoro Bay was helping these guys."

"But why?" They'd slowed their pace to a crawl. "Why would someone want a private cruise stop to be raided by criminals? What was their plan?"

"It definitely feels as if something more is going on here...and we got stuck in the middle of it."

As they headed to the comms shack, the bluff stretched out in every direction—exposed, silent, empty. It gave them an understanding of how isolated they actually were.

But it also gave him perspective—and none of it looked accidental.

This wasn't some chaotic prison break.

It was a setup.

DAY TWO

10

S kylar woke with a sudden jolt. For a moment, she couldn't remember where she was. Then reality crashed back as she blinked against the light streaming through dirty windows.

The casita. Saint Marielle. The chaos at Tesoro Bay. The ship leaving without her.

She sat up slowly, wincing as her body protested. Despite years of sleeping on rocky ground during climbing expeditions, the cheap mattress on the rudimentary wooden bunks was a different kind of punishment. Beneath her borrowed Meridian staff polo, her bikini had dried stiff with salt, creating an uncomfortable chafing against her skin.

What she wouldn't do for a shower and some clean clothes.

The others were still asleep. Mark snored next to his wife. Diego, who'd probably only finished his watch shift an hour ago, adjusted his position on the recliner. Vanessa, in the bottom bunk below her, probably looked elegant even while sleeping. Only Noah was missing from the group.

Skylar found him by the east-facing window, silhouetted

against the early first light of dawn. He stood perfectly still, his profile outlined, attention fixed on something outside. The gentle sunlight highlighted features she hadn't really noticed yesterday—his strong jawline, the way his dark hair fell across his forehead. Strange how the adrenaline and confusion had made her miss how attractive he was.

"Couldn't sleep?" She asked softly after quietly climbing down from the bunk and joining him at the window.

He glanced over, the shadows under his eyes confirming her guess. "Not much. You?"

"On and off." Skylar didn't mention the nightmares that had plagued her—vivid replays of Pascal being shot on the beach, except in her dreams, it was her brother, Ethan, falling face-first into the sand.

"What are you looking at?" she asked, following his gaze through the grimy window.

"How beautiful it is up here. Everything looks so peaceful. I can almost pretend nothing's happened."

From their elevated position on the bluff, Seashell Beach and the watersports dock were visible among swaying palms and the blue-green ocean glittering beyond. It did look deceptively normal.

Behind them, the others were beginning to stir. Diego stretched and yawned loudly, while Julia murmured something to Mark. Vanessa, true to form, transitioned from sleep to alertness in seconds, immediately reaching to smooth her hair.

"Good morning," she greeted them. "Anything interesting out there?"

"We really need to get that communication equipment working," Noah said, sidestepping her question. "The longer we wait, the greater the chance those convicts find us."

"I can help," Skylar offered. She didn't know a thing about

radio systems, but doing something—anything—felt better than sitting around.

"Hopefully by now the ship's contacted the authorities and given them a list of who's missing," said Diego. "The cruise line's not going to leave us stranded."

"But we're the ones on the ground," Noah said. "We know what happened. If we want to survive this, the Coast Guard needs real-time information. Getting word to them is our best shot."

Diego shook his head. "You think the Coast Guard showing up against a bunch of armed convicts is going to help? That could blow this whole thing wide open. What if it turns into a firefight? How do we survive that?"

Vanessa coolly stepped between the two men, grabbed a Styrofoam cup and the instant coffee from the counter and said, "Anyone know where I can get some hot water?"

The interruption brought down the temperature in the room.

"Eh, do whatever you want. Not like I can stop you." Diego got up out of the recliner and went to start the camp stove to heat some water. "I keep thinking about the watercraft down by the beach. If we could only grab one of those boats...we could cruise to the mainland in less than an hour. I know where they keep the keys."

"Tesoro Bay is swarming with armed lunatics," said Julia, sitting on the edge of the bottom bunk and testing out her ankle. "I'd rather wait for the Coast Guard."

Diego shrugged and poured the now-boiling pot of water into Vanessa's waiting cup. "To each his own. A small group late at night? I think we could sneak across to the beach...those creeps have to sleep some time, don't they?"

"Well, I'm behind Noah's plan," Skylar said. "Didn't you say you'd almost put together a transmitter or something?"

"Almost." Noah grabbed his own cup of instant coffee. "I couldn't get it running last night, but I was burned out. This should help." He raised his cup and dropped into the nearest seat.

"I think Diego's plan has merit," Vanessa said. "We could be out of here by tonight if we played our cards right."

Skylar noticed Noah's back stiffen. Probably not nice to hear your former girlfriend take sides with a stranger.

Breakfast was a quiet affair of protein bars and instant coffee. It hadn't taken long for fractures to appear in their patched-together group. Alliances were quickly forming—and shifting. Whatever sense of unity they'd had the day before was already wearing thin.

After a tense, awkward breakfast, the group split up to handle different tasks. Vanessa took charge of organizing their food supplies, intent on rationing what was left. Diego claimed he needed a walk to stretch his legs after spending the night in the recliner. Mark stayed in the casita with Julia, keeping her ankle elevated and managing her pain meds. Noah and Skylar walked down to the station to try again.

Since Noah had woken up that morning, his mind had been spinning with the wiring sequence he hadn't finished the day before. He'd thought Vanessa had been on board with his plan, since she'd been eager to help him yesterday with restoring communications, but something must have changed her mind.

Should he really be so surprised? When had she ever really been on his side in anything from business to their relationship?

When they entered the building, he snapped on the solar-powered light and headed right to the workbench where the half-assembled transmitter waited.

"How can I help?" Skylar stared at the twisted web of cables and salvaged circuit boards. It probably looked like a garbage heap to her.

"Here." He handed her a penlight they'd found in one of the drawers yesterday. "Can you hold this for me? The lighting isn't that great in here."

"Sure." Skylar pulled up a stool and pointed it at his project.

Although he'd liked building stuff out of components he salvaged from old VCRs and desktop towers when he was a kid, this was next level. He wasn't an expert in radios or signal transmission, but he understood enough about circuits, voltage, and grounding to improvise. The transceiver he'd cobbled together was a Frankenstein of scavenged bits and pieces. He could almost hear his dad's voice in his head, criticizing his mess of jumpers and spliced lines.

"It's close," he muttered. "I've got power flowing through the primary relay, but the signal's not hitting the uplink."

"Is that a good close or a one-spark-away-from-smoke close?"

He cracked a tired grin. "Bit of both."

With her help, they rechecked the ground lines and rerouted the feed through a backup signal converter Noah had pulled from an old weather station module. The moment he switched the line over, a faint whine came from the transceiver. Noah went still. After hours of dead silence from the equipment, that sound was music.

"There," he said, smiling. "That's what I was hoping to hear."

"Did you fix it?"

Maybe this would work. If he could get a clean enough signal out, someone might pick it up. It wouldn't fix everything, but it could buy them a way out. He glanced at Skylar, still holding the penlight steady, focused and calm. He hoped like hell she'd be impressed—not because he needed the validation, but because her opinion was starting to matter to him.

"I sure hope so."

Noah reached for the dial, adjusting the frequency slightly, and suddenly a voice crackled through the speaker.

"...repeat, situation on Saint Marielle remains contained. Escaped prisoners have established control of Tesoro Bay resort area but have not moved beyond that perimeter."

Noah froze. Clearly, this is some kind of official communication. He adjusted the frequency slightly, improving the reception.

"Latest intelligence suggests the prison break was orchestrated to provide cover for a museum theft. Artifacts valued at over twenty million were taken, including the Saint Marielle Cross. We believe this was the primary objective."

The voice on the other end continued. "Coast Guard has established a five-mile exclusion zone around the island. No vessels in or out until control is restored. Military option being considered, but hostage situation complicates extraction. Will update at 1400 hours."

Noah tried the handheld radio unit he'd scavenged from one of the shelves along the far wall, pressing the call button experimentally. "This is Tesoro Bay, requesting assistance. Do you copy?"

Only static answered him. The receiver was working, but the transmitter wasn't operational. They could hear but not be heard.

Dammit.

"I don't know who's listening," he said, voice low as he leaned toward the mic, "but this is a distress call from Tesoro

Bay. We're survivors from the Meridian Voyager—repeat, Meridian Voyager. Limited food, no weapons. We need help."

He kept speaking, repeating the message slowly, clearly, adding anything he could think of that might help someone triangulate their position.

The transmission cut out suddenly, leaving only empty static and a wisp of smoke. Noah tried several frequencies, hoping to pick up more information, but found nothing but atmospheric noise.

He sat back, breathing hard. "Signal's out. Not sure how long it held."

"But someone could've heard it," Skylar said.

"Dammit." He unplugged the headset and looked at the scorched terminal. "All that work for nothing."

No wonder Vanessa had sided with Diego. Had she already sensed failure yesterday when she'd been in the shack with him?

Skylar touched his arm gently. "You sent your message. That's more than we had yesterday."

"We don't know if it reached anyone." He shook his head and stared at the scorched panel. "If I'd had twenty more minutes—maybe even ten—I could've stabilized the damn voltage."

"You did what you could," she said quietly. "It was our best shot."

He didn't answer right away. The silence in the shack pressed in around him. No hum, no static—nothing but the echo of failure in his own head. He'd poured everything he had into that signal, pushed the equipment further than it was ever meant to go, and now it was dead. No way to know if anyone had heard them. No way to fix it. For all his technical skill, for all the hours he'd spent trying to prove he could make a difference—this might still end with them stranded.

Skylar, who must have sensed his shift in mood, stood and crossed to the doorway, looking toward the east. "What do you think of Diego's idea to try for the beach? Take a boat?"

Noah scoffed. "I really hope that's not our only option."

Diego meant well, but he moved fast—too fast. He wanted to jump into action before thinking it through. A late-night dash across open sand in hopes of having enough time to find the right keys to an unsecured boat? Not when one wrong move could get them all killed. Noah had never been the type to gamble on long odds without a backup plan.

"It's not," she said. "Not yet."

He exhaled and joined her near the door. The ocean shimmered faintly in the distance.

"This place has a good vantage point," he said. "It's elevated, defensible. We have shelter, some supplies, and eyes on the water when help shows up."

Skylar nodded. "And we can rotate watches. Night patrols."

"We hunker down," he said. "Give it a day or two. Let them come to us."

A woman's scream shattered the calm.

Skylar's head snapped toward the sound. "That was nearby."

"Help! Somebody help!"

The sound froze them both for an instant—raw, desperate, unmistakably Mark's voice. Noah pushed through the partially open door and sprinted toward the sound with Skylar close behind.

They found Mark standing at the lip of a steep drop-off on the far side of the ridge, staring down in horror.

"She said she wanted to get some fresh air and sunshine," he sobbed, his voice cracking. "I was getting her a blanket from the cabin. I left her right here."

They approached the overlook. Noah crept to the edge carefully, his gut clenching at the sheer drop, and looked down. Jagged rocks loomed below. At first, Noah didn't see anything but rocks and crashing waves.

Then—

"There," Skylar whispered.

He followed her gaze.

A figure lay at the base of the rocks. Sprawled. Motionless.

"It's Julia." Skylar's face paled.

Julia's blonde hair fanned across the stone, a bloom of red spreading beneath her body.

Noah stared.

Her arms were bent at unnatural angles. Her neck—

His stomach dropped.

No movement. No breath. Just the wind blowing her hair.

"She's dead," he said.

Skylar pressed a hand over her mouth and stepped back. Noah kept looking. Forced himself to.

The image burned itself into his mind.

They were hiding from killers. Running to survive.

Now one of their own was gone.

Vanessa burst out of the casita. Diego appeared over a rise further away.

"What happened?" Vanessa gasped when she joined them, taking in the scene with widening eyes.

"Julia," was all Noah could say, nodding grimly toward the drop-off.

Vanessa approached cautiously, her face paling as she looked over the edge. "Oh no," she whispered.

"I don't understand," Mark kept repeating, pacing back and forth only a foot or two from the cliff. "She was feeling better. Why would she get so close to the edge?"

Diego arrived, took one look and frowned. He let out a slow

breath. "That's... awful." But his voice was flat, as if he didn't quite know how to react.

Noah's mind churned, even through the shock. The situation didn't add up. Julia's ankle was healing, so why would she have wanted to walk so far after yesterday's grueling hike? And why to this dangerous stretch of the ridge without Mark to keep her steady?

He turned from the body and caught sight of Diego.

His expression wasn't quite right. Not blank, not broken. Just... guarded. Something in it gave Noah pause.

Skylar had noticed too. As she stood beside him, she watched Diego with the same quiet focus.

A few paces behind them, Mark had gone still, his expression vacant. Then, slowly, the disbelief gave way. He dropped to his knees with a ragged sound, one hand pressed to his mouth as if trying to hold something in.

Vanessa rushed over to the older man, kneeling beside him, her voice low and steady as she helped him up and guided him back from the ridge, out of full view of the body.

Noah turned away, thinking it through. Vanessa he could rule out—he'd known her for years. Mark seemed entirely focused on Julia, had talked about nothing but their anniversary cruise and the pool he was building her. Skylar had been with him in the comms shack all morning until they heard the shouts for help.

But Diego?

Helpful. Calm. Observant. And a complete unknown.

Diego had been the one to encourage them to come up to the ridge in the first place...to a communications station that appeared to have been sabotaged.

Noah wasn't drawing conclusions. Not yet. But he was starting to watch more closely.

They turned back toward the casita, a slow, subdued

procession. Skylar caught his eye. No words passed between them, but they didn't need any.

Behind them, Mark's sobs broke the quiet. Vanessa stayed close, trying to keep him from unraveling completely.

Across the clearing, a quiet Diego had drifted beyond the casita.

Noah watched him go, a flicker of unease tightening in his chest.

They didn't know who they could trust. Not really.

11

M ark sat hollow-eyed and silent on the edge of the bunk where he'd slept with his wife less than a few hours ago. Vanessa hovered nearby, saying little, but kept busy by dividing the food stores into five piles instead of the six she'd made earlier that day. No one brought up lunch. No one asked the obvious question—what now?

Skylar couldn't let her mind linger on Julia's death, or she'd lose it.

The whole thing was so awful, and it hit a little too close to home...

Six months ago, she'd fallen too. Not off a cliff, but close enough—a rock face in southern Colorado, slick with a late spring frost, during a solo climb. Her boot slipped, her harness lagged by a second, and she dropped nearly thirty feet before hitting the rock shelf below. The snap of her femur and pelvis still echoed in her memory, sharp and final. Her body still knew the feeling—cold stone against her spine, ears full of nothing, and the horrifying certainty that she couldn't move. The pain was instantaneous. The waiting afterward was worse.

She hadn't even screamed, only landed hard, stunned, staring up at the sky while pain wrapped around her like a vise. Although she had an emergency beacon within reach, it had taken hours before help reached her. That part was what stuck with her the most—the stillness. The waiting. Knowing she was vulnerable and couldn't do a damn thing about it.

Panic fluttered in her chest. It had been a while since she'd felt this way—walls closing in, not enough air, lungs tight.

"Excuse me," she managed to say, and scrambled for the door. She needed sunlight, a breeze, something other than this too-close cabin with too many bodies in it.

"Skylar—" she heard Noah say behind her.

Before she could hear anything more, the door slammed shut.

Something drew her to the cliff again. Even knowing Julia's body was still there. As a child, she'd always been fascinated with climbing—trees, monkey bars, ladders. Being up high gave her a feeling of freedom and escape. Right now, she wanted more than anything to escape this place. She wanted to see her brother again, to laugh at his bad jokes, to feel his bear hug around her shoulders when she needed a pick-me-up. He'd been the only one who really understood why she took the risks she did.

Her parents had wanted her to quit climbing. Saying she needed to find a 'real job' and put away such a dangerous 'hobby.' But Ethan knew she needed to climb, as much as someone else needed air to breathe or food to eat. The six months of recovery she'd put in after the accident had been the most difficult period of her life. Without climbing, her mental health suffered. So she'd poured it on...done twice the exercises her physical therapist recommended, even returning to the climbing gym earlier than recommended to work on her grip strength and flexibility.

Ethan had been hoping the wedding cruise would be relaxing for her by taking her out of her element and giving her back the spark he said had been missing since her fall. But look what it had turned into—a living nightmare of guns, criminals, and the threat of death. Climbing the Nose on El Capitan in Yosemite National Park would've been a far better way to find her spark.

Now, walking past the spot where Julia had been found, she tensed. She didn't know what had happened to the poor woman, but she couldn't stop herself from studying the terrain with a climber's eye. Something about the scene bothered her.

She walked straight to the drop-off. At the top of the cliff, the footing was solid. No loose rock, no crumbling edge that might give way unexpectedly. A stable platform like that didn't simply collapse under someone's weight.

Where the ground fell away, there were no signs of struggle —no scrape marks, no torn plants, nothing to suggest someone had clawed for a handhold on the way down. It looked pristine. But the narrow stretch of packed earth and loose stone leading up to it told a different story. Scuff marks that looked as if something—or someone—had been dragged across the rocky ground.

"Are you all right?" asked Noah behind her.

How long had he been standing there?

She turned away from the sheer cliff to face him. "I can't stop thinking about her fall."

Noah's brows drew together.

"Why would she go so close to the edge?" Something wasn't adding up. "Her ankle was still a mess. She could barely walk after she made the climb up here."

Noah leaned forward a little as if to remind himself how far a drop lay below.

"Nothing about it makes sense," he said. "I haven't been able to shake it either."

"She wasn't disoriented. She was only waiting for Mark to come back," she said.

"Where was Diego going anyway? His whole story doesn't make sense," Noah said. "He said he thought he heard a weird noise coming from the jungle to the north, according to Vanessa."

The only other way back down to the beach was the northern route. The more modern 'road' that Diego told them was being built to replace the crumbling path they'd taken yesterday.

"Do you think he pushed her?"

Noah met her eyes. "I don't think we know him. Not really. That's enough to worry me."

Skylar didn't answer right away. Her mind flicked back to the way the Meridian employee had reacted to the news.

"Diego...do you think he looked guilty?" Skylar asked.

"Maybe. Also, he's been acting strange since then. Nervous. Jumpy."

She nodded.

Noah ran a hand through his hair. "Back down in the maintenance building, he's the one that came up with the idea to hike up here. He knew we'd be isolated and trapped on one side by the ocean. Plus, the trail almost killed us; it was so steep."

"But why would he do it?"

"Maybe he was supposed to bring us here for a reason." He gave her a pointed look.

"The museum heist we heard about on the radio? The prisoners landing here? You think Diego could be involved in all of that?"

"The kind of people who plan a prison break as a distraction for a theft could be extremely dangerous." His gaze flicked to the cliff. "And if Diego is working with them—"

"Then Julia's death makes more sense," Skylar said quietly. "Maybe she saw something. Or he was afraid she would talk."

"Agreed." Noah puffed up his cheeks with air and then blew it out. "About the radio—no one else should know we heard those transmissions. If Diego is working with them, the less he knows, the better."

Acid churned in her stomach at the thought that Diego may have pushed Julia off the cliff. How horrible.

"I should head back to the transmitter," said Noah, "and take another crack at fixing it. We need to send out our distress signal now more than ever."

"I can keep Diego occupied," Skylar said, looking over her shoulder at the casita behind them. "He's been asking about your progress—says he might be able to help since he's familiar with the systems here."

"Definitely keep him away," Noah said. "The last thing we need is more sabotage."

As they were about to part ways, Skylar hesitated. "Noah—" His gaze met hers.

"Be careful," she said finally. "I... we need you." Her face heated.

"I will," he said, then shifted his weight as if he had something else to say—but instead headed back in the direction of the comms shack.

When Skylar returned to the casita, she found Vanessa seated outside, face tipped toward the sun. She looked composed at first glance, but her tight grip on the edge of the bench told a different story.

"Any progress on the radio?" Vanessa coolly asked without opening her eyes. It was as if Julia's death hadn't disturbed her at all.

"Some," Skylar said. "Noah thinks he's close to patching something together."

She sat beside Vanessa on the rough bench, its slats sun-warmed and splintering. The pearl necklace at Vanessa's throat caught a glint of the early afternoon light. Not flashy—elegant, old. Skylar guessed antique, maybe inherited. Didn't Noah say she came from a wealthy family? The sort of piece someone wore without thinking, as if it belonged around her neck.

"Those pearls—you've got good taste," she said, nodding at the necklace.

Vanessa cracked one eye open. "Vintage Mikimoto," she said. "Estate sale in Zurich. I couldn't resist."

Of course, she couldn't. Skylar smiled faintly. Even now, with the world narrowed to survival and uncertainty, Vanessa still carried the air of someone who thrived in boardrooms and auction houses.

It made Skylar feel a little boorish by comparison.

"You collect a lot of antiques?"

"When I have the time and the budget." Vanessa gave a dry smile. "Lately it's been more of a browser's hobby.

Skylar paused, then said, "Ever hear of the Saint Marielle Cross?"

Vanessa's eyes opened fully now, but her tone stayed light. "Local legend, isn't it? Gold, emeralds. Colonial something-or-other. I think I saw a replica in a hotel lobby once."

As she spoke, she reached up to adjust her necklace—a quick shift against her sweaty skin.

Skylar nodded slowly, letting it drop.

"You and Noah," she asked, shifting gears, "worked together long?"

"Five years," Vanessa said. "Two of those... closer than just work."

Skylar nodded, pretending it didn't dig somewhere under her ribs. "Didn't seem to have affected your working relationship."

"We're both professionals." Vanessa glanced over, assessing. Always assessing. "He's brilliant with tech. People, less so. Though I think he's made a rare exception."

Skylar didn't look at her. "Excuse me?"

"I know it feels real, honey," Vanessa said quietly, "but this is typical Noah."

There was something gentle in the warning. Not territorial —just honest. Skylar didn't argue. They both knew this wasn't normal life. Probably anything that happened here wouldn't survive whatever came next.

She turned the conversation to keep up her end of the deal with Noah. "Any idea where Diego went?"

That got Vanessa's attention. "You don't trust him."

Wow, she was perceptive.

"Do you?" Skylar asked.

"I don't trust anyone I've known for less than three days," she said smoothly, giving Skylar a pointed look. "But Diego's been...strange. Tense. More so since Julia."

Skylar was about to reply when a figure appeared from around the far side of the casita.

Diego.

He was walking toward them with purpose, brushing dust off his hands.

"How's Mark?" he asked.

"He said he needed space," Vanessa said. "So I've been outside for a while now."

Skylar kept her expression neutral, but her mind was spinning. Had Diego looped near the comms shack?

"And the radio?" he asked, looking at her.

"Noah's working on it," she said noncommittally. "Takes time."

"We should check on him," Diego offered. "Maybe he needs help."

Skylar tensed. She didn't want him anywhere near that shack.

"He prefers to work alone," Vanessa said. "He always has. Yesterday when I was in there with him, he practically bit my head off."

Diego's expression tightened momentarily before he forced a smile. "Gotcha. Guess I'll check the water levels in the cistern instead." He took a bandana out of his back pocket and wiped the sweat from the back of his neck. "I can't stand sitting around doing nothing."

"Need any help?" Skylar asked, starting to rise from the bench. Maybe working alongside the Meridian employee would be the best way to keep tabs on him for Noah.

He waved a hand at her. "Nah, it's not rocket science."

As he walked away, Skylar chewed on her bottom lip.

"Walk with me." Vanessa stood and smoothed out the wrinkles in her linen pants. "I need to stretch my legs."

They took the outer loop trail that led to the southern end of the high plateau they'd turned into their emergency refuge. Once they were far enough from the casita—and the comms shed—Vanessa stopped.

"I mention Diego's been acting strange, and suddenly you want to buddy up with him out of nowhere. What's going on?"

Skylar hesitated. She wanted to trust her. She was sharp, loyal to Noah, and she didn't miss much. But caution had become second nature since yesterday's shocking events.

"I don't think Julia's death was an accident."

"You think she killed herself?" Vanessa said with a horrified gasp.

"No, that's not what I meant."

"Someone pushed her?" She placed a hand in front of her mouth, her eyes wide.

Skylar nodded. "I don't know what happened on that ridge, but the evidence I saw makes me think someone was involved."

Vanessa didn't blink. "Diego?"

"His story's off... and his behavior since..."

"He was too smooth afterward," Vanessa agreed. "As if it barely bothered him."

The confirmation landed heavily.

"Something really weird about him." Had they hitched their hopes to someone who had been involved with the theft at the museum? The prisoners now roaming Tesoro Bay? He'd been so insistent they take refuge up here... were they trying to divide and conquer any remaining cruise passengers?

"If he thought he had a reason to kill Julia, he might find a reason to go after someone else next."

The conversation confirmed one thing for Skylar—whatever complex feelings existed between Vanessa and Noah, the woman wasn't working with Diego. Her concern seemed genuine; her suspicions aligned with Skylar's own. One potential ally in their shrinking circle of trust.

That thought stayed with Skylar long after they turned back toward the casita to prep some kind of afternoon meal out of the odds and ends they'd collected. She glanced toward the communications shed in the distance, a small square shadow sitting out in the middle of a grassy plain, whipped by the afternoon winds. Noah was in there, trying to call for help, working with half-dead equipment and borrowed time. Was he making progress? Had he heard any more transmissions?

She had to believe he'd reach someone. The alternative wasn't worth considering.

12

"Almost there," Noah muttered to himself, connecting the final wire to the makeshift transmitter. His back ached from hunching over the workbench. He'd thought the same thing a few hours ago, right before the whole system had sparked and smoked and died. This time, he triple-checked every connection. With one more adjustment, they might have their lifeline out of this nightmare.

As the heat of the day grew more intense, the shed became uncomfortably warm. If they were still on the cruise with the rest of the passengers, the heat and sunshine would've been welcome. Especially after an abnormally cold and wet New Jersey autumn. Although he didn't agree on Vanessa's idea about a 'relaxing' team getaway—he'd rather be kayaking alone in the Delaware and Raritan Canal State Park for a week—he knew most of the higher ups in Reed Security Systems loved a good social event.

He wondered how his new 'team' was doing. The immediate aftermath of Julia's horrific death had created a fragile truce among them, but Noah knew it wouldn't last. Not with what he and Skylar now suspected about Diego. If it were true, that meant there was a killer among them, disguised as a helpful Meridian employee. Just how much did he know about the prisoners who managed to reach Tesoro Bay? And the heist at the museum? Was he being paid off by someone to ensure none of the stranded passengers interfered with their plan?

Their fastest and safest way out of here was communicating with the outside.

"Come on," he whispered, adjusting the final connections. "Work this time."

He powered up the system and held his breath as the components hummed to life. The improvised frequency display flickered. Looked as if this repair was holding. Heart pounding, Noah picked up the microphone.

"This is Noah Reed at Tesoro Bay communications relay station. Mayday, mayday. Five survivors stranded, one confirmed casualty. We need immediate evacuation. Do you copy?"

Static answered him. He repeated the message, adjusting the tuning slightly. On the third attempt, the static broke.

"—receiving...signal. Very weak. Repeat location."

Relief hit him like a wave—it worked. "Tesoro Bay communications station on Saint Marielle. Five survivors stranded. Northeast side of the peninsula. We need immediate evacuation."

"Understood. Maintain position. Situation fluid and—"

The transmission cut off with a high-pitched whine that faded to silence. Noah's hands froze on the dial. The frequency indicator had gone dark, and no amount of adjustment brought it back.

"No, no, no." He opened the main panel, fingers moving frantically through the wiring. The culprit revealed itself almost immediately—the oscillator crystal had cracked, probably from the humidity or the stress of being pushed beyond its limits. Without it, the transmitter was just a box of useless parts.

"Damn it!" He slammed his palm against the workbench, then stood and paced the small space, running both hands through his hair. So close. Had the transmission been clear enough?

The door opened, and Skylar slipped inside. "I was sent to collect you for an early dinner. Any progress?"

"Crystal's cracked. Transmitter's dead." He rubbed his face with both hands, unable to hide his frustration. "I got a message out, but I don't know if it was enough."

She surveyed the damage. "Did they respond at all?"

The hope in her voice twisted the knife a little deeper. He hadn't realized how much he wanted to give her something that worked.

"Briefly. They acknowledged receiving our signal, but the connection was weak. I don't know how much they understood before that."

Her crestfallen look gutted him more than the blown circuit. His shoulders sagged, frustration and fatigue catching up to him all at once.

"Hey, you got something through." The corners of her mouth lifted, just barely. "That's more than we had before."

He wished he could be as pragmatic as she was. Systems integration was supposed to be his strength—diagnosing failures, rebuilding from the ground up, making broken things work again. But none of that mattered when everything around him was falling apart. In his real life, he would've had a clean workspace, time to think through contingencies, access to every part he needed. Here? He looked across the room at warped shelves stacked with salt-eaten cables and rusted components.

Nothing matched. Nothing fit. Trying to build a transmitter from this mess had been like repairing a watch with a hammer.

He turned back to the ruined transmitter, but there was nothing left to try.

"If we had a spare crystal, maybe I could rebuild it." He set the cracked piece on the workbench. "But we don't. I've gone through everything in this place twice. There's no way to bring it back."

"One problem at a time," she said, echoing words he'd used yesterday on the beach.

The callback landed harder than it should have. Her hand settled on his shoulder—steady, warm—and lingered just long enough to register.

Her touch anchored him in a way he hadn't expected.

What surprised him was how much he didn't want her to leave.

Diego burst into the building, his expression tense. "Storm coming," he announced without preamble, gesturing eastward. "Big one, building fast."

The warmth of her hand vanished the instant the door opened. She pulled away as if it meant nothing. He wouldn't have been able to say the same.

The moment broke as quickly as the weather. Outside, the sky had shifted in only a few hours. Dark clouds massed on the eastern horizon, advancing rapidly toward the island. The clear blue sky of morning had given way to an ominous gray mass, and the wind had strengthened, carrying the electric scent of approaching rain.

Could that be what the voice on the radio meant by 'situation fluid'?

"How far out?" Noah asked.

"Two hours, maybe less." Diego nervously scanned the

horizon. "Tropical systems move fast this time of year. We should secure the casita."

"That doesn't look good." Skylar's brows came together.

The way the treetops bent under the wind spurred him to action. "We'll need to batten down. Block the windows, secure loose equipment." Of course. The moment he'd been close to fixing their communication problem, another obstacle was rolling in.

Somewhere in the trees, a flock of birds lifted all at once—sharp wingbeats vanishing into the darkening sky.

Noah made sure to secure the door to the comms shack with the hope that he could come back to his project after the storm blew past. He hoped a second round with Mother Nature didn't damage things further.

Then, all three of them crested the ridge together, the wind rising at their backs as the casita came into view. Dry leaves skittered over the dirt, chased by larger bits of palm frond that tumbled like paper across the clearing.

Then came a sound—thin but clear—threading through the gusts.

Voices.

Male.

Carrying up from the trail below.

The same unstable switchback they'd barely managed to climb themselves.

Noah froze, locking eyes with Skylar. The Coast Guard couldn't have arrived this fast—not even if the transmission had gone through clean. Which meant...

"Inside," he said sharply. "Now."

They bolted for the cabin. Mark and Vanessa looked up, startled, as the door flew open. Diego shut it behind them and threw the bolt.

"Someone's coming up the trail," said Skylar.

Noah moved to the small window that faced it. What he saw turned his stomach. Four men had reached the top of the trail, weapons in their hands, orange prison-issue clothing bright against the darkened sky. Two of them he knew—the bald prisoner from the pier with his rifle, and the massive tattooed one who'd been searching the maintenance compound and had chased them in the jungle. He moved with the lazy confidence of a man who had nothing left to fear.

"Shit," he breathed. "They came for us."

"How many?" Diego joined him.

"Four. At least two guns that I can see—a rifle on the bald one, a pistol on another. One has a baseball bat." Noah scanned the room. They had no weapons—only tools. The simple slide-bolt lock on the door wouldn't hold long, not against men that size with that kind of intent.

"We need to leave. Now. Before we're boxed in."

"Leave?" Vanessa asked, voice high.

"There's nowhere to go—"

"The new road," Diego said. "It's not finished, but it curves around the back side of this mountain." He jerked his chin northwest. "First half is a mess—downed trees from the hurricane, dirt and mud, but it leads to the northern beach, above the tourist zone."

"What's on the northern beach?" Mark asked, his voice hollow.

"Hopefully, no men in orange. It's our best option right now."

"Pack what you can carry," Noah ordered. "Water, food, first aid. Two minutes, then we move.

They scattered. Noah grabbed his makeshift pack—the vinyl tool bag from the maintenance building—and stuffed it with supplies. Mark already had his canvas bag strapped across his chest, the same one he'd been carrying since the maintenance shack. He stood frozen for a moment, staring at the bunk where Julia had slept, before Vanessa pushed a water bottle into his hands.

Everyone moved fast. A pile of protein bars clattered to the floor. Vanessa shoved the extra water bottles into her satchel, hands unsteady. Skylar zipped the med kit closed and handed it to Diego, who still had room in his backpack. Her eyes flicked to the door.

"They're too close," Mark said. "They'll catch up."

Noah slung his bag over his shoulder and crossed to the window.

The prisoners moved through the clearing, less than a hundred yards away, headed toward the communications shack.

No rescue on the horizon. No cavalry coming over the ridge. Just four dangerous men about to find them.

"We need to go," Noah said. "Now."

They shoved open the back door and rushed into the wind. Rain hit sideways, sharp and cold. The trees bent under it. Every second mattered now.

A shout cut across the clearing.

One of the convicts pointed—right at them. Another raised his weapon.

"This way!" Diego motioned northwest toward a barely visible path that disappeared into the dense foliage behind the casita. "Stay close. It might be rough."

They ran.

Noah took up the rear where he could keep everyone in sight. Skylar's suspicions about Diego echoed in his head. They had no choice but to trust the man. But for all he knew, the Meridian employee could be leading them toward an uncertain escape route.

As they entered the trees, tall palms swayed violently in the wind, offering some protection from the rain but shrouding the trail in shadow. Overhead, the sky rumbled low and angry.

Noah's heart pounded. The path ahead was a gamble—he had no way of knowing if Diego was leading them to safety or straight into trouble. So he focused on Skylar, who was just ahead of him, moving fast but limping slightly. He'd be damned if he let her fall behind now. Not after everything. And Vanessa—whatever history lay between them—she was his responsibility too.

A shout cracked through the storm behind them, followed by the distinctive snap of a gunshot. A bullet whizzed over their heads. Vanessa let out a scream, clamping her hands over her ears.

The prisoners had moved faster than he'd anticipated.

"Run!" Noah shouted.

Adrenaline surged through him, fast and blinding. This was a fear like he'd never experienced before. A rabbit must feel this way being chased by a coyote. Panic, a rush of energy, thoughts heading in all directions at once.

The trail dropped into a steep descent, forcing them into a chaotic, stumbling slide down the muddy slope. Rain lashed their faces. Roots and rocks became hazards underfoot. Noah's aqua shoes slipped twice, but he kept upright—barely.

Flashlight beams cut through the murky jungle behind them. Another shot rang out, this one splintering bark off a tree just inches from Diego's head.

"Keep moving!" Noah yelled. "Stay together!"

Panic wanted to scatter them. But if they broke formation, someone would fall behind. Someone would die.

The path forked unexpectedly, splitting into two narrow trails vanishing in opposite directions.

"Which way?" Mark asked, panic edging his voice.

Diego skidded to a stop. "Left!" he pointed. "Steeper, but

more jungle to hide in, and we'll eventually hit the road. It reconnects near the beach."

Vanessa didn't wait. She bolted left, shoes kicking up mud. The others followed.

Behind them, the voices and flashlight beams grew closer.

Another gunshot cracked through the jungle.

Ahead of him, Skylar staggered—her leg giving out mid-stride—and went down hard. She cried out as her body slid down the right fork.

"Skylar!" Noah lunged for her, caught her arm, only to lose his own footing with her. The mud gave way under both of them, sending them sliding fast and out of control.

"Noah!" Vanessa's voice echoed above them, tight with fear. He looked up in time to see her frozen on the trail, eyes wide. But another burst of gunfire sent her running.

"I've got you," Noah said, gripping Skylar tighter as they tumbled down the right path together. His shoulder slammed hard against a tree trunk, and his breath was punched out of him.

"Keep running!" he shouted to the others, even as he and Skylar tumbled farther down. "We'll circle around!"

He wasn't sure how. Who knew where this trail led? But one thing was certain—he wasn't dying on this island.

13

The last thing Skylar saw before she tumbled down the steep, muddy slope was Diego pulling Vanessa and Mark toward the left fork. The three of them disappeared into the rain and creeping darkness as beams of light slashed through the trees behind them.

She and Noah continued sliding down the muddy incline, unable to gain purchase on the slick ground. The trail—if it could even be called that—immediately deteriorated into little more than a game trail with rivulets of rain creating deeper and deeper ruts in the soft ground. The rain fell harder, which turned the slope into a cascade of mud and loose stones.

When they finally stopped sliding, Skylar found herself pressed against Noah, her hip throbbing. They lay still, catching their breath, listening for any sign of pursuit.

Her heart wouldn't slow. She'd never been this scared—not even during the fall that shattered her body.

"Are you hurt?" Noah asked, his voice barely audible above the storm.

She didn't want to make him worry, so she covered up the truth. "Bruised, but nothing serious. You?"

"Same." His gaze held hers in the dim light, sharp with concern.

As if he didn't quite believe her.

His arms were still around her. She could feel the warmth through soaked clothes, the steady rise and fall of his chest against hers. Part of her wanted to stay right there, only for a minute—to rest, to breathe, to forget how close death was. But that wasn't an option.

Bad men with guns were after them. What happened once they realized she and Noah were right below them off the main trail?

Somewhere in the back of her mind, she could hear Misty —her physical therapist—rattling off reminders about slow progress, controlled movements, avoiding reinjury. Sliding down a muddy jungle trail during a tropical storm probably wouldn't be on Misty's list of rehab exercises.

"What about the others?" she asked.

"They'll be okay." His deep voice rumbled through her. "Diego knows the terrain."

Maybe he was trying to reassure her, but even he didn't sound convinced.

She nodded anyway. Diego possibly couldn't be trusted but seemed frightened of their pursuers. Maybe she'd misjudged him. What choice did she have but to hope Vanessa and Mark were safe with him? Their immediate priority had to be their own survival.

Above them, shouts indicated their pursuers had discovered the fork. One of them shouted orders to the group in a language she didn't understand.

She didn't need a translation to know they were out of time.

"There." Skylar pointed to a narrow ravine cutting across

their path, hidden by a mess of tropical vegetation. "If we can get down there, we might lose them."

They pushed through the undergrowth until the ravine came in to view. Noah knelt next to her at the edge, his clothes plastered to his body, chest heaving from the run.

She assessed the steep descent. Under normal circumstances, she would never attempt such a treacherous climb, especially not with a leg that wanted to cramp when pushed too far and without the proper equipment. But nothing about this was normal, and the alternative—being caught by armed men—was unquestionably worse.

"You first," he said. "I'll follow your line."

Skylar nodded and pushed forward, ignoring the protest in her hip as she lowered herself onto the slick rock. The first few footholds held, but the angle was punishing. Her leg trembled by the third step, muscles tightening in warning.

Noah noticed. "You okay?"

"Keep moving," she said through her teeth, unwilling to admit just how much it hurt.

When she glanced back, he was still standing at the top, watching her with a furrowed brow. Finally, he followed. His foot slipped almost immediately, sending a spray of rocks rattling past her into the darkness below.

He froze for a second, trying to find his footing again. His fear of heights had gotten the better of him.

"Hold on," she said quietly, bracing herself despite the burn in her leg. "Let me help."

Her fear of the scary men chasing them disappeared as her mind focused on the route down. *Just like any other climb*, she told herself. *You got this.*

In a few swift moves, she reached the paralyzed Noah clinging to the canyon wall. She took his hand and guided it to a more secure hold. "Just like on the ridge yesterday," she murmured. "One move at a time."

He nodded, steadied. They kept climbing—slow, careful, side by side. Her shoulder brushed his arm. His breath was ragged. So was hers.

By the time they reached the bottom, her leg was shaking and her hip pain was nearly unbearable. She leaned against the rock wall for support. Noah stood close, his hands braced on his knees, rain dripping from his hair.

She glanced at him—and caught herself staring.

He looked different now. Or maybe not different...just clearer. Warmer. Stronger. There was something in the way he'd trusted her in that moment, how he hadn't questioned her strength, even when she'd barely believed in it herself.

That pull between them—whatever it was—was still there.

When Noah dropped the last few feet into the ravine, he landed hard. His legs burned. His hands were scraped raw. But he was down—and Skylar was there.

He stared up at the slope they'd descended, half-expecting gunfire to rain down from above. Nothing yet. Just wind and rain and the sound of his own breathing.

Skylar stood a few feet away. Mud streaked her pants. Water ran down her face. She was breathing as if she'd barely outrun death. And, damn, if she wasn't the most compelling thing he'd ever seen.

Something in him shifted—sharp, unexpected. Maybe it was adrenaline, or maybe it was her. But it hit hard.

Without thinking, he stepped toward her. She looked up, startled at first, but didn't move.

He kissed her.

It wasn't planned. Wasn't clean or careful. But it was real. Her lips were cold from the rain, but she leaned into him, and that was all the answer he needed. He slid a hand under her jaw, deepening it just slightly—enough to forget, for one stolen second, where they were and what was coming.

Then the voices came—shouts from above, urgent and closing in.

They pulled apart. Skylar touched her mouth as if she didn't trust what had just happened.

Neither of them said a word. There wasn't time.

Noah tugged her hand, pulling her back into motion before the voices above them grew any closer. She was his to protect now. His to keep safe.

And just like that, everything changed.

Before, he'd been focused on survival—how to escape this island, how to make it home in one piece. But that moment had reset something in him. Now he knew—if it came down to it, he'd trade his life to make sure she got out of here alive.

They ran, aqua shoes slipping on the slick stones of the streambed now filling with rainwater. The ravine twisted and widened, opening into a narrow valley choked with underbrush. The storm was in full force now—sheets of water, wind howling as if it wanted to tear the jungle apart.

"We need to find shelter!" Skylar shouted over the roar.

He scanned the hillside. A dark cut in the rocks caught his eye—maybe a shallow cave, maybe nothing at all. But it was better than staying exposed.

"There," he said, pointing. He tightened his grip on her hand and led them toward the shadow in the rock.

The cave wasn't much—only a shallow recess in the cliff face, barely deep enough for shelter—but it was dry.

They ducked inside. Neither of them spoke. Wind screamed through the ravine outside, and rain battered the jungle with relentless force. Whatever sounds might have followed them were swallowed by the storm.

Noah listened anyway. Every snap of wind made his nerves twitch.

Skylar slid down the rock wall beside him, legs stretched out in front of her, one hand massaging her thigh. He didn't need to ask if she was hurting. He could see it in the tightness of her jaw, the way she shifted slowly, managing her pain without complaint.

She wrung out her braid and broke the silence. "Do you think the others made it?"

He wanted to say yes. To believe it. Instead: "Diego knows the terrain."

It wasn't enough. He knew it. She knew it.

Noah stood and moved to the back of the cave, doing a quick sweep. The floor was rough-packed dirt. Craggy rock walls. No signs of any wildlife. No other exit. Just a dead end with better odds than the open jungle.

"If he were really trying to help..." he added.

He didn't finish the sentence. He didn't have to. If Diego was working with the prisoners, Mark and Vanessa could already be in trouble.

A hollow unease settled in his chest. He and Vanessa hadn't been a couple for a while, but they'd built something once—trust, history. He still felt a responsibility to her. And Mark? The man had lost his wife earlier that day. The idea of their being led into a trap made Noah's stomach twist.

"We'll find them once the storm passes," Skylar said. She'd perched on a rock that gave her some elevation, her eyes scanning the opening as if she half-expected one of the criminals to appear at any second. "Right now, we rest and regroup."

She was right.

They had shelter. They'd outrun the men for now. They were soaked, scraped, and exhausted—but alive.

He settled beside her again. Close, but not quite touching.

He hadn't meant for any of this to happen. Not the kiss. Not the pull he felt toward her now, even with everything falling apart around them. But he couldn't deny it anymore.

No matter what came next, he wouldn't leave her behind. Her safety had become more than a mission. It was personal now—lodged somewhere deep, in a place he hadn't let anyone near in a long time.

The air inside the cave was cool and carried the faint scent of damp stone. Outside, the storm raged, the sound of rain on the rock like static. With each minute that passed, the light dimmed further, until the world beyond the entrance blurred into gray.

While sitting on her rock, Skylar sorted through their meager supplies by touch and instinct. She checked water bottles, counted energy bars, tested their flashlight with a quick flick of her thumb.

Noah watched her work. "Thank you," he said quietly. "For helping me on that climb."

She looked up, a strand of hair plastered to her cheek, her eyes catching what little light remained. "You would've made it without me."

He huffed a breath, something close to a laugh. "Maybe. But it was better with you."

He shifted, trying to mask the thought that followed— everything lately seemed better with her.

She held his gaze a beat too long, and the cave felt smaller for it. Darker. Closer. The memory of their kiss flickered through his mind, vivid as lightning—heat against the cold, impossible to forget.

Then she broke eye contact. "We should dry off. Hypothermia's a real thing, even in the tropics." Skylar's practical nature reappeared stronger than ever.

He nodded, forcing his focus back to the moment. "Right."

Maybe he imagined the connection, the warmth beneath her calm exterior. Maybe it was one-sided, a trick of adrenaline and proximity. He'd misread things before.

Vanessa's voice surfaced uninvited from some distant place in his mind. Their breakup over sushi had been quiet, almost polite. A business transaction disguised as an ending.

"You're like an app that updates itself," she'd said, chopsticks poised over her plate.

He'd blinked, thrown off balance.

"Same version," she'd added with a smile, "fewer features every time."

The memory stung more now than it had then. Maybe because made him realize he wanted to be more.

He glanced toward her again. She'd spread her damp Meridian polo over a rock to dry, hugging herself to keep warm in her bikini top and oversized pants. The last of the light died, plunging the cave into darkness. They sat close enough to feel each other's warmth, two survivors waiting for dawn.

14

Neither of them spoke. Outside the cave's narrow opening, the storm continued its assault—wind funneling down the ravine in violent gusts, rain falling in sheets that turned the jungle into a gray blur. It had covered their escape from the armed men, buying them precious time. But now it had become another kind of trap, pinning them in place with mud and rising water and nowhere to go.

Skylar pulled her knees closer to her chest, still waiting for her shirt to dry. After a while, she glanced toward Noah. He'd closed his eyes, head tipped back against the stone. To anyone else he might have looked like a man resting, but she'd spent the last thirty hours with him—running, hiding, surviving—and she'd learned to read the subtle signs. The tension in his shoulders. The faint crease between his brows that never quite smoothed away. The way his fingers tapped an irregular rhythm against his thigh.

He wasn't resting. He was thinking.

That engineer's mind of his was working through scenarios,

contingencies, probabilities. Searching for the solution to keep them alive until rescue came—if it came at all.

Out here, stripped of technology and the controlled environments where he thrived, all that problem-solving intensity had focused entirely on their safety.

She found it easier to study him when his eyes were closed. With the rough stubble darkening his jaw, the capable hands resting loosely on his knees, he wore his quiet strength like a second skin. He wasn't the kind of man who drew attention in a crowded room—no flash, no swagger—but out here, stripped down to essentials, his steadiness had become her anchor.

Yesterday morning, he'd been nobody to her. Another cruise passenger. Another snorkeler stranded out at sea. Now she couldn't picture surviving this without him beside her. That shift should have unsettled her—how quickly he'd become necessary, the flutter in her pulse whenever he looked at her. But for some reason, it didn't.

Not to mention the kiss.

She let the memory rush back—the shock of his mouth on hers in the ravine, rain pouring down around them, his hand sliding under her jaw to pull her closer. It had been impulsive, desperate, and exactly what she'd needed. The memory sat warm in her chest even now, with the storm showing no mercy and danger waiting beyond the cave entrance.

"The transmission," Noah said suddenly, opening his eyes to find her watching him. "Right before the equipment burned out...there was a window. A burst, maybe. Enough to flag that we were in trouble."

Skylar studied him, catching the flicker of stubborn hope in his eyes. "Then we hang on to that," she said. "Until we know otherwise."

"Maybe." He exhaled slowly.

He rubbed a hand across his face. "I keep replaying it— every choice we made since swimming back to Tesoro Bay. Letting Diego lead us up here. Assuming Vanessa was a good judge of character. I'm supposed to be able to see this kind of thing coming."

Skylar sat quietly beside him, her expression unreadable in the fading light.

"You didn't do this," she said finally. "We both made those choices. Together."

She shifted closer in the half-dark, settling beside him on the dirt. Their shoulders brushed, a shared pocket of warmth in the damp chill.

He wanted to believe her, but the knot of guilt in his chest wouldn't loosen. She'd trusted him, and now they were hiding in a hole in the side of a mountain while armed fugitives hunted the rest of their group.

Outside, thunder cracked, echoing off the ravine walls.

"If we get through this," he said, "I'm done letting anyone else call the shots."

No more quiet competence while the loudest voices in the room rewrote his vision. No more retreating into code and numbers because speaking up felt like noise. They'd called him distant, cerebral, safer behind a screen than in front of a crowd. Fine. They'd stripped the title, kept the company, and thought that would be the end of him.

It wasn't.

When he walked back into that building (and he would walk back in), it wouldn't be to ask for his old seat. It would be to take the whole damn table. He was finished apologizing for the way his mind worked. The board wanted a showman?

They'd get a force. He'd spent years building something no one else could have dreamed up; from now on they'd feel the weight of the man who dreamed it.

He was done being a ghost in his own life.

"One problem at a time," she said softly. "We made it off the ridge. We're safe. We're dry—mostly."

For a moment he could only look at her, rain clinging to her lashes, her voice a calm thread in the middle of the turmoil in his head. In less than a day, this almost-stranger had seen him at his worst. She'd watched him dig his fingers into the ravine wall, cursing the drop, fighting vertigo with every step. She hadn't flinched. She'd stayed with him, trusted his half-baked plans, yanked him forward when his nerve broke.

Her gaze met his. "And we have each other."

That last part caught him off guard. Tension bled from his jaw. He couldn't look away. A current snapped taut in the air— fragile, electric, undeniable.

Thunder rolled, sudden and close. The cave shuddered with it.

Skylar flinched beside him, and that's when he noticed the fine tremor running through her. She was soaked to the skin, teeth barely holding back the shiver.

"We need to warm you up." He slid an arm around her and drew her in. "I've got you."

A sharp inhale broke the quiet between them.

"Cramp," Skylar said through clenched teeth, her hand gripping her thigh.

Noah shifted instantly. "Here—let me." He reached for her leg, his fingers finding the tense muscle just above her knee. "Breathe through it."

She did, her breathing shallow, teeth clenched. His hands moved in slow circles, coaxing life back into the cramped muscle beneath her borrowed pants.

He told himself it was only about keeping her warm, but the truth sat heavier in his chest.

The muscle was knotted hard as rope under his palm. Each slow press dragged a faint tremor through her leg. He could feel the exact shape of her fatigue, the way she'd pushed past every limit for him without complaint, and now here it was, trembling under his fingers like proof.

He kept the pressure steady, deliberate, but he didn't rush. Not when the curve of her thigh fit his grip, as if it had been waiting there. Not when every small hitch in her breathing told him the pain was easing. Not when he realized he didn't want to let go.

"Better?" he asked after a moment.

She nodded but didn't move away. He didn't either.

His world had shrunk to just Skylar: the quick, shallow pull of her breath, the small, stubborn pulse jumping at the base of her throat, the quiet fire that burned in her even when she was half-frozen and shaking. He knew he should say something safe, something that would put distance between them again. Instead, he kept his hand on her leg, thumb resting against the fading knot of muscle, and met her eyes without a word.

He wasn't ready to let go. Not yet.

Before he knew what he was doing, he leaned in, drawn by some force he didn't have the will to fight. Their lips met— tentative at first, then deepening, urgent, as though the fear and exhaustion of the last two days had found one outlet they both understood.

The world beyond the cave disappeared. Wind, thunder, the threat of pursuit—all of it fell away. Nothing existed but her warmth against him, the soft drag of her mouth, the taste of rain on her skin.

When she finally pulled back, her forehead rested against

his, their breaths unsteady, mingling in the narrow space between them.

"I didn't expect this," she whispered.

"I know." His thumb brushed her cheek, lingering at the corner of her mouth. "Neither did I."

He hadn't anticipated needing her—not like this. But in the dark, something inside him gave way. Cupping the back of her neck, he traced the damp strands of her hair that had come free of her braid. He wanted to keep her close for one moment longer.

She didn't pull away.

He kissed her again—slower this time, conscious, a choice instead of an impulse. Her hand pressed against his chest. He breathed her in, trying to memorize the sensation before the storm—and everything else waiting for them—could take it away.

Noah's kiss was better than she'd imagined—controlled at first, then deepening with a heat that caught her off guard. Beneath his staid exterior, something passionate and raw had been waiting for the right moment to break free. As his lips moved against hers, she couldn't help but wonder how Vanessa had ever let a man like this slip away.

Her fingers slid into his hair. He groaned softly into her mouth before easing her down until she lay against the cool cave floor. Braced on either side of her, he hovered close, as his lips traced the curve of her neck.

Moments ago she'd been shivering. Now, heat pooled low and steady inside her, spreading outward until she forgot the cave, the cold, the dirt. For once, her mind didn't race ahead—it drifted, floating somewhere between fear and release. After twenty-four hours of running and six months of recovery, she needed this brief escape.

Rehab had consumed her—hours spent forcing her body to cooperate again, pushing harder than her therapist thought wise. Her work, her passion, her sense of self all depended on her strength returning. Guiding others up a cliff, watching fear turn into triumph—that was the high she'd lived for.

Her romantic life had withered in the process, and what little it had offered came from men cut from the same cloth: climbers, thrill-seekers, adrenaline chasers. Noah was none of those things, yet as he slid one strap of her bikini top from her shoulder and pressed a tender kiss against her collarbone, she realized she'd underestimated quiet men. His touch was deliberate, reverent. Each brush of his lips stripped away another layer of fear, leaving only the aching need to feel alive again.

His lips teased his way from her collarbone to her bared breast. She cupped the back of his head, fingers tightening as her leg bent, drawing him closer.

Each touch dulled the throb in her hip, softened the pain that had shadowed her since the accident. The image of Julia's body on the rocks, the gunfire on the trail, the question of whether rescue would ever come—all of it slipped further away. There was only Noah. Only the steady heat of him and the quiet certainty that he was real, that this moment was theirs.

He lifted his head, searching her face as if asking permission without words. She answered with a touch, a breath, a whisper that wasn't really a word at all.

And then there was nothing but the warmth of skin against skin, the soft hitch of breath, and the surrender to something that had been building since the moment they met—until the world outside ceased to exist.

By the time words returned between them, the rain had softened to a steady hiss. The storm hadn't passed, not really, but the urgency that had driven them together had burned itself down to a quiet hum. Skylar sat up first, tugging her bikini top into place and getting up to grab her Meridian polo shirt. Noah watched her in the faint light, struck by how quickly the world could tilt—from survival to something far more complicated.

Once she was dressed, Skylar sat next to him and leaned her head against his shoulder.

"Do you think Diego betrayed us?" she asked after a while, voice low, shattering whatever spell had settled over them. "Suggesting that incomplete road as our escape route..."

Noah exhaled and raked a hand through his hair. "I don't know." He took her hand, lifted it to his mouth, and brushed a kiss across her knuckles. "It seemed as if he genuinely wanted to help. And if he wanted to hand us over, why not lead us straight to them?"

"To isolate us? Lead us somewhere with no way out?"

"Maybe," Noah said. "But the road gives us options—faster travel, easier navigation. If he wanted us trapped, he could've suggested we head deeper into the jungle."

"Unless the road leads exactly where they want us to go."

"It's possible." He stood, brushing grit from his palms, and started pacing the narrow strip of ground. Movement seemed to help him think—or perhaps it kept him from thinking too much. "Or maybe he really was trying to help."

Skylar studied him. His lips had twisted when he said 'maybe.' If Diego had been working with the prisoners, he'd had countless chances to betray them already. So why wait until now?

"Where does that leave us?" she asked quietly. "If not Diego, then who killed Julia?"

"I don't know," he admitted. "But right now, survival comes first. We sort the rest out if we make it off this island alive."

When we make it off, she wanted to say, but the uncertainty in his tone stopped her. His doubt shook her more than the danger itself.

"We've made it this far," she said instead. "We'll make it the rest of the way."

He stopped pacing. Maybe her conviction pulled him back from his negative thinking. She reached out, a small, deliberate movement, and his hand met hers halfway. Their fingers laced together, a silent agreement. The warmth of his palm grounded her as much as it seemed to ground him.

He sank down beside her again.

The memory of what they'd just done still hung thick in the small cave—skin sliding on skin, her back against cool stone, his mouth hot on her throat. She could feel the faint burn where his stubble had scraped her, the ache low in her body that proved it hadn't been a dream. Something between them had cracked open, and she wasn't ready to look straight at it yet.

She began sorting their few supplies, speaking in practical tones about food, the climb down, possible rendezvous points. But she could feel his eyes on her as she worked, that quiet intensity she'd come to recognize. When she glanced up, he was watching her with an expression she couldn't quite read.

When she whispered that her fingers were still freezing, he simply tightened his grip and slid his other hand over theirs, rubbing slow, deliberate circles—friction, warmth, and something far less innocent building between their layered palms.

"Better?" he asked.

"Much," she said softly.

They stayed like that, hands locked, until the wind outside thinned to a low moan and finally died.

The jungle had gone silent, as if the world itself were holding its breath. No sound of pursuit reached them. The reprieve seemed fragile, like everything else they'd built in the past two days.

Noah shifted, drawing her in until her shoulder tucked under his and her head rested against the steady drum of his heartbeat. She let herself sink into the solid warmth of his chest without resistance. Outside, the storm would pass, and the danger would circle back soon enough. But right now, in this pocket of darkness that belonged only to them, the world could wait.

DAY THREE

15

Skylar woke with a start, disoriented by the pitch-dark stillness. For a fleeting second, she didn't know where she was—the smell of wet earth, the weight of damp air, the uneven ground beneath her. Then memory returned. The cave. The storm. The desperate flight through the jungle.

A weak gray light seeped through the narrow entrance. Her body ached from the cold floor, her clothes still faintly damp, but she realized she'd slept—really slept—for the first time since the nightmare began.

Noah's arm draped over her waist, his breath warm against her neck. They'd curled into each other through the night, first for warmth, then... something more. A memory flickered—soft kisses tracing the curve of her neck—intimate and electric in the pre-dawn darkness.

Careful not to wake him, she shifted a little to study him. His face, softened by rest, looked almost unfamiliar without the furrow of concentration she'd grown used to. A lock of hair had fallen across his forehead, and she had to stop herself from brushing it away.

Noah stirred. His eyes opened, meeting hers in the muted gloom. Neither spoke at first.

"Hi," he murmured, voice rough.

"Hi," she replied softly, the single word carrying an unexpected hint of shyness.

His fingers brushed a damp strand of hair from her cheek, lingering there. "I thought I might've dreamed last night."

"Not a dream," she said, leaning slightly into his palm.

He studied her for a long moment—eyes drifting to her lips. Somewhere in the distance, a bird called out, sharp and real, dragging them from their fragile bubble.

"We should get moving." Skylar pulled back. "Find water. Get our bearings."

His hand gripped hers as she rose, a quiet promise that lingered even after he let go.

Noah stood, rolling the stiffness from his shoulders with a low grunt. "Storm's passed. Full daylight soon. We can use the sun to navigate."

They moved in the half-dark, slow and deliberate. Skylar dug through her pack first: one bottle of water left between them. She took the smallest sip, then passed it over. Noah drank, wiped his mouth with the back of his hand, and handed it back without comment. Next came the last of the dried mango someone had stuffed in a side pocket in their scramble to leave the casita—three leathery slices each, chewed slowly so the sweetness lasted.

She wiped the grit from her pants and shirt while he crouched at the cave mouth, listening. Nothing moved outside except wet leaves dripping.

She swallowed, letting the faint sugar settle on her tongue, and allowed herself one thin thread of hope. If Mark, Vanessa, and Diego had made it through the night, they could already be waiting at the north beach. According to Diego, that stretch of coastline was undeveloped and wild—separated from the tourist zone by difficult terrain. The convicts had taken over the resort areas, but the north beach appeared to be isolated, unreachable. If they could find their way there, they could stay hidden until the authorities arrived.

Skylar slid her arms through the pack straps and cinched them tight. Noah met her eyes, gave the smallest nod. Together, they stepped out of the cave into the pale, clean light of morning.

Once outside, Skylar scanned the jungle beyond the ravine, orienting herself.

"North should be that way," Noah said, pointing down the ravine where the last of the storm drained away. "If this drainage keeps heading downhill, it ought to take us toward the coast."

"And hopefully to the others," she said. *If they made it out.* The image of gunfire flashing through the trees came back sharp—the shouts, the upheaval, the panic. For all she knew, the men in orange had caught up with them already. She pushed the thought down and kept moving.

"That's what I'm counting on." His voice carried a thread of forced confidence. He glanced up through the trees, where the last wisps of fog drifted toward the clearing sky. "With any luck, they managed to evade those escapees with Diego's help."

The odds didn't look good after what they'd witnessed yesterday. But what would be the point of being negative? They had to hope the three of them managed to get away. To think anything differently was too awful to consider.

As they followed the drainage to the northwest, the silence stretched between them. Finally, Noah said quietly, "Maybe they found shelter closer to the beach. We'll catch up." It sounded less like reassurance and more like a hope he was clinging to.

"I keep thinking about Julia," Skylar said quietly. "How she died right there on the rocks, and we just... left her."

"We didn't have a choice."

"I know," Skylar said. "But I keep thinking—why her? What if she saw something she shouldn't have when Mark went back for that blanket?"

"Then Vanessa might be in more danger than we thought." A muscle jumped in Noah's cheek. "If Diego's involved somehow..." He trailed off, then pushed forward with more urgency. "We need to reach that beach. Make sure they're okay."

Skylar heard the helplessness in his voice. "Let's just hope we're not too far off course."

Their unexpected slide off the main trail could've dumped them miles from the beach. For all they knew, they were headed toward a cliff, a stretch of jagged rocks, or nowhere the Coast Guard would ever find them.

"They'll be at the beach," Skylar said, half to him and half to herself. "They have to be."

Noah's gaze slid toward her. "You don't sound convinced."

"Neither do you."

The storm had left its mark everywhere. Mud and debris had washed out the faint path they'd been following for the last hour.

"Did you lead a lot of expeditions in Colorado?" Noah asked after they navigated over a fallen tree blocking the trail.

Skylar smiled at the hint of admiration in his voice. "Expeditions? I wasn't exactly an Arctic explorer."

Noah laughed.

"Some guided climbs," she continued, "but mostly weekend

escapes. The mountains were my sanctuary whenever the real world got too complicated."

"What complications were you escaping?"

"Relationships, mostly." She tested her footing on a slick rock. "I have a talent for picking men who claim to love my independence until they actually experience it."

Noah glanced at her, curious.

"My last boyfriend said he was excited about dating a 'fearless adventurer.'" She rolled her eyes at the memory. "Then he spent six months trying to convince me that weekend climbing trips were 'immature' and I should focus on 'building a real future.' Which apparently meant moving into his condo and taking a desk job."

"Let me guess—he lasted exactly six months?"

Skylar laughed. "Just about. I came home early from a climbing trip with a sprained ankle, and he launched into this lecture about 'reckless behavior' and 'growing up.' I packed my bags that night."

"His loss," Noah said simply.

The straightforward response made her cheeks heat. She was acutely aware of his presence beside her, the memory of his touch in the cave still vivid. She cleared her throat. "What about you? Had to be hard working alongside your ex."

A flicker of something guarded passed across his face. "Sometimes. But she's good at what she does. I couldn't afford to lose her just as the company was starting to take off."

"Seems as if she still has a thing for you." The words came out before Skylar could stop them. Since they'd met, Vanessa had inserted herself into everything Noah was doing.

He looked genuinely surprised. "Really?"

"She can be a little hard to read..." Maybe she'd said too much. Vanessa had seemed intelligent enough, but she'd kept herself separate from the group—detached, coolly clever. Skylar mentally winced at her own uncharitable assessment.

"That's accurate." He held back the branch of a tropical shrub and let Skylar pass. "Vanessa comes from old money—the kind where emotions are messy and therefore not to be trusted. Everything gets filtered through logic and control. Even relationships."

"That sounds exhausting."

"It was." His eyes found hers with an intensity that made her breath catch. "Last night was the opposite of exhausting."

Heat flooded her face, but she didn't look away. The intimacy they'd shared in that cave—desperate and tender and overwhelming—had changed something fundamental between them.

"We just met," she said softly—not quite a protest, more an acknowledgment of the improbability of what was happening between them.

"I know." Noah reached for her hand, his fingers intertwining with hers. "Doesn't make it any less real."

Her fingers tightened around his. Whatever this was, it wasn't one-sided. They'd crossed a threshold last night that went beyond simple attraction. She'd let herself be vulnerable with him in a way she hadn't with anyone in a long time.

His thumb traced circles on her palm.

"I think I need someone who can pull me out of my head occasionally," he said quietly.

Skylar squeezed his hand. Around them, the jungle had begun to wake—birds calling through the canopy, insects buzzing in the humid air. The storm had washed everything clean, leaving behind the rich scent of wet earth and green growth. Ahead, the drainage continued its descent toward the coast, toward rescue or more danger or both.

She didn't know what awaited them at the beach. Didn't

know if Vanessa, Mark, and Diego had made it, if help was coming, if they'd survive another night. But she could count on the feel of Noah's calloused palm against hers, the steady rhythm of his breathing as they walked, the way he kept glancing back to make sure she was still there.

For now, that was real. That was something to hold on to.

They kept moving, one step and then another, into whatever came next.

Noah wiped sweat from his face with a muddy forearm, breathing in the thick jungle air. His life in New Jersey—the climate-controlled office, the catered lunches, the parking garage—seemed oddly distant now, almost as if it had been someone else's existence. The endless meetings, the technical challenges, the corporate politics—all of it felt hollow compared to this. Somehow the events on this trip had clarified everything. What did success mean without someone to share it with?

"What happens after?" he asked suddenly. "With us."

Skylar glanced back at him. "If we get off this island, you mean?"

"When," Noah corrected, forcing optimism into his voice. "When we get off this island."

"Look who's being hopeful now," she said with a hint of warmth in her voice.

She was quiet for a moment, her aqua shoes crunching over fallen palm fronds. "I don't know. You go back to your life; I go back to Colorado. We...call each other?"

"I'd like that," Noah said, the understatement almost comical given the intensity of his feelings. "The calling part.

And the visiting part. And maybe...exploring whatever this is between us."

Skylar paused on the trail, turning to face him fully. Her hair was tangled, her borrowed clothes torn and stained, but she'd never looked more beautiful. "You mean that?"

"Colorado's not that far from New Jersey." Now that he'd found this woman who'd turned his life upside down, he wasn't about to let her disappear. "Reed Security has clients all over the West. I could arrange more business trips in that direction."

A smile played on her lips. "I've always wanted to climb the Gunks in Minnewaska State Park."

The normalcy of the conversation—planning visits, discussing geographic proximity—felt surreal against the backdrop of their situation. Yet Noah needed this reminder that life might continue beyond this moment. That they might have a future.

"First, we have to reach that beach," Skylar said. "How much further do you think it is?"

"A few miles, if we're lucky." Noah raked his fingers through sweat-matted hair. "But I keep thinking—an isolated beach means no pier, no easy landing for the Coast Guard. They could sail right past without seeing us."

"So, what do we do?"

"Make ourselves visible. Spell out SOS with rocks or driftwood on the sand, build a signal fire if we can manage it." His mind worked through the logistics. "Anything that stands out from the air or water."

"If we have time before someone else finds us first."

"Yeah," Noah said quietly. "That's the gamble."

The terrain gradually shifted. The dense jungle began to thin, allowing more sunlight to filter through. Gulls wheeled in the widening patches of sky, their cries thin and lonesome. The beach couldn't be far.

The prospect of reaching their destination brought mixed emotions. On one hand, they might find Vanessa, Diego, and Mark safely waiting for them. On the other hand, the beach could expose them to anyone searching—Coast Guard or escaped prisoners alike. And if Diego was involved with the plot somehow, they could be walking straight into an ambush.

As the trees thinned further, Noah caught glimpses of white sand and turquoise water through the gaps in the foliage.

So close.

"Wait." Skylar stopped abruptly, her hand shooting out to grip his arm. "Voices."

They froze. The murmur of conversation carried on the breeze—not from the direction of the beach, but deeper in the jungle to their left. Multiple voices, some raised in argument.

"We should check it out," Noah said quietly. He hoped it was their friends, but his gut told him otherwise. "Carefully."

They moved as silently as possible up a gradual rise, the ground beneath their feet shifting from soft jungle soil to exposed rock and hard-packed earth. Skylar led the way, her climber's balance evident in how she navigated the uneven terrain without making a sound.

As they climbed higher, the landscape changed dramatically. The dense jungle gave way to sparse ground cover—low scrub brush, scattered palms, and sun-bleached grasses that offered little concealment. The volcanic rock beneath showed through in patches, dark and pitted.

Noah's pulse quickened as the slope steepened into the final crest. They would be out in the open up here, visible to anyone below who happened to look up.

As they drew closer, the voices grew clearer—rough, aggressive tones punctuated by occasional laughter. Not the sound of their friends from the bluff.

They both dropped to a crouch as they approached the top.

A cluster of wind-twisted shrubs marked the edge. They crawled the last few feet on their bellies, peering down into the depression below.

.What Noah saw made his blood run cold.

A makeshift camp occupied the clearing below—tarps strung haphazardly between trees, some still flapping loose where the wind had torn them free, puddles pooled in their sagging centers. A small fire burned in a sheltered pit ringed with damp rocks, smoke curling through branches still dripping from the night's storm. Supplies were scattered around: water bottles rolling in muddy ruts, resort towels streaked with dirt and leaves, a cache of food packages torn open and half-consumed, their wrappers plastered to the wet ground.

But it was the people that seized his attention.

At least ten men in orange prison uniforms moved through the camp, some carrying makeshift weapons—sharpened sticks, rocks, what might have been a guard's baton—a few had rifles. Their movements were casual, confident. Broken branches, trampled ferns, and a freshly hacked path at the edge of the clearing made it clear they'd carved this place out in a hurry and claimed it. This wasn't a group on the run—this was a group in control of their territory.

And huddled in the center of the clearing, watched over by two guards, were approximately twenty civilians. Cruise passengers, Noah realized with growing horror. Men and women in resort wear, some streaked with mud and rain, all terrified. They sat close together on the churned, waterlogged ground, some with their hands bound, others simply too afraid or exhausted to attempt escape.

"Oh, God," Skylar breathed beside him.

Noah scanned the faces of the captives, searching desperately. His heart lurched as he studied each person—the elderly couple huddled together, the middle-aged woman with blood on her shirt, the two men sitting with their heads in their hands.

No Vanessa. No Mark. No Diego.

Relief flooded through him, immediately followed by guilt. These people were someone's family, someone's friends. But at least Vanessa wasn't among them. At least she was still out there somewhere, possibly safe.

Beside him, Skylar had gone rigid, her breathing shallow and quick.

Noah turned to look at her and saw the color drain from her face.

"Ethan," she whispered.

16

Skylar's breath caught painfully in her throat.

The world contracted to a single point—a man sitting against a tree trunk at the far edge of the camp. Tall, athletic build, sandy hair matted with blood down one side of his face.

"It's Ethan." Her voice cracked on her brother's name.

Every instinct screamed at her to move, to run to him, consequences be damned. She shifted forward, but Noah's hand locked around her wrist.

"Wait," he whispered urgently. "Look at the guards."

Her brother was supposed to be safe on the ship with his fiancée and the rest of the wedding party. If she'd known he'd been stranded like her, she never would've run off with Noah. Despite everything that had happened between them yesterday, she would've chosen her brother. No question.

Tears burned behind her eyes.

Get your crap together, Skylar. Ethan needs you.

Noah's words forced her to focus. Too many armed men. Too many hostages who could get hurt in any confrontation. No clear escape route.

"We need a plan," she admitted.

"We'll help him," Noah said. "But rushing in gets us all killed."

Her eyes never left her brother's bloodied face. "He's hurt."

"The bleeding looks like it's stopped." Noah's voice remained steady. "He's conscious, sitting upright. Those are good signs."

A guard approached Ethan, saying something they couldn't hear. Skylar tensed, ready to reveal herself if necessary. But the man simply handed Ethan a water bottle before moving on.

"They're keeping them alive," Noah observed. "They need them for something."

"Bargaining chips?" She thought about what they'd over-heard on the radio. "They don't want to go back to prison. Maybe they want to trade hostages for safe passage off the island?"

"Maybe. Which means your brother isn't in immediate danger."

Logic warred with emotion as Skylar watched Ethan shift position, wincing. He'd always been her protector growing up —the one who faced down bullies, who taught her to ride a bike, who cheered loudest at her first climbing competition. Seeing him hurt and vulnerable unsettled her on a funda-mental level. His fiancée, Kayla, must be frantic not knowing what happened to him.

"We should head to the beach," Noah suggested quietly. "See if we can find Vanessa and the others. Come back with a real plan."

"What if they move him?" Skylar countered. "What if we can't find this place again?"

"Skylar." Noah's voice was gentle but firm. "We can't help him if we're caught too."

She knew he was right. "He's my brother."

"I know. But charging in there—"

"Can we at least watch for a while? Figure out exactly how many guards there are, when they move around?"

"One hour. Then we go to the beach."

They settled into better positions behind the scrub, cataloging everything: guard rotations, the number of hostages, weapons count, the layout of the camp.

Skylar's gaze kept returning to her brother. Even injured and captive, he was checking on the other hostages, especially a frightened-looking younger man beside him.

"He's keeping up morale," Noah said, sounding impressed.

"That's Ethan. Always taking care of everyone else."

"Like his sister." Noah's hand found hers, his thumb brushing across her knuckles.

The simple comparison nearly broke her composure. She bit the inside of her cheek to keep it together.

"Hour's up," Noah said eventually. "We need to move."

Every cell in her body rebelled against leaving, but Skylar nodded. They needed help, resources, a better plan than two unarmed people against a team of armed thugs.

"We're coming back for him," she said, the words somewhere between promise and threat.

"I know," Noah agreed, squeezing her hand. "We will."

They retreated carefully, putting distance between themselves and the camp before speaking at normal volume again. Leaving Ethan there was like tearing off a piece of herself. She burned to sprint back, call his name, pull him into her arms. After days alone with practical strangers, she longed for the comfort of family.

If the others didn't agree to help rescue her brother, she'd find a way to do it herself.

She glanced back toward the camp.

As if reading her mind, Noah stopped her with a hand on her arm. "I need you to promise me something."

She raised an eyebrow.

"No solo rescue attempts. We do this together."

Skylar bristled. "I wasn't planning—"

"Weren't you?" His voice remained gentle. "I saw your face when you spotted him. If I hadn't been there..."

She couldn't deny it. How did this man read her so well after only a couple of days? "Fine. Together. But I'm not leaving this island without my brother, Noah. Non-negotiable."

"Understood."

His respect for her decision hit harder than any rational argument could have.

"I'm sorry," she said suddenly. "I'm being selfish. Vanessa is still out there somewhere. You must be worried sick."

A shadow crossed his face. "It's not the same. You and Ethan are family."

"But she matters to you." Skylar's conscience pricked. "And I'm making you wait here when we should be trying to find her and the rest of our friends."

"The plan doesn't change," Noah said firmly. "We reach the beach, meet up with everyone. Then we come back for Ethan with more people, better odds."

They resumed their trek, backtracking until they reached the drainage. The sun climbed higher, turning the humid air into a furnace. Sweat soaked through Noah's borrowed shirt within minutes. Beside him, Skylar had gone quiet, all her energy focused on maintaining pace.

The terrain shifted as they neared the ocean, with sandy soil replacing the muddy path. They stopped twice to rest in whatever shade they could find, rationing the last of their water. Noah's legs burned. His feet had gone numb in the aqua shoes that were never meant for this kind of distance. But Skylar never complained, never asked to stop longer than necessary, so neither did he.

The sound reached them first—the distant rhythm of waves against shore. Then the salt smell on the breeze. The scrub thinned further, transitioning to coastal grasses and wind-sculpted trees.

When the first stretch of white sand finally became visible through the palms, Skylar stopped walking. Noah turned back to check on her, concerned about her leg, but she was staring at the wild, beautiful beach. They'd made it.

A smile broke across her face, tired but genuine. He found himself smiling back.

Noah stood at the edge of the sand, staring at the empty beach ahead.

How the hell were they supposed to rescue a hostage from an armed camp? Two people against ten guards with weapons. No guns, no backup, no resources beyond their wits and what-ever they could scavenge. The odds were insane.

Yet he'd promised Skylar they'd find a way.

Pristine white sand stretched in a crescent curve before them. Noah scanned the shoreline for any sign of their companions—footprints or even disturbed sand. Anything that might indicate the rest of their group had reached the rendezvous point.

Nothing.

"They should have been here by now," he said, unease building. "Even with the storm and rough terrain, they had a head start."

Skylar's gaze traveled across the sand to the water's edge.

"No tracks, but the tide's been in and out. Rain too. Could've erased everything."

"Or they never made it at all."

"Then we search. But those armed men were right behind them when we split up. If they followed them here..." She didn't finish the thought. "We need to be careful."

They moved parallel to the beach, keeping to the shadows where jungle met coastline. Big chunks of driftwood and exposed volcanic rock concealed them as they worked their way north. The beach curved gradually, the pristine sand giving way to even more sharp volcanic formations along the water's edge.

"Wait." Skylar stopped, hand on his arm. "There. Beyond the rocks."

Noah followed her gaze. In a small cove on the far side of an outcropping, partially hidden from the main beach, three figures stood close together. Even at this distance, he recognized them—Vanessa's rigid posture, Diego's compact frame, Mark's larger build.

Relief hit him hard. They'd made it. All three had survived.

Then the relief soured. Vanessa's arms were crossed defensively. Diego was gesturing sharply, his movements agitated. Mark stood too close to both of them, his stance aggressive.

"Something's wrong," Noah said quietly.

As they crept closer, fragments of conversation reached them, carried on the salt-tinged breeze.

"...can't wait any longer," Diego was saying, his voice urgent. "That boat—it's our way off this island. We need to leave now."

Boat?

Noah shifted position behind the rocks, straining to see past the three figures. There—a small fishing vessel pulled onto the sand, its hull scraped and weathered, partially hidden by beach grasses.

Where had that come from?

"Nobody's leaving," Vanessa said, her voice carrying the same controlled tone she used when closing difficult deals. "Not until I see the Cross. Then we discuss terms."

The Cross? Terms?

"That's not how this works," Mark snapped. He reached inside the canvas bag he'd been carrying since they left the resort—the one he'd guarded so carefully, the one that had seemed oddly important even in the middle of their escape. "I need payment now. My contact won't hand over the merchandise without it."

"What contact?" Diego asked, confusion clear in his voice. "Mark, what are you talking about?"

"You still haven't figured it out?" Mark's voice dripped with contempt. "Vanessa hired me to broker a deal for the Saint Marielle Cross. Vanessa pays me. Then, he hands it over when I pay him. Simple."

Mark's hand lifted out of the bag. When it came back up, metal glinted in the sunlight.

A gun.

Noah's chest tightened. Mark was armed. Mark—the grieving husband, the man who'd seemed shattered after Julia's death—was aiming a gun at Vanessa and Diego.

Beside him, Skylar went rigid.

"Mark, what are you doing?" Diego demanded, backing away.

"Insurance," Mark replied, his voice flat. "You two know too much. Can't have you running to the authorities when we reach the mainland."

"We had a deal," Vanessa said, raising her hands slowly. "I pay you, you deliver the Cross, everyone walks away clean."

"Had," Mark emphasized. "Past tense. The whole arrangement depended on a wire transfer. Two million, clean and untraceable. But those prisoners knocked out the cell tower, and now there's no signal anywhere on this damn island. No Wi-Fi, no cell service, no way to move money. My entire payment plan is dead."

"Then take these." Vanessa's hand moved slowly to her neck, to the multi-strand pearl necklace she'd somehow kept through everything—the one with the distinctive luster of natural pearls. "They're antique. I'm sure they're worth two million, maybe more. Your contact can verify their authenticity in five minutes."

Mark's eyes flickered to the pearls, and Noah saw the hesitation—the greed warring with frustration.

"My contact wanted cash," Mark snarled. "Clean money he can move without a trace. Jewelry means he has to fence it, find a buyer, take risks he didn't sign up for. He's not going to like it."

"Cell service is dead, Mark. You just said it yourself." Vanessa's voice stayed steady despite the gun pointed at her. "Cash isn't an option anymore. These pearls are real; they're here, and they're worth what you owe him. Take them or walk away with nothing."

"You think I don't know that?" Mark's desperation finally broke through. "That's exactly the problem. Without payment, he won't hand over the Cross, and I'm a dead man." He gestured sharply with the gun. "The prison break destroyed my timeline. My Shell Beach pickup fell through—I had to scramble to arrange this boat. Do you know what that cost me? Everything is falling apart, and pearls aren't what he asked for!"

"They're better than showing up empty-handed," Vanessa said coolly. "Because right now, that's your only alternative."

Diego took a step back, hands up. "I don't understand what's happening—"

Mark's jaw clenched. "Get on the boat. Both of you."

"And if I refuse?" Vanessa asked.

Mark gestured with the gun toward Diego, who had gone very still. "Then, our helpful guide here pays the price. And you're next. I can't let either of you walk away knowing what you know."

Noah struggled to process what he was hearing. This wasn't about escaping the island—this was about smuggling. Stolen artifacts. Black-market deals.

"Nothing personal," Mark said, his voice cold. "Business. Nothing more."

Diego lunged forward, going for the gun. The two men grappled, a brief tangle of limbs before a sharp crack split the air.

Diego stumbled backward. A dark stain spread across his shirt, blooming fast. He stared down at it with something like confusion before his knees buckled and he dropped to the sand.

"No!" Vanessa started forward.

Mark swung the gun toward her. "Don't."

Skylar's hand clamped around Noah's wrist, her grip iron-tight. He could sense the tremor running through her, the effort it took to stay still, to not reveal their position.

They'd been wrong. Catastrophically wrong. Not Diego—Mark. Mark was behind Julia's death. All this time, they'd suspected the wrong person.

"Get in the boat," Mark ordered, gesturing with the weapon. "Now. You're coming with me to make the exchange."

Vanessa didn't move. Her hands trembled at her sides. Her eyes were fixed on Diego, the man who'd saved all their lives at the resort by leading them through the jungle to safety, shot dead because Vanessa's hunger for some priceless artifact had put them all in the crosshairs.

"I said, move!" Mark barked.

Her hand went to her necklace. "Not until I see the Cross. That was the deal."

"The deal," Mark said through gritted teeth, "is whatever I say it is now. But here's the truth—I need you there. My contact doesn't know pearls from plastic. You do. You're the collector, the expert. You're going to look him in the eye and convince him these are worth what you say they are." His laugh was harsh. "So congratulations, Vanessa—you get to make the pitch in person. If he believes you, you get your precious Cross. If he doesn't?" Mark shrugged. "Then we're both dead, and it won't matter anymore. Hand over the pearls."

Vanessa's head turned toward Diego one more time. Her shoulders rose and fell with a deep breath. When she looked back at Mark, something had hardened in her posture. "And if your contact doesn't accept the pearls even with my authentication?"

She removed the necklace and handed it to Mark.

"Then I suggest you be very convincing." Mark tucked the pearls in his bag. "Because I'm not dying on this island for anyone. Not you, not him, not anyone. Move."

"You won't get away with this," Vanessa said, but she began backing toward the vessel, her eyes never leaving the gun.

Mark kept the gun trained on her as she moved. "I don't have a choice anymore. The prisoners ruined everything. It's the pearls or nothing, and nothing gets us both killed. So we're doing this together—you, me, and your fancy necklace. Now get in the boat."

Diego lay motionless on the sand, blood darkening the ground beneath him. The wet stain spread, soaking into the white sand, turning it rust-red. Mark kept the gun trained on Vanessa as he forced her toward the boat, his attention split between her and the surrounding jungle.

Julia had witnessed something. Diego had been in the

wrong place at the wrong time. Mark was cleaning house, eliminating anyone connected to his smuggling operation. And Vanessa—despite whatever deal she thought she had—was walking straight into a death sentence. Once she'd authenticated the pearls and Mark had his artifact, he wouldn't need her anymore. She'd be the last loose end.

17

Noah's shoulder pressed against Skylar's as they crouched behind a driftwood log. Tension radiated through him as they stared at his ex-girlfriend held at gunpoint. Diego lay motionless in the sand nearby, blood spreading through his shirt in a dark, irregular stain. Skylar forced herself to breathe slowly, fighting every instinct screaming at her to rush in.

"We have to help them," she whispered, her gaze moving between the wounded Meridian employee who had been so helpful to them all and Vanessa. "They're in worse danger than Ethan right now."

The thought caught her off guard. Earlier today, she'd been ready to abandon everything to rescue Ethan the moment she'd seen him in that camp. Now she was putting Noah's ex-girlfriend ahead of her own brother. A woman she barely knew and hadn't particularly liked.

Noah nodded, his eyes locked on the standoff. "I know. But what do we do? He's got a gun and we've got nothing."

Vanessa's voice carried on the salt breeze, controlled despite the weapon aimed at her. "I'm not going to run, Mark. Where would I go? You have the boat, you have the gun, and Diego..." Her eyes flicked to the bleeding man on the sand. "Diego needs help. Can we at least stabilize him before we leave? I still intend to honor our arrangement, but I need you to meet me halfway."

Not a tremor in her voice, as if she were negotiating in a boardroom rather than for her life—and for the first time, Mark's shove toward the boat stalled, his gun hand wavering as he weighed her words.

"The arrangement changed the second this island went off the rails," Mark snarled. "This was supposed to be simple— your cover story, my transfer, the Cross changes hands, and we walk. Now every cop in the region's going to be sniffing around, and my contact is beginning to think I set him up."

"You knew the risks when you reached out to me about the Cross," Vanessa replied. "I created a legitimate reason to be in the Caribbean. I was discreet. I held up my end. Not my fault your jailbreak idiot idea blew up in your face."

Skylar glanced at Noah. Shock registered on his face as understanding dawned, before his expression hardened into something cold.

"She was buying stolen goods," he whispered. "The company cruise was her cover story to get here. Paid for by Reed Security Systems."

"Noah," Skylar started, but movement from the boat caught her attention.

A dark-skinned man in his sixties emerged from the cabin, his face lined with concern. He wore faded cargo pants and a stained fishing shirt, his close-cropped gray hair peppered with white at the temples.

"Hey now," the boat captain called out, his accent thick with island inflections. "What's all dis? You said passenger pickup, nothin' 'bout no guns and shootin'!"

Mark's head snapped toward the interruption, the gun wavering. "Shut up and go back in the cabin."

"I don' want no part in murder," the captain protested, but froze when Mark turned the weapon on him, the barrel now pointing at his chest instead of Vanessa's.

Skylar's breath caught. Mark was facing away from them now, fully occupied with the captain. Beside her, Noah went rigid.

His hands were trembling. She watched him curl them into fists, his jaw tight, his whole body coiled as if he was about to do something stupid.

"Stay here," he whispered. "If something happens—"

She grabbed his wrist. "Wait..."

Their eyes locked. Then he kissed her—quick, fierce—and before she could react, he tore himself away and bolted down the beach.

No, no, no.

She wanted to scream at him to stop, to come back, but her voice caught in her throat. This was insane. Reckless. He was going to get himself shot, and there wasn't a damn thing she could do about it.

Noah bolted silently down the beach, sprinting straight for Mark's exposed back.

The gunman whirled at the crunch of sand.

Vanessa's face went white

Skylar's heart stopped. Noah kept running. She could see every detail with horrifying clarity—Mark's startled expression, the boat captain frozen at the rail, Diego's motionless body sprawled near the waterline.

And Noah, charging straight at a man who'd already proven he would kill without hesitation.

Everything happened in seconds. Mark whirled as Noah barreled toward him, his grip on Vanessa loosening. Noah's ex took the opportunity to slam her heel down on his instep. He cursed, swung the gun wildly, and fired.

The bullet splintered wood on the boat's railing. The captain dove for cover, shouting something in patois.

Skylar's hand closed around a chunk of driftwood at her feet. She started forward, the makeshift club gripped tight—two steps, maybe three—when footsteps crunched in the sand behind her.

Before she could turn, strong hands grabbed her from behind. The driftwood dropped from her grasp. She drove her elbow backward on instinct, aiming for ribs, but her attacker was ready. A massive forearm locked around her throat, cutting off her air before she could scream.

"Well, well," a rough voice rasped in her ear. "Looks like we got ourselves another player."

Then the stench hit her—unwashed body, something rancid. She twisted, clawed at the arm crushing her windpipe, but the grip only tightened. Black spots bloomed at the edges of her vision.

"Move, and I stick you," the voice warned. Something sharp pressed against her side—a kitchen knife that bit through her shirt. "Mark's gonna be real happy to see you."

Farther down the beach, Noah slammed into Mark with all his weight, sending them both tumbling across the sand. The collision knocked the breath out of his lungs, but adrenaline kept him moving. He had no technique, no strategy—only raw instinct as he grappled with the older man.

One thought cut through the chaos:

The gun—where was the gun?

Mark's hand shot out, fingers closing around the grip. Noah grabbed his wrist as the weapon came up. They struggled for control. The gun fired; the crack was deafening. Vanessa cried out.

The gun skittered away, knocked loose in their struggle. Noah caught a glimpse of it, barely out of reach.

By some miracle of momentum, Noah found himself on top, pinning Mark beneath him. He couldn't believe it had worked. Years hunched over a keyboard hadn't prepared him for this kind of physical confrontation, yet here he was, actually restraining an armed man.

Vanessa staggered toward them, clutching her upper arm where blood seeped between her fingers. The wild shot had caught her.

"Noah." Her voice was tight with pain.

Running purely on adrenaline, Noah managed to land a solid punch that snapped Mark's head to the side. The impact sent pain shooting through his knuckles—no one had ever told him how much it hurt to hit someone. For a heartbeat, victory seemed possible.

Then a cry reached his ears—a sound that made his blood run cold.

He turned to see Skylar being dragged by a hulking man. He'd trapped her in a crushing bear hug from behind, one arm banded across her ribs, the other pressing a knife into her side.

Recognition hit Noah like a punch to the gut. The tattoos on both arms. The build. This was one of the men from last night —one of the convicts who'd chased them through the jungle in the rain.

"Skylar!" The name tore from Noah's throat.

That split second of distraction was all Mark needed. He bucked upward with surprising strength, throwing Noah off-balance. Their positions reversed in an instant, Mark now looming over him, one knee driving the air from his lungs.

Mark's split lip curved into a bloody smile as he glanced toward Skylar's captor. "Perfect timing, Russo."

"Found her hiding by those rocks." Russo maintained his iron grip on Skylar despite her struggles. He forced her down the remainder of the beach, her feet dragging in the sand as she fought each step.

"Nice work." Mark looked down at Noah with mocking contempt. "Amateur hour is over, Reed. Did you really think you could play hero? What was your plan exactly—take me down with your bare hands and save the day?" He chuckled. "You should stick to computers."

Noah tried to push Mark off, but the older man was heavier than he looked, his knee digging painfully into Noah's sternum. Each breath came with effort, his ribs compressing under the weight.

Skylar continued fighting against Russo's grip, but her movements lacked their former strength. The toll of the last two days—the constant running, climbing, fighting—had finally caught up with her. Each struggle made her wince, pain evident in the tight lines around her mouth.

"Let her go," Noah choked out.

"Not a chance," Mark replied. "She's coming with us—insurance against any further heroics."

He glanced toward Vanessa, who had sunk to her knees in the sand. The sleeve of her once-immaculate blouse was soaked with blood, the fabric darkening with alarming speed. Her normally composed features had gone slack with pain and shock.

"Looks like your ex got more than she bargained for," Mark noted, sounding almost pleased. "Should've gotten in the boat when I told her to. We could already be at the watersports dock if she'd cooperated."

"Noah," Vanessa whispered, pressing her hand against the bleeding. "It wasn't supposed to go like this. I wanted the Cross. The prisoners taking over...that wasn't part of our plan. Mark said it would be a simple transaction."

Russo revealed a cruel smile. "The Boss promised me passage off this rock if I helped him. Better deal than rotting in that prison." He adjusted his grip on Skylar, making her wince. "Plus, I get to enjoy the company of this pretty little thing."

Nausea twisted Noah's stomach. They should have known the men who'd chased them through the storm wouldn't give up. And he'd left Skylar unguarded and vulnerable while he focused on Mark.

Now she was paying the price for his tunnel vision.

Russo's arm tightened around Skylar's chest, and suddenly she was back on that cliff in Colorado—handhold crumbling beneath her fingers, the sickening lurch of freefall. The same paralyzing fear gripped her now, squeezing the air from her lungs.

"Stop squirming," Russo growled in her ear, the knife pressing deeper against her side. "You're only making this harder on yourself."

She made herself go limp, conserving energy, assessing options. The climber's mindset kicked in. But unlike a sheer rock face, her captor's vulnerabilities weren't obvious. No handholds. No way up or out.

She locked eyes with Noah. His face was a mask of anguish—jaw clenched, eyes wide with helpless rage. Vanessa was bleeding in the sand, Skylar was caught in the grip of a convicted felon, and Mark was in control of everything.

She tried to convey something with her gaze, some flicker of defiance or hope:

Don't give up. We'll find a way.

But even as she held his stare, doubt crept in. The massive man in orange had committed God knows what crimes to land in a Caribbean prison—and now she was trapped in his arms. The possibilities made her stomach turn.

Mark had regained his feet and retrieved his gun. He aimed it casually at Noah's head, his finger resting on the trigger.

"Perfect replacement hostage," Mark announced, gesturing toward Skylar with his free hand. "Much more manageable than your ex, I expect."

Russo's grip tightened. "Want me to bring her to the boat?"

Mark nodded. "We've wasted enough time. The Boss, as you say, won't wait forever."

Ice spread through Skylar's veins at the casual way they discussed her fate—as if she were cargo, not a person, which made her an expendable piece of their exit plan.

The boat's engine roared to life. The captain had been forced back to the helm, his reluctance evident in every stiff movement. Vanessa sat crumpled in the sand nearby, blood pooling beneath her arm. The bullet had done more damage than a graze.

Noah had to make a decision.

Vanessa needed immediate medical attention—that much was clear. The amount of blood she'd lost in minutes was alarming. Without help, she might not survive much longer.

But Skylar... God, Skylar was being dragged toward that

boat by a convicted prisoner, about to be taken who knows where by a killer.

Mark watched dispassionately as blood seeped through Vanessa's fingers.

"Didn't mean to shoot you," he said, almost conversationally. "But it simplifies things, doesn't it? I've got the pearls." He patted the canvas bag at his side. "You're in no shape to follow, and now I don't have to hand over the Cross after all." He shrugged. "I'll find another buyer on the mainland. Someone who can pay cash. Funny how things work out."

Mark's gaze landed on Skylar with renewed interest. "Now, her—she's still useful. Leverage, in case your boyfriend gets any more heroic ideas or thinks he can send the Coast Guard after us."

"Let's go." Mark backed toward the boat, gun trained on Noah.

Russo dragged Skylar across the beach. Despite her struggles, he maintained his grip, half-carrying her toward the waiting vessel.

Noah scrambled to his feet, torn between rushing to Vanessa's side and making one last desperate attempt to reach Skylar.

Diego, still somehow conscious despite his wound, reached weakly for Noah's ankle. "Don't..." he whispered, his voice barely audible. "He'll kill you... then her... no matter what."

Noah hesitated for only a heartbeat. Then he lunged forward anyway.

The ground exploded at his feet as Mark fired. The warning shot stopped him mid-stride. Noah froze, painfully aware of how exposed he was on the open beach.

"Stay with her, Reed," Mark said, gesturing toward Vanessa with the weapon. "She's bleeding bad." His smile was cold, calculating. "Or chase us and let her die. Your choice."

Russo dragged Skylar onto the boat, shoving her down hard onto the deck.

Noah's eyes met hers one last time. Mark barked an order to the captain, who reversed the engine. The propeller churned sand and water as the boat slowly backed off the beach, then turned and began to pull away.

The look on her face nearly destroyed him.

The captain steered the vessel away from shore. Skylar twisted around for one final glimpse of Noah, and the terror in her eyes cut straight through him. She reached toward him— one hand extended, fingers spread—as if she could somehow bridge the widening gap of water between them.

The boat disappeared around a rocky point.

Noah dropped to his knees and let out a sound somewhere between a roar and a raw, agonized sob. He'd never been so completely, devastatingly powerless in his life.

18

Skylar sat on the deck of the boat, unrestrained but trapped all the same. The ocean stretched around them in all directions, and Mark had the gun. As she watched the shoreline recede, Noah's desperate figure grew smaller with each passing second. A hollow ache opened in her chest, threatening to overwhelm her, but she forced it down, replacing it with the cool rationality that had saved her life before.

Breathe. Assess. Plan.

It was the mantra she'd developed during her years of climbing—the same mental discipline that had kept her alive when she'd fallen six months ago and nearly lost her life. She could still recall that heart-stopping moment at Devil's Canyon: the anchor point disintegrating, the sickening weightlessness, the impact that shattered her pelvis and broke her leg in two places. What she remembered most clearly wasn't the pain— though that haunted her nightmares—but Ethan's face when he arrived at the hospital. Her older brother, who'd always looked up to her fearlessness, saw her broken for the first time. Her climbing friends had rallied around her during those brutal months of recovery, but it was Ethan who'd pushed her hardest, refusing to let her quit. "You're not done climbing," he'd insisted. "This doesn't get to be your ending." She'd promised him she'd get back on the rock. Now she had to survive long enough to keep that promise.

That same discipline rose in her now, automatic as muscle memory.

Mark paced the small deck like a caged animal. His carefully maintained façade cracked completely, revealing the calculating predator beneath. The man who'd seemed so devastated by his wife's death was gone, replaced by something far more dangerous—a desperate man with nothing to lose.

"Faster," he snapped at the captain, who stood rigidly at the helm. The older man's face remained impassive, but Skylar noticed his white-knuckled grip on the wheel, the rigid tension in his shoulders. He was terrified, with no choice but to comply.

Mark had the gun and hadn't been afraid to use it. That was all that mattered.

Skylar studied her surroundings, cataloging every detail that might prove useful. Life vests stowed beneath the bench. A locked cabinet that likely contained emergency flares or other safety equipment. A marine radio mounted beside the helm—probably disabled, but worth remembering. Two oars lashed against the gunwale. A fishing gaff hanging from a bracket near the stern.

Each item represented a possibility—a tool or a weapon, depending on the situation.

Russo, the tattooed escapee, leaned against the exterior cabin wall with his arms crossed, watching her with half-lidded eyes that never quite closed. Unlike Mark, whose attention kept darting between the shoreline, his captive, and the distant horizon, Russo appeared almost bored. His focus was probably fixed on whatever payment 'The Boss' had promised him rather than on Skylar herself.

"We need to stay close to shore," Mark muttered, more to himself than anyone else. "Can't risk deeper waters with the Coast Guard patrolling this area."

The captain grunted in acknowledgment, adjusting their course slightly to hug the coastline. Salt spray misted across the bow as they cut through the chop, the engine's constant growl the only sound besides Mark's restless pacing.

Mark's hand kept drifting to the canvas bag, checking and rechecking that the pearls were still inside. His mouth pressed into a thin line.

"Should've made her transfer the money at the spa. Had a perfect signal there, everything ready." His voice rose with agitation. "But the escape turned into a free-for-all, and some idiot took out the cell tower. Now I'm stuck with jewelry instead of cash."

Skylar watched him come apart in real time. His plan was collapsing, and men whose schemes fell to pieces became unpredictable. Dangerous in new ways.

Mark resumed his agitated pacing, talking half to himself. "Laurent better accept those pearls." He checked his watch. "Thirty minutes to make the rendezvous."

Laurent.

Skylar's ears pricked up. The Boss's name was Laurent. The man behind all of this.

He glanced at Skylar, seeming to remember her presence. "That little stunt your boyfriend pulled? He's lucky I didn't kill him. But as long as you're with me, he won't risk it again."

"He's not my boyfriend," Skylar said quietly.

"Whatever he is, he clearly cares whether you live or die. That's enough to keep him in line."

Mark pulled a bulky satellite phone from his bag and punched in numbers with sharp, aggressive movements.

Skylar's breath caught. Mark noticed and shrugged. "Rule number one of operating in unstable regions—never rely on the local infrastructure. This thing works anywhere on the planet."

Anger flared hot in her chest. He'd had that the entire time. While Noah had spent hours fixing broken equipment with scraps and spare parts to send a signal for rescue, Mark had a working satellite phone in his precious canvas bag. All that danger, all that effort—and this bastard could have called for help at any moment.

Instead, he'd let them all believe they were stranded.

As the call connected, Mark's shoulders drew up and his body language shifted into something more controlled. The ocean breeze carried salt spray across the deck, forcing him to turn his shoulder against it. The shift gave Skylar a clearer view of his face as he spoke into the satellite phone.

"Laurent," he said. "We have a complication."

She strained to catch every word. On the rock when she was new to climbing, her instructor had taught her to read every crack, every shift in the stone. The same principle applied here —understand the route before you commit to the climb.

"You have it, right? The Cross is secure?" Mark paused, listening. The tight line of his mouth eased. "Good. That's good. But there's been a problem with the buyer. She took a bullet..."

Another pause, longer this time. Color crept up Mark's neck, darkening the skin above his collar.

"The Wi-Fi network is completely dead—the prisoners took out everything. No signal anywhere on the island. Wire transfer is impossible." Mark's free hand clenched and unclenched at his side before he kicked at a coiled line on the deck. "But I have something better. Pearls. Antique natural pearls worth at least two million—probably more. The buyer handed them over before she got shot."

The boat rocked gently beneath them, the engine's steady drone a backdrop to his increasingly agitated voice.

"I know it's not cash. But these are real, Laurent. Your people can verify them easy. They're worth more than you're owed. Take them as the final payment, and we complete the exchange."

An angry voice erupted from the other end—loud enough that Skylar caught the cadence if not the words. French-accented. Harsh.

"Your 'controlled distraction' turned into a goddamn island-wide disaster," Mark shot back, his composure fracturing. "But I'm still bringing payment." He listened, his scowl deepening. "I don't care if it got messier than planned—I need the Cross."

His voice dropped lower, taking on an edge that made the hair on Skylar's arms stand up. "Because I have people waiting for payment back home who don't accept excuses... Yes. Exactly those kind of people." Another pause. The boat hit a swell, and Mark braced himself against the railing without breaking stride in the conversation. "So I need this to go smoothly, too. We both walk away clean."

The engine growled low and constantly. Waves slapped against the hull. Russo still hadn't moved from his spot by the cabin bulkhead, idly surveying the deck and everyone on it. The captain kept his gaze fixed on the horizon, his wrinkled hands steady on the wheel even as everything around him spiraled into anarchy.

When Mark finally ended the call, he stood at the railing, staring at the distant shoreline. A man watching his carefully constructed plan hang by a thread—and knowing that thread could snap at any moment.

Skylar pressed her fingernails hard into her palms, the sharp bite grounding her. Panic wouldn't help. She needed to think. To plan.

The meetup was thirty minutes away. Thirty minutes to figure out how to survive whatever came next.

She decided to risk asking a question. "What's so special about this Cross that it's worth killing for?"

Mark turned. His eyebrows lifted slightly. She braced for him to lash out or ignore her completely. Instead, a glint of genuine pride flashed in his eyes.

"The Saint Marielle Cross," he said, and his voice took on a different quality—reverent, almost tender. "Five hundred years old. Solid gold, encrusted with emeralds and rubies the Spanish conquistadors brought to this island. Worth millions to the right collector."

He moved closer, crouching down to bring his face level with hers. "And it would have been a clean operation if not for those damn prisoners."

"And now they're running loose all over the island," Skylar said, keeping her tone flat, conversational.

Mark's laugh came out harsh. "A simple distraction—that's all it was meant to be. Six, maybe seven inmates escaping, sowing chaos in the capital while Laurent's people slipped the Cross out of the museum in the confusion." A vein pulsed at his temple. "It wasn't supposed to spread like wildfire. The whole island wasn't supposed to descend into martial law. We needed enough disorder to cover the theft while Laurent's crew accessed the museum. Then the Cross would be delivered to us at the spa while the cruise ship was docked—Vanessa makes the bank transfer, everyone gets paid, she gets the Cross. We'd be back on board before the authorities even realized it was missing. Clean, simple exchange."

"So what went wrong?"

"What went wrong," Mark said, the words coming out clipped and sharp, "is that Laurent's prison contact got greedy. One injured guard became three dead guards. Six inmates became forty-three." He turned his gaze toward Russo. "And the chosen few who were supposed to help with the theft and stay in the capital? They decided to spread out across the island instead."

Russo's mouth curved into something that might have been a smile. "Couldn't help myself. All those tourists at the resort, wandering around in their fancy clothes, no security..." He shrugged. "Sitting ducks."

Mark's nostrils flared. "You were supposed to create a distraction in the capital. Not hunt cruise passengers all the way out here."

"Made it more convincing, didn't I?" Russo said, unbothered. "Authorities thought it was a full-scale riot instead of your little art heist."

"A controlled distraction became..." Mark swept his arm toward the island. Smoke rose from multiple points along the coastline, dark columns against the blue sky. "This disaster."

He stood abruptly, moving back to scan the waters ahead. The boat rocked gently beneath them. Russo shifted his weight against the cabin wall, with that half-smile still playing at his lips. The captain's knuckles stayed white on the wheel.

"And Julia?" Skylar asked softly. "How did she fit into all this?"

Mark went still. Then he turned, slow and deliberate. His eyes narrowed for a heartbeat. His shoulders dropped slightly. Apparently, he'd concluded it no longer mattered what his captive knew.

"Bad timing," he said, his voice flat and empty. "She overheard me discussing final details with Laurent when I thought she was asleep in the casita." His mouth twisted. "Once she figured that out, she started asking questions. Why I had a satellite phone. Why I hadn't told anyone. Why I'd let everyone believe we were stranded when I could've called for rescue the whole time."

The timeline clicked into place.

"She threatened to turn you in," Skylar said.

"Twenty-five years of marriage, and she couldn't give me this one thing. Said she couldn't live with herself knowing I was stealing a national treasure. Said she'd go to the authorities the minute we reached civilization." His gaze drifted toward the horizon. "It was her or me. Simple calculation."

The cold detachment in his voice—describing his wife's murder like a business decision—made Skylar's stomach sour. Mark hadn't snapped in a moment of rage. He'd weighed the options and chosen murder because it solved a problem.

"And now?" she asked. "What's the plan?"

"We meet Laurent at the security fence. I hand over the pearls, he gives me the Cross, and we're done." He patted the canvas bag across his chest. "Then I find another buyer on the mainland who'll pay cash. Maybe bump it up to five million."

The possibility of more money animated him. His grip on the phone tightened with barely contained anticipation.

"And me?" Skylar kept her voice steady.

Mark's smile didn't reach his eyes. "You're a problem. You've heard Laurent's name, the location, the whole damn plan. I can't leave you behind to talk." He shrugged, casual as discussing the weather. "The pearls should satisfy him. If they don't, well... I'll improvise. Either way, your part in this ends tonight."

Skylar nodded as if accepting her fate.

Mark's casual shrug lingered in her mind. The pearls might satisfy Laurent, or they might not. It didn't matter. Once the exchange was done and Mark was safe, her knowledge of the heist, the names, the route off the island—all of it made her a risk he wouldn't tolerate. She'd end up like Julia: gone, erased, forgotten.

There had to be a way out.

Russo pushed off from the cabin wall, clearly bored with talk about crosses and money. "What about me?" he demanded. "You promised passage to the Dominican Republic."

"And you'll get it," Mark replied smoothly, not bothering to look at him. "Once we complete the transaction."

Russo's eyes narrowed. His hand drifted to the knife at his belt—a small movement, but deliberate. Mark either didn't notice or didn't care.

Tension hummed between them. Russo didn't trust Mark, and Mark viewed Russo as a temporary tool, useful now but destined to be abandoned once his purpose was served.

Another crack in their alliance. Another potential opening.

The captain's voice cut through. "We're approaching the southwest point."

Mark checked his watch. "How long until we reach the dock?"

"Maybe ten minutes," the captain answered, his face impassive.

Ten minutes.

Skylar scanned her surroundings again. The tools she'd already spotted—vests, oars, gaff—took on new urgency. Thirty seconds of distraction might be all she needed. If the right moment came, she might have a chance.

The boat rounded a rocky point, the hull rising and falling with the increasing swell. A new stretch of shoreline came into view. In the distance, the white buildings of the resort complex emerged. They were nearly back to the same beach where she and Noah had first struggled ashore after the evacuation. Two days ago. It seemed like years.

A flash of sunlight on metal caught her attention farther out on the water. Coast Guard patrol boats—at least three of them —their distinctive white hulls and orange stripes unmistakable against the distant blue horizon.

Mark saw them too. "Dammit." Color crept up his neck. "Laurent said they'd be scrambling to the northeast—a distress call came in. That boyfriend of yours must've actually gotten the radio working." His eyes flicked to Skylar.

"Military vessels too," Russo pointed out, gesturing toward several larger ships in deeper waters. "Big ones. They might have helicopters in the air soon."

Mark spun toward the captain. "Keep us tight to shore. Stay close to the rocks."

The captain nodded without comment, adjusting the wheel to bring them closer to the treacherous shoreline. The change was immediate—the waves became choppier, less predictable. Stronger currents pulled at the hull from different directions. The captain made small adjustments to keep them from being pushed into the rocks that lurked beneath the surface.

One wrong turn and they'd rip the hull open. The captain knew it.

With every lurch and dip, Mark divided his focus—scanning for patrol boats, snapping orders at the captain. Russo had moved to the bow, scanning for rocks ahead.

For the first time since they'd shoved off the beach, neither man had eyes fixed solely on her.

Then the captain adjusted their heading, drifting nearer to the jagged rocks than necessary, his eyes flicking briefly to hers.

Was he trying to help?

Skylar couldn't be certain, but the possibility was enough.

Mark joined Russo at the bow, their voices dropping to angry whispers as they argued about what to do next. The satellite phone emerged from Mark's bag again, and he placed another tense call to Laurent, updating him on their position and the unexpected Coast Guard presence.

Skylar shifted on the deck, easing herself closer to the starboard side in small, careful increments. Life vests within reach. Gunwale three steps away, maybe four. She mapped the route the way she'd map a climbing sequence—hand here, foot there, explosive push to clear the rail.

The shore wasn't far—maybe two hundred yards at most, closer in spots where the rocks jutted out. But those currents looked vicious where they churned around them, and her hip already ached, the old injury protesting after nearly three brutal days of climbing, running, surviving. Too little sleep. Not enough food.

She might not make it.

The alternative, however, was certain death.

The choice was obvious.

A distant mechanical whine drew everyone's attention skyward. A Coast Guard helicopter, still miles off, tracking along the northern coastline. The distinctive thwop-thwop of rotor blades carried faintly across the water.

"They're sweeping the coast," Russo said, real panic edging into his voice. "If they swing this way—"

"Shut up," Mark snapped, spinning toward the captain. "Get us closer to shore. Tuck in behind those rocks before they turn."

The captain nodded. Then he spun the wheel hard to port —far harder than the maneuver required.

The boat lurched violently to the side, hitting an oncoming wave at the worst possible angle. The deck tilted sharply. Both

Mark and Russo staggered, their hands shooting out to grab the railing to keep from falling. The satellite phone flew from Mark's grip, skittering across the wet deck.

The captain's eyes met Skylar's for a split second. She saw it then—clear as day—the deliberate nature of the maneuver, the almost imperceptible nod he gave her, the slight tilt of his head toward the water.

He was giving her the opening she needed.

Skylar didn't allow fear to paralyze her.

In one fluid motion born from years of trusting her body on vertical rock faces, she lunged forward, grabbed a bright orange life vest from beneath the bench, and rushed toward the starboard rail.

"Hey!" Russo reached for her, his fingers grazing her shoulder, catching briefly on her shirt.

Mark whirled around, his hand grabbing for the gun tucked in his waistband. "Stop her!"

But Skylar was already at the gunwale, her momentum carrying her forward. She planted one foot on the low rail and vaulted over it with the kind of explosive movement that had once carried her up impossible routes. With the life vest clutched tight to her chest, she launched into empty air, away from the boat, toward the churning water and the distant shore beyond.

For a heartbeat, she was weightless—suspended between the boat and the sea, between captivity and freedom, between certain death and possible survival.

The last thing she heard was Mark's enraged shout, followed by the sharp crack of a gunshot as she hit the cold, dark water below.

19

Noah stayed where he'd fallen, knees in the wet sand, watching the empty horizon. The real pain wasn't in his bruised ribs or his scraped palms. It was the hollow that had opened in his chest the moment that boat disappeared and Skylar with it. Three days. That's all it had taken for her to become someone he couldn't imagine losing.

Now she was gone, and the memory of his own helplessness hurt worse than any bruise.

He'd spent his career building systems to protect people—firewalls, encryption, layers of digital defense. None of it meant anything here. Mark had beaten him with brute force and a gun, and Skylar had paid the price. But staying on his knees wouldn't change that.

Vanessa lay sprawled beside him, her face draining of color with each passing minute. Blood soaked through the sleeve of her blouse where the bullet had torn through her upper arm. The wound was still seeping despite the pressure he'd applied, and her skin had taken on a grayish cast that made his stomach turn.

Diego lay a few feet away near the waterline, his chest barely rising with each labored breath. The wound in his torso was far more severe, and his blood had darkened the white sand to rust-red.

Mark had engineered an impossible choice: stay with Vanessa and let Skylar be taken or pursue Skylar and leave Vanessa wounded and alone. The rational part of Noah's brain knew there had been no realistic way to catch that boat—Mark had a gun, Russo was twice his size, and the vessel was already pulling away before Noah could reach the water. But rationality offered no comfort. His mind kept screaming that he should have done something. Anything.

For the first time in his life, no amount of clever engineering could solve the problem in front of him. Vanessa and Diego needed something he couldn't code or design. They needed him to act.

His hands were steady despite the adrenaline still pumping through his system. That surprised him. As a teenager, he'd taken a first-aid course at his mother's insistence—one of her many attempts to prepare him for a world she worried he wasn't equipped to handle. At the time, it had seemed like overkill for someone destined to spend his life behind a keyboard. Now he silently thanked her for it.

"Skylar would tell me to focus on what I can control," he muttered to himself.

First priority: stop Vanessa's bleeding before she went into shock. He stripped off his Meridian polo shirt and tore it into makeshift bandages. The material wasn't sterile, wasn't even particularly clean, but it was all he had. He gathered handfuls of seawater to rinse away enough blood to see the wound clearly. The bullet had passed cleanly through the fleshy part of her upper arm—a through-and-through that had missed the bone. It looked horrific, but could have been worse. Blood loss was the immediate danger.

He folded strips of fabric into thick pads and pressed them firmly against the entry and exit wounds. Vanessa's eyes fluttered open, unfocused. She tried to speak, but only a weak groan emerged. He wrapped another strip around her arm to hold the pads in place, pulling it tight enough to slow the bleeding without cutting off circulation.

The same focus he brought to debugging complex code now applied to keeping someone alive. Break the problem into components. Address each one systematically. Don't think about the big picture—think about the next step, then the next. What had seemed overwhelming moments before now resolved into distinct, manageable tasks. Stabilize Vanessa. Check Diego. Assess the situation. Form a plan.

The fear didn't go away, though. It sat like a stone in his chest. But the work gave him something besides terror to focus on.

A weak voice interrupted his concentration. "Reed..."

Diego was looking at him with glazed eyes, blood bubbling at the corner of his mouth. The Meridian employee was dying —his complexion gray, his breathing wet and labored, each exhale producing a faint rattling sound.

Noah moved quickly to his side. The metallic smell of blood was overwhelming this close.

"In my pocket..." Diego's voice was barely a whisper, each word clearly costing him. His hand twitched weakly toward his chest.

Noah waited, hoping for more, but Diego's eyes fluttered closed. His chest rose once more, then fell, and didn't rise again. The final breath escaped in a soft sigh, and then nothing. No more movement. No more sound.

Noah paused, his hand resting on Diego's shoulder. The

skin was still warm beneath his palm. They'd suspected this man of being involved in Mark's scheme, had questioned his loyalties, and in the end he'd been innocent—a good man only trying to help them survive. He'd died trying to stop Mark, and Noah couldn't even remember his last name.

Pushing aside the guilt that threatened to choke him, Noah searched Diego's pockets. He found a well-worn pocket knife with a three-inch blade in the cargo pants, and a folded paper tucked inside a pocket of his blood-soaked shirt.

It was a map of Saint Marielle—the entire island, not the sanitized cruise port area tourists saw. This was a working map, water-stained and creased from frequent use, with topographic lines showing elevation changes and hand-drawn notations marking trails and landmarks. Noah unfolded it carefully, spreading it on a dry patch of sand and weighing down the corners with small rocks to keep the ocean breeze from tearing it away.

The island's full geography laid itself out before him, far larger than he'd realized. This cove—the beach where they'd agreed to rendezvous—was marked on the northern coast. The private resort complex and cruise ship terminal occupied a small southeastern section, isolated from the island by miles of dense jungle and mountainous terrain. Far to the south, beyond vast stretches of wilderness, sat the capital city—the real Saint Marielle, where the island's actual population lived and worked, worlds away from the manicured tourist zone. That's where Mark had said the prison break happened, where the museum theft had gone down.

His eyes traced the central area, following the route he and Skylar had taken from the ravine when they'd stumbled across the hostage camp. That's where Ethan was being held, along with roughly twenty other cruise passengers. If Noah could somehow reach that camp, free Ethan and the others, they might have the numbers to mount some kind of rescue for Skylar.

But the more he turned the idea over, the more impossible it seemed. How could he infiltrate a camp full of armed escaped prisoners with nothing but Diego's pocket knife? Even if he managed to free Ethan—Skylar's brother, a stranger he'd never met—what chance did two unarmed men have against Mark, Russo, and whoever else was involved? The questions multiplied, each one more daunting than the last.

And what about Skylar? Where was Mark taking her? Back to the resort area? To some other extraction point? Every minute that passed, she was getting farther away, facing God knows what.

Noah stared at the map, then at the horizon where the boat had disappeared. Where the hell did he even start looking? Mark had a boat and access to the entire coastline. He could be heading to the resort, to some hidden cove, to a rendezvous point anywhere around the island's perimeter. Without knowing Mark's destination, searching would be pointless.

His fingers dug into the sand until they ached. There was no right answer, only degrees of wrong, and the clock on Skylar's life kept ticking down.

Noah tucked the knife and map into his pants pocket and turned back to Vanessa. He gathered her into his arms, surprised at how light she seemed, and headed up off the beach.

As he carried her out of the blazing sun and toward the cooler shelter of the jungle, he thought about the years they'd spent together. This woman had been his partner in every sense—they'd built a company together, shared an apartment in Princeton, discussed long-term plans. But even in their best moments, something fundamental had been missing. She'd treated their relationship like another acquisition in her portfolio, something valuable to own rather than cherish. Every conversation had been a negotiation. Every decision analyzed for optimal outcomes. He'd told himself that was her personality, that not everyone showed affection the same way. Looking back, he realized he'd been making excuses for someone who'd never really let him in. He didn't want Vanessa to die—he wouldn't wish that on anyone—but beyond that basic human concern, he had nothing left to give her.

What he had with Skylar after only days was already more real, more visceral than anything he'd experienced with Vanessa during their two years together. Skylar didn't calculate her responses or manage his perception of her. When she'd kissed him in that cave, it hadn't been strategic—it had been raw and honest in its intensity. The realization should have been shocking given the circumstances. Instead, it was simply acknowledging an obvious truth he'd been too cautious to admit before.

Noah found a small clearing several yards into the vegetation, protected by dense foliage that filtered the harsh sunlight. He gently laid Vanessa down on a patch of relatively dry ground between two large ferns, checking her wound again. The bleeding had nearly stopped, the makeshift bandages holding. Her color looked marginally better—less gray, more of a normal pallor. Her breathing had steadied, growing deeper and more regular.

She would survive if she got proper medical attention within the next few hours.

That was the problem, wasn't it? He couldn't get her medical attention. Not out here. The resort was miles away and swarming with convicts. The hostage camp was inland through rough terrain, and who knew when the authorities were coming. He could leave Vanessa here, hidden and resting, while he went for help. But what if he didn't make it back? What if he was captured trying to free Ethan, or killed, or simply lost in the jungle? She'd die here alone, and no one would ever find her body.

He couldn't leave her.

As he checked her bandages one more time, still second-guessing the decision, her eyes fluttered open. She stared up at the trees overhead for a moment, disoriented, before her gaze found his face.

"Noah?" Her voice was barely audible.

"Don't try to move," he said, kneeling beside her. "You've lost a lot of blood. The wound's stabilized, but you need to stay still."

He pulled out his water bottle—mostly empty—and tilted it carefully to her lips. "Drink. Slowly."

Vanessa took a few small sips, grimacing as she swallowed. Some of the water dribbled down her chin, but her eyes showed gratitude. When she'd had enough, she turned her head slightly to the side.

"Skylar..." Vanessa's brow furrowed with effort as she tried to piece together what had happened. "Where is she?"

"Mark took her. On the boat. They left maybe ten minutes ago."

Vanessa's eyes closed briefly. When they opened again, they glistened with unshed tears. "This is my fault." She tried to sit up, but the movement sent a visible shock of pain through her —a sharp gasp, her body going rigid. She fell back immediately, breathing hard. "I need to tell you everything. You have to understand—I never wanted anyone to get hurt."

"Bit late for that, don't you think? Julia's dead. Diego's dead. Skylar's been kidnapped. Tourists are being held hostage. All because of your little art collecting hobby."

"I know." With surprising strength, she caught his hand, fingers clamping around his wrist as if she was afraid he'd pull away. "Listen to me, Noah, please. The Cross is the crown jewel of the Saint Marielle collection—pure sixteenth-century Spanish workmanship, carried here by the conquistadors themselves. To the right buyer, it's worth a fortune." She stopped, dragging in a shallow breath as if every syllable cost her. "I wanted it for my private collection. A few months ago, Mark found me through a middleman. He had connections on the island, inside information. All I had to do was finance the operation."

"What the hell were you thinking?" Noah pulled his hand away, needing distance from her touch. It made no sense to him. She came from old money—real wealth, not the nouveau riche tech money he'd made. She had a top-tier education and ran a successful company as CEO. "Why would you do something like this?"

Her tears spilled over, tracking down her dirt-streaked face. "Since we broke up, my interest in collecting rare artifacts became... more than a hobby. An obsession, I suppose. My therapist would probably say I was trying to fill a void, acquire things I could control when I couldn't control my personal life." A bitter, broken laugh escaped her. "When Mark told me about the Cross, showed me photographs, research about its history... I couldn't resist. I told myself it was a transaction. A business deal. I didn't think it through. I didn't consider what could go wrong. Who could get hurt."

Her hand went limp on the ground beside her, the confession seeming to drain what little energy she had left. "Forgive me, Noah."

Noah shook his head, struggling to reconcile this confession with the composed, intelligent woman he'd known for five years. He remembered her passion for antiquities all too well— she'd pulled him through museum halls and private viewings, spent quiet weekends poring over auction catalogs with a focused gleam in her eye. But this crossed a line he'd never pictured. "Financing a heist?" His voice came out rough. "Diego's body is lying over there. Julia's gone. This thing you wanted—it cost lives, Vanessa."

"The prison break was meant to be contained," Vanessa said, her voice cracking. "A small distraction. A few prisoners wreaking havoc on one side of the capital while Mark's contact removed the Cross from the museum on the other side. Minimal risk. No one was supposed to get hurt. A few minutes of confusion to distract the police, and then it would be over." Her voice dropped to barely a whisper. "I never thought people would die. I never wanted those cruise passengers caught in the middle of this nightmare."

"But they were," Noah said flatly. "And Julia was murdered."

"Mark killed her because she found out about the plan. She overheard him on his satellite phone, talking to Laurent about final logistics." Vanessa's eyes drifted closed, exhaustion washing over her features like a wave. "He panicked. Made a decision in the moment."

"Laurent?"

"His partner. Laurent Baptiste. The one with all the connections in Saint Marielle—government officials, museum security, prison guards." She dragged each word out as if it hurt. "Laurent organized everything on the ground. They're meeting tonight where the resort's security fence cuts Tesoro Bay off from the rest of the island. Laurent has the Cross."

The southern edge of the resort area lay a long hike from where they stood now—and an equally brutal trek from the prison camp holding Ethan. How could he possibly coordinate rescuing Skylar's brother, getting Vanessa to safety, and intercepting Mark? The logistics felt impossible. Three separate locations. No transportation. Nothing but Diego's pocket knife for a weapon.

"I'm sorry, Noah," Vanessa whispered, her voice fading. "For everything. For betraying your trust when we were together. For being so selfish and greedy that I put all these innocent people at risk. I wanted something beautiful and rare, and I didn't care about the cost. Now, people are dead because of me."

Noah studied her face, searching for the manipulation he'd come to expect during their relationship—the calculated vulnerability she'd used in business negotiations, the strategic displays of emotion. Her mask had cracked. The tears on her cheeks weren't for show. The tremor in her voice wasn't performance. Perhaps facing death had a way of stripping away pretense, forcing people to confront who they really were.

"The best way to make it up to me," he said after a long moment, "is to help me fix this disaster you created. And that means I need to find someone first."

"Who?" Vanessa asked weakly.

"Skylar's brother. Ethan." Noah stood, offering her his hand. "He was taken hostage when the prisoners first escaped. Skylar and I spotted their camp earlier today—maybe twenty hostages heavily guarded by some of the convicts. We had to leave to make the beach rendezvous, but I know roughly where it is." He helped Vanessa to her feet, noting how unsteady she was despite the bleeding having mostly stopped. She swayed slightly, her weight pressing against his supporting arm. "And you're coming with me. I can't leave you here alone."

"Noah, I'll only slow you down," Vanessa protested, her free hand clutching her wounded arm. "You should go without me. I can wait here."

"I can't leave you alone out here." The thought of walking away and leaving her wounded twisted something sharp in his gut. "If something happens to me, at least we're together. We'll take it slow."

He pulled out Diego's map again, orienting himself. The hostage camp was roughly half-a-mile inland, maybe less if they could find the trails Diego had marked. Through dense jungle. Uphill. With an injured woman who could barely stand.

But Ethan was there. Skylar's brother. And maybe freeing him and the other hostages would give Noah the numbers and the leverage he needed to get Skylar back.

It was a long shot, but it was the only shot he had.

Noah bore most of Vanessa's weight as they pushed inland, leaving the exposed beach behind. She leaned heavily against him, her injured arm cradled protectively across her body, her free hand gripping his shoulder for balance. The jungle swallowed them within minutes—dense foliage closing in from all sides, the temperature rising as they moved deeper. Every few steps, she'd stumble or gasp in pain, and he'd have to pause, let her catch her breath, adjust his grip to keep her upright.

He tried to retrace the morning path he'd taken with Skylar, searching for the drainage they'd followed, the distinctive rock formations he'd committed to memory. But everything looked different now—unfamiliar, deceptive. Had they climbed up through here, or farther north? The trees blurred together. The faint trails—if that's what they were—vanished into thick walls of green. The landscape refused to match what he remembered.

Vanessa's breathing grew labored within the first hundred yards. They stopped frequently, her hand pressed against a tree trunk for balance while she fought to stay conscious. Sweat plastered her hair to her forehead, dripping down her face to mix with the dirt. The wound on her arm had started seeping again, fresh blood darkening the already-stained bandage.

Noah pulled Diego's map from his pocket, orienting himself by the slope of the land and the distant sound of surf behind them. The hostage camp lay somewhere to the southeast through this tangle of jungle. A half mile that might as well be twenty, given Vanessa's condition and the terrain. Already his legs burned from the climb, his shoulders ached from supporting her weight, and they'd barely covered a tenth the distance.

His mind churned through scenarios, each one worse than the last. Twenty hostages held by armed men. Vanessa slipping toward shock. Skylar somewhere on the water, a bargaining chip in Mark's desperate play for the Cross. Three impossible problems, zero good options, and a skill set that had never prepared him for any of it.

The wrong move could get them all killed. But no move guaranteed it.

Noah pushed himself to his feet.

A branch snapped somewhere in the jungle behind him.

He froze, his hand dropping instinctively to the pocketknife in his pocket. The three-inch blade wouldn't stand a chance against a gun, yet he eased it open anyway, the small click loud in the sudden quiet.

Nothing. Maybe an animal. Maybe his paranoia.

The adrenaline spike left him jittery, his nerves frayed to the edge. Noah folded the map with unsteady hands and kept walking, half-carrying Vanessa deeper into the green maze, toward a prison camp he'd only glimpsed once and wasn't entirely sure he could find again. Sweat ran into his eyes. His aqua shoes—designed for poolside lounging—slipped on the muddy incline.

Vanessa stumbled, nearly taking them both down. He caught her, his arms burning with the effort of keeping her upright.

"I'm sorry," she whispered, her voice barely audible. "I'm slowing you down."

"We keep moving together," he said. "End of discussion."

She'd brought this disaster down on all of them. But leaving an injured woman alone in the jungle to die—that was Mark's playbook, not his. If he started making those kinds of choices, he'd lose something he couldn't get back.

They pressed on, climbing higher, following a trail that might not even be a trail toward a camp that might not even be there anymore.

20

Noah tested Diego's knife as they walked, checking the edge against his thumb. Sharp enough to cut, but nothing he'd want to bet his life on. The three-inch blade was meant for cleaning fish, not fighting armed men. Along the way, he'd also fashioned a crude club from a fallen branch. The wood was solid, dense—it would crack bone if he swung hard enough. He gripped it tighter and hoped he wouldn't have to find out what that felt like.

As they climbed inland, the terrain grew steeper. He knew this stretch now—the ridge to the hostage camp overlook, exactly where he'd been with Skylar before. They were heading the right way. Vanessa struggled with the incline, leaning into him with each step, but she didn't complain. Her silence worried him more than protests would have. She moved like someone measuring out every ounce of effort, her jaw tight, her breathing controlled.

Seeing Vanessa like this—wounded, struggling—made his thoughts circle back to Skylar. Was she still alive? Had Mark already completed his transaction with Laurent and disposed of her? The possibilities clawed at him, each one worse than the last. The image of her face when she'd looked at him from the boat stayed burned in his mind. She hadn't screamed or begged—just reached for him, fingers spread, until the boat disappeared.

Something twisted behind his ribs. He forced the thoughts away—Skylar hurt, Skylar bleeding, Skylar dead—and focused on the immediate problem. Find Ethan. Free the hostages.

After that, he'd tear this island apart until he found her.

When they reached the steepest section, Noah stopped. This was the spot. The prisoner camp should be just over the other side... "Wait here." He helped Vanessa settle behind a grouping of boulders that offered both concealment and shade. "I'm going up to scout the camp. Ten minutes, maybe less."

"Noah—"

"I promise I'll come back." He made sure she had the water bottle within reach. After a moment's hesitation, he pressed Diego's knife into her palm. "Just in case." He'd wanted to keep it, but she needed it more.

She stared at the small blade as if it were a live grenade. Her fingers closed around it weakly.

"Stay quiet. Stay hidden." He kept the club and started up the steep slope, using roots and rocks for handholds. His muscles protested—as if he had any other choice. Pain was only noise now. Background static.

The observation point where he and Skylar had hidden that morning was exactly as he remembered it—a natural shelf of rock concealed by overhanging ferns. He dropped to his stomach at the crest, peering down into the depression below.

He counted six guards, maybe more out of sight. Smoke curled from a fresh cookfire, prisoners lounging on salvaged lounge chairs while a woman in torn cruise wear heated up some kind of food in a pot, her movements mechanical.

Although it was obvious they'd attempted some clean-up by stacking some storm-felled branches haphazardly nearby, the camp hadn't changed much. Same positioning, same setup. The guards still had every advantage.

How the hell was he supposed to extract Ethan from that?

Noah studied the clearing, trying to think it through. There had to be... something. Some pattern, some opening. The guards traded spots, looped back, crossed paths—he wasn't sure if there was a system to it or if they were only restless. One of them was smoking, not paying as much attention as the others. Another kept looking toward the trail on the left side— waiting for someone? Worried about something?

Noah had no idea what he was looking for. What would a weak point even look like? In code, he knew how to find the vulnerability and exploit it. But this wasn't code. These were armed criminals who'd already killed people, and he was a guy with a stick.

He turned his attention to the hostages. Some were lying down. Others sat with their heads in their hands. A few stared at nothing.

He scanned the faces, searching for Skylar's brother. It didn't take long—Ethan was in the same spot where Skylar had pointed him out earlier. He sat with his back against a tree, sandy hair matted with dried blood on one side of his face. One leg was stretched out in front of him at an awkward angle— injured, maybe twisted or worse.

Then, a boat engine cut through his thoughts, distant but growing louder.

Noah turned, scanning the coastline visible from his elevated position. There—approaching the resort area from the north—a small fishing vessel cutting through the water at speed. Even from this distance, he could make out the weath-ered hull, the distinctive silhouette.

Mark. It had to be.

Before he could process what that meant, a voice spoke directly behind him.

"On your feet. Slow."

Noah's blood turned to ice. He rolled onto his back to find a man in a filthy prison uniform standing three feet away, solidly built with heavy arms, shaggy hair, and a gold tooth visible in his sneer. The stench of stale cigarettes rolled off him in waves. Behind him, another prisoner with matted dreadlocks had Vanessa in a chokehold, a sharpened piece of metal pressed against her throat. Her eyes were huge.

"You off that cruise ship?" The gold-toothed man stepped closer, all muscle and prison-yard violence. He had at least thirty pounds on Noah, none of it fat. Scars crisscrossed his knuckles—the kind earned from years of fights.

Noah's mind emptied. Every plan, every calculation, every careful consideration—gone. They were caught. Vanessa was seconds from having her throat cut, and he was holding a stick against men who'd survived years in a Caribbean prison. His mouth had gone dry. His palms were slick with sweat.

The club was a joke now.

He had maybe three seconds to decide: fight and watch Vanessa die, or surrender and hope he could talk his way out.

Neither option would save Skylar.

Neither option would rescue Ethan.

But doing nothing guaranteed failure for everyone.

The gold-toothed man's hand moved toward his waistband, toward whatever weapon he had tucked there. Metal glinted in the filtered sunlight.

Three seconds.

Two.

21

When Skylar launched herself from the boat, her body arced through the air. For one suspended heartbeat, she was weightless—free from Mark's grip, free from the gun, free from the certainty of what he'd do once he had the Cross and she'd outlived her usefulness.

Then gravity reasserted itself, and she hit the water hard.

The impact ripped the life jacket from her hands. Warm saltwater forced itself up her nose, down her throat, burning as she plunged beneath the surface. The transition from the boat's solid deck to the yielding sea disoriented her completely—up became down, left became right, sound became muffled and distorted. Above her, Mark's bellowing rage, Russo's panicked shouting, the boat engine's mechanical growl, all filtered through layers of water as if she'd descended into another world.

Her lungs screamed for air, burning with the need to breathe, but she forced herself to stay submerged. The water was her only protection from Mark's gun.

Her leg sent a vicious spike of pain shooting through her

hip as she kicked and began swimming. Hitting the water had jarred everything—old fractures that had barely healed, rebuilt muscle that was still weak, scar tissue that pulled and burned with every movement. She gritted her teeth against it and pushed through, drawing on the same bone-deep stubbornness that had gotten her through months of brutal, often agonizing physical therapy. Those endless hours in the rehab center's pool were paying dividends now.

She swam beneath the surface using powerful strokes, her arms doing most of the work, until her lungs threatened to collapse and black spots danced at the edges of her vision.

When she finally broke the surface and sucked in fresh air, Mark's voice cut across the water.

"There, I see her! Turn the boat around now!"

Skylar dove again before he could take a clean shot. The engine pitch changed behind her, revving higher, more urgent. They were maneuvering to pursue her. She swam hard, angling away from the sound, trying to put as much distance as possible between herself and her captors. She surfaced only when her vision started to gray out again, when her body absolutely demanded oxygen.

Breathe. Dive. Swim. Breathe. Dive. Swim.

The pattern became everything.

On her fourth time surfacing, treading water while she pulled in ragged breaths, the vessel was completing a wide, sweeping turn. Mark stood at the bow, gun raised and extended, scanning the choppy waves with the intensity of a hungry predator who'd lost his prey. The captain remained at the helm as he carefully navigated the increasingly rough water near the rocky coastline.

The gunshot, when it came, was shockingly loud even across the distance.

The bullet struck the water close enough that the entry

point appeared in perfect detail—a small explosive eruption of spray, followed by the silvery streak of its underwater trajectory as it passed maybe three feet to her left before losing momentum. Pure terror flooded her system. She dove again, forcing herself to think past the fear that screamed at her to give up. Mark was shooting blind. He couldn't track her clearly in these conditions, not with the waves and the chop and the way the late afternoon sun was reflecting off the water's surface.

More shots followed in rapid succession—crack, crack, crack—each one sending her deeper, making her swim harder. But even through her panic, a pattern emerged. The captain kept steering the boat away from her position, pulling back whenever the vessel got within seventy or eighty yards. He wasn't pursuing her aggressively. He was worried about something.

The rocks.

He was worried about the submerged volcanic formations that lurked beneath the surface near the shoreline, the ones that could tear through a fiberglass hull like paper.

She surfaced again, lungs burning, arms leaden. The boat hovered fifty yards out, coming no closer. Mark squeezed off two more shots that splashed harmlessly into the water. Then he stopped firing and started watching—binoculars raised, tracking the waterline where she'd gone under. He wasn't leaving. He was waiting for her to surface.

A sideways pull tugged at her body—subtle at first, easy to miss in her exhausted state. The surrounding water changed color, shifting from the deep sapphire blue of the open ocean to an increasingly pale, almost translucent green. The hidden current seized her and dragged her toward shore.

Skylar swam perpendicular to the pull, the way every beach safety course instructed to escape a riptide or lateral current. Swim parallel to shore; don't fight it directly; let the current release you. But her leg had other ideas. The muscle in her right thigh suddenly cramped with vicious intensity. Her rebuilt body was finally giving out, pushed beyond its limits.

She tried to stretch it out, pointing her toes and flexing, but that only made it worse. The pain was blinding, all-consuming. All the while, the current pulled her inexorably toward the rocks. The dark volcanic formations jutted up from the foam like the teeth of some ancient predator. Waves crashed against them with enough force to pulverize anything caught between stone and sea.

The current was winning. Panic set in. She'd been so desperate to escape Mark's gunfire that she hadn't seen this coming. Her injured leg had locked up, muscles clenched tight, every attempted kick a spike of pain that stole her breath. The ocean didn't care how hard she'd fought to get here. It would take her anyway.

The rocks loomed closer. Twenty yards. Ten. Waves exploded against them in thunderous crashes. White foam churned where the ocean's power turned lethal.

Then, her climber brain kicked in, overriding the panic.

She made herself go limp, surrendering to the current.

Think. Assess. Solve the problem.

She studied the water's movement with an analytical eye— the direction of the waves, the way foam patterns revealed underlying currents, how the water flowed around and between the rocky formations.

The current wasn't simply pulling her toward the rocks in a straight line. It was following the coastline, moving parallel to the shore, using the underwater topography to channel its power. If she stopped fighting it, if she worked with it instead of against it...

Skylar angled her body, letting the current carry her side-ways along the coast rather than straight into the jagged formations. Allowing the water to take her seemed like surrender. But sometimes, surrender could be its own strategy.

Through the spray, she spotted her objective: a narrow gap where the water appeared calmer, protected from the worst of the crashing surf by the rocks themselves. It was exactly like finding a good ledge on a climb—a safe harbor where you could rest, catch your breath, reassess your route.

Her muscles had moved past screaming into a dull, pervasive agony that made her wonder if she was doing permanent damage. Each attempted kick sent lightning bolts of pain radiating from her hip all the way to her toes.

But she'd climbed through worse. Pain was information. It couldn't stop her unless she let it.

Skylar used the last reserves of her strength to swim toward that gap.

Ten feet. Five.

The protected water was right there.

The current released her suddenly, the way it always does at the boundary between different water zones. One moment she was being dragged helplessly along; the next she was drifting into calm water that lapped gently against the sand. The contrast was so immediate, so complete, it seemed surreal— like the strange stillness inside the eye of a storm.

Skylar's hands found bottom. She crawled the last few feet, her arms shaking so badly they barely supported her weight. When she finally dragged herself fully onto the narrow strip of beach, she collapsed face-down in the sand, gasping, trembling, alive.

For several long moments, she lay there. Her lungs stopped burning. Her heart rate slowed. Her cramped leg gradually, agonizingly, released its death grip.

But despite everything—the pain, the fear, the utter depletion—a smile spread across her face. She'd made it. Against all odds, despite Mark's bullets and the ocean's fury and her own body's betrayal, she'd survived.

She wasn't going to give up now. Couldn't give up. Ethan was out there somewhere, being held hostage by escaped prisoners. Noah was out there, too, probably trying to do something heroic and stupid. They needed her.

She was going to survive this, dammit. All of them were.

When her breathing finally steadied enough, Skylar forced herself to move. She crawled toward a gap between two large rocks and flattened herself against one of them, peering out toward the water.

Mark's boat lingered in the distance, carving wide search patterns across the water where she'd gone under. She spotted Mark at the bow, gesturing wildly, no doubt screaming at the captain to keep looking. But the vessel drifted farther from shore with each pass, abandoning the dangerous shallows.

She tracked their movements for another five minutes. The search patterns grew wider, more random. They were giving up. Probably convinced she'd drowned or been smashed against the rocks, her body swept away by the current.

Finally, the boat turned and headed toward the resort area. The watersports dock was visible in the distance, maybe a mile down the coast, and the white buildings of the resort complex behind it. Mark was going there to meet Laurent, to get the Cross, to complete whatever transaction had already cost so many lives.

Good. Let him think she was dead. Let him think he'd won.

Skylar leaned back against the sun-warmed rock, closing her eyes for a moment. She was done with Mark's schemes, done with stolen artifacts and black-market deals and whatever else he had planned. None of that mattered anymore. This wasn't about historical crosses or smuggling operations or money.

This was about survival. Hers, her brother's, Noah's. Everything else was noise.

She'd give herself another minute to rest, to let her leg recover enough to walk. Then she'd start moving inland, find her way back to that prison camp where Ethan was being held, and get him out.

She'd find a way. She always did.

22

The minute she'd promised herself turned into five, then ten. Skylar couldn't move yet—her body refused. So she stayed hidden in the rocks and watched Mark's boat work its way down the coastline, the engine's drone fading to nothing.

Noah's face flashed through her mind—the devastation in his eyes when Mark had dragged her onto the boat. Was he okay? Had he gotten Vanessa help? The questions hit her all at once in a wave of worry.

Her vision blurred.

Their night together in the cave during the storm came back to her in fragments. The way he'd held her when she'd been shaking from more than cold. How he'd listened when she'd finally told him about her accident—the real story, not the sanitized version she gave to most who asked. The gentle way his fingers had traced the surgical scar on her thigh in the darkness, not with pity but with something like reverence. When he'd kissed her, something had clicked into place she hadn't known was missing. Now she might never see him again.

And he would blame himself. Of course he would. The

thought of him carrying that guilt—for her—made her eyes sting. None of this was his fault. She needed to survive, if only to tell him that.

Then there was Ethan, held captive somewhere in the island's interior by men who had nothing to lose.

Her only sibling. Her protector.

When kids at school had mocked her for being the weird girl who preferred climbing trees to playing with dolls, Ethan had defended her with a loyalty that had gotten him into more than one schoolyard fight. During the nightmare of her recovery, he'd shown up at the hospital every single day—bringing her favorite mystery novels, telling terrible jokes, holding her hand through those early physical therapy sessions that left her sobbing. He'd never once suggested she should give up on climbing.

She'd returned that loyalty when their parents had objected to his fiancée, Kayla. Too frivolous, they'd said, not serious enough for their ambitious son. When his college friends had written her off as shallow, Skylar had been the one to see what Ethan saw: someone who brought out the best in him.

Kayla came from a completely different world—sorority sisters and country club brunches, a life of careful planning and social calendars. Not Skylar's world at all. But Kayla made Ethan happy, and that was what mattered.

Skylar couldn't fail them. Wouldn't fail them.

Other hostages were in that camp with Ethan. If she could reach them, get word out somehow—that was more than a dozen people who might survive this.

The cramping in her leg finally eased enough for her to stand. She moved along the shoreline, staying low among the volcanic rocks, working her way north. Barnacles scraped her palms raw, the salt water stinging the fresh cuts. Her knee throbbed with each step, hot to the touch even through the fabric of her pants—the scrape from days ago, the one she'd never cleaned properly. She pushed the thought aside. She had no plan yet, no clear idea where the camp was or what she'd do when she got there, but more rest wasn't something she could afford.

Far to the north, something caught her eye. A small Zodiac inflatable with distinctive orange and white Coast Guard markings cut through the water. The craft moved with purpose.

Thank God.

Professional help. People with weapons and radios and the training to handle situations like this.

Skylar squinted against the glare, judging distance. They were too far away to hear her voice, even if she screamed. But if she could find something reflective, catch the sunlight, signal them somehow...

Scanning the rocks, she searched around her for anything that might work—a piece of metal, glass, anything with a surface that could flash.

Voices drifted up from behind.

Male voices. Close.

Skylar froze mid-reach, then dropped into a crouch behind a massive rock. Blood roared in her ears.

Two men in orange emerged from the direction of the resort area, moving along the rocky beach like trackers closing in on a trail. Both carried crude weapons—one had what looked like a tire iron, the other a golf club from the resort's small driving range. She couldn't look away or make herself smaller. She could only watch them come closer and feel her window of escape sliding shut.

Even if the prisoners spotted the distant Zodiac now, the boat was still too far away to help. No immediate rescue, no witnesses. Skylar remained at their mercy.

Pressing herself deeper into the shadow of the formation,

she made herself as small as possible. Their conversation carried clearly across the rocks.

"Boss said sweep this whole section." The taller one was gaunt and mustached, with a voice roughened by years of cigarettes. "She might've slipped past us."

Not searching at random, then. Hunting. For her.

"We find her," the shorter one said in a thick island accent. He was built like a bull with a shaved head.

The tall one spat into the rocks. "Mark's got something cooking with Laurent and needs this girl. If we find her, we get an extra cut."

The shorter one laughed—a mean sound without humor. "How much we get?"

"Enough to get off this rock. Enough to disappear somewhere they'll never find us."

Mark had reacted quickly after she'd jumped. He must've mobilized a search party before she'd even dragged herself out of the water. The man didn't miss a beat.

Her eyes darted northward, fixing on the Coast Guard Zodiac. The boat was still visible, but barely—a small speck against the glittering water. They were so close, salvation within sight. But not for her. Not here, hidden on this stretch of beach, out of their view. No one on that boat knew she was missing, let alone trapped. The realization hit hard and cold: rescue so near, yet oblivious to her.

The men were closing in. They searched methodically, checking behind every boulder, every crevice large enough to hide a person.

Skylar's breath came shallow and quick. She willed herself to slow it down, to quiet the ragged gasps that might give her away. Her injured leg throbbed where it was folded beneath her, threatening to cramp again.

Nowhere to run. Nowhere to hide. With the ocean on one

side, prisoners on the other, and the Coast Guard too far to matter.

The compact, muscular man stopped walking. His head turned slowly, scanning the uneven terrain of volcanic stone and tidal pools.

She pressed herself deeper against the rock, willing them to pass by without looking too carefully at the shadows.

"You hear dat?"

"Hear what?"

"Tink I hear somethin'."

Skylar stopped breathing entirely, her lungs burning with the effort of absolute stillness.

The seconds stretched. Waves crashed against rock. Seabirds cried in the distance. Her pulse hammered in her skull.

Then a piece of loose volcanic rock, disturbed when she'd pressed back against the boulder, skittered down toward the waterline.

The sound was tiny. Insignificant.

Fatal.

Both sets of footsteps stopped. They turned toward her hiding spot.

"Well, well." The tall one said. His words dripped with satisfaction. "What do we have hiding back there?"

"Come on out, sweetheart." The shorter one's voice came from her right as he moved to flank her, cutting off any route toward the jungle. "We know you dere. Don' make dis harder dan it need to be."

Skylar risked a glimpse around the edge of the boulder. The tall one stood maybe ten feet away, tire iron in his hand. The shorter one was circling wide, his golf club raised and ready.

Her mind raced through the options.

Run?

Her leg was barely functional.

Fight?

She had no chance against two armed men.

"We ain't gonna hurt you," the shorter one said as he crept closer. His harsh laugh was worse than his words. "Not too much. Mark wouldn' be likin' dat."

The tall one laughed too. The sound made her stomach turn.

Then strong fingers dug into her shoulders, hauling her upright. She tried to twist away, but her exhausted muscles had nothing left to give. The tall prisoner jerked her out from behind the boulder, his breath hot and rancid against her ear.

"Look what we caught," he said, genuine pleasure in his voice. "Boss is gonna be real happy about this."

In the distance, the Coast Guard disappeared behind another outcropping of rocks. The orange and white markings vanished from view.

Rescue had been so close. Now it was gone.

Her desperate swim to freedom had bought her nothing but a few minutes of hope before Mark's net closed around her again. The taste of bile rose in her throat. Every cut, every bruise, every agonizing kick through the water had been for nothing.

This time, he wouldn't give her another chance to escape.

The shorter prisoner grabbed her other arm, and together they began dragging her south.

Back to the resort.

Back to Mark.

Back to whatever he had waiting.

23

One moment Noah had been surveying the hostage camp from the ridge, the next he was staring down two armed escaped prisoners. He froze, the makeshift club suddenly useless in his hand. The gold-toothed prisoner with the Elvis sideburns stood five feet away. Behind him, his dark-skinned companion held a sharpened piece of metal to Vanessa's throat. A thin line of blood already marked where the point pressed into her skin.

"You one of them cruise people?" Gold Tooth repeated, taking another step that narrowed the gap between them.

"Easy," Noah said, raising his free hand while keeping the club low and non-threatening. His voice came out steadier than he expected. "I don't want to go back to that hellhole any more than you do."

The lie came easier than it should have. Desperation made liars of everyone, apparently.

Gold Tooth's eyes narrowed as he conducted a methodical assessment—taking in shirtless Noah with scratches covering his arms from days of jungle survival and the general look of someone who'd been fighting for his life.

Something shifted in the man's posture. The aggressive tension eased slightly, his shoulders dropping an inch.

"Don't recognize you," he said, his tone still suspicious but no longer immediately hostile. "What cell block you from?"

Noah's stomach dropped. He had no idea about prison hierarchies or the internal dynamics of Saint Marielle Correctional. One wrong answer and this conversation would end with his blood soaking into the jungle floor.

"Was in processing when everything went down," Noah said, hoping the vague explanation would cover his ignorance. "New transfer."

Gold Tooth studied him for another long moment, his head tilting slightly. Noah could see him weighing the explanation, looking for tells. Sweat ran down Noah's naked back despite the shade.

Before the prisoner could respond, a voice cut through the air from the direction of the hostage camp.

"Ramirez, what the hell are you doing out here?"

Another prisoner emerged from the undergrowth—younger with a double teardrop tattoo under his right eye and long scraggly hair pulled back in a ponytail. But instead of joining forces with the first two, his body language immediately signaled conflict. His stance was aggressive, territorial. This wasn't backup. This was competition.

"Taking my prize to Baptiste," Gold Tooth—apparently Ramirez—replied, his tone shifting to defensive. His weight redistributed as if preparing for a confrontation.

"*Your* prize?" The newcomer laughed, harsh and mocking, gesturing toward Vanessa with his weapon—hedge trimmers with the safety guard ripped off, exposing the serrated double blades. "Since when do you work alone, old man? And who decided Baptiste gets first pick of the rich tourists?"

The dynamic shifted completely. Vanessa's capture had ignited some kind of internal power struggle. Prison politics playing out in real time.

"Been hunting strays all morning," Ramirez shot back, his grip tightening on the rebar, his makeshift weapon of choice, until his knuckles went white. "Found her fair and square, Walker. Baptiste will get his cut, like we planned."

"Baptiste isn't running this show anymore," Walker said. "Russo claimed the south camp. Things are changing, and you old-timers better get with the program."

The prisoner with dreadlocks, who'd been holding Vanessa, shifted nervously, the shiv lowering slightly from her throat. "Russo? Since when?"

"Since he collected every weapon he could find after the breakout and decided he wants to be in charge now," Walker replied, his attention now fully focused on Ramirez. "Clubs, pipes, blades—anything that can crack a skull. Game's changed, and loyalty's got a new price tag."

The tension coiled tighter between the prisoners. Years of prison hierarchy and gang politics were playing out in front of them. Vanessa had inadvertently become the catalyst for what was building into an inevitable clash.

If they started fighting each other, Noah might have only seconds to pull Vanessa away before someone remembered he existed.

"Russo can kiss my ass," Ramirez snarled, spitting into the dirt. "We've been loyal to Baptiste for five years. We're not switching sides because some punk makes a move."

"Then you're going to have a problem," Walker replied.

Out of the corner of his eye, Noah caught movement— several more figures stepping from the jungle behind the younger man. Three, four, five. Reinforcements. All armed with improvised weapons. All watching Ramirez like wolves circling a wounded deer.

The math had changed. Ramirez was outnumbered.

"This rich lady comes with us," Walker declared, lunging for Vanessa.

Ramirez stepped between them, rebar raised. "Like hell she does."

The deadlocked prisoner holding Vanessa was so focused on the standoff that he didn't notice her hand sliding toward the small pocketknife Noah had pressed into her palm earlier. In one swift motion, she slashed backward with the blade, catching him across the forearm. He yelped and released her, stumbling backward as blood streamed from the cut.

"Bitch!" He swung wildly in his rage and pain, catching Walker across the jaw with a vicious right hook that snapped the younger man's head sideways.

Within seconds, all pretense of negotiation shattered. The gang of escapees launched into brutal combat—fists, weapons, raw violence. A couple more prisoners emerged from the jungle—some loyal to Baptiste, others aligned with Russo's faction—and the fighting spread like wildfire. Grunts of impact. Cursing in Spanish and English. The wet sound of fists hitting flesh.

Noah didn't waste a second. As the prisoners grappled and cursed, he grabbed Vanessa's wrist and pulled her away from the melee.

"This way," he whispered, his eyes catching an opening between trees and shrubs where the prisoners had emerged.

Amid the screams and the crack of makeshift weapons against bone, two more moving bodies went unnoticed.

Barely more than a game track, the narrow trail offered a way down. Vanessa gripped his shoulder and leaned heavily against him, each step a careful negotiation. The path wound steep and treacherous through dense foliage. When they reached the bottom, Noah oriented himself toward the camp.

More shouts erupted from the direction of the camp itself. The violence was spreading. What had started as a localized dispute over one hostage was part of something larger—a fracturing within the prisoner hierarchy that had been building since they'd taken over Tesoro Bay.

The screams reached them through the undergrowth. Vanessa stiffened. "What's happening?"

"Our chance," Noah said grimly. "Sounds as if the gangs are turning on each other."

The fighting grew louder as they approached the camp perimeter. When they finally reached the edge of the clearing, Noah's pulse spiked.

The prison camp was in upheaval.

The damage from last night's storm was worse than it had looked from the ridge above, and now the prisoners were tearing through what remained. They had broken into factions and were fighting running battles across the compound. Some wielded crude weapons: glass shards wrapped in cloth, golf clubs, kitchen knives. Others fought with bare fists. In the far corner, a man stuffed rags into plastic water bottles filled with something that caught the light like gasoline. Several shelters were already burning, sending columns of black smoke into the sky. Even at this distance, the heat pressed against Noah's face.

The cruise passengers huddled in the center of the compound, momentarily forgotten as the prisoners focused entirely on destroying each other. Guards who'd been watching the hostages minutes before were now engaged in the fight, their attention completely diverted.

"There," Noah said to Vanessa. "That's Ethan."

Skylar's brother was easy to identify even from this distance

—the same straight nose, the same sandy brown hair. Despite an obvious leg injury causing him to limp, he helped shield an elderly couple from the violence erupting around them, positioning himself between them and the fighting.

"How are we supposed to get through that?" Vanessa stared at the war zone before them.

She was right. But Noah noticed something else—the hostages were no longer surrounded. Their guards had joined the brawl or scattered into the jungle. Twenty terrified tourists sat huddled and unattended near a collapsed shelter. If he and Vanessa could reach them before the fighting ended, before the victors remembered their leverage...

"We go around the edge," Noah said. "Stay low, move fast, and pray they're too busy killing each other to notice."

Slowly, they skirted the edge of the compound, acrid smoke stinging their eyes and screening them from view. The battle was everywhere.

The hostages came into view through a break in the smoke
No time for subtlety.

"Ethan!" Noah called out.

Skylar's brother turned toward the sound. For a moment he just stared, not comprehending. Then Noah waved, and Ethan's eyebrows shot up, his body already shifting toward them.

"Who are you?" Ethan called back.

"I'm with Skylar," Noah shouted. "She sent me to find you."

Ethan's rigid posture broke. Something between a laugh and a sob escaped him as he hobbled toward them, favoring one leg. He didn't come alone—he grabbed arms, hauled others up, and brought them with him as he limped toward Noah and Vanessa.

"Skylar's alive?" Ethan's voice cracked with emotion as he drew closer. "Where is she?"

"She's alive, but she's in trouble," Noah said as Ethan led a small group of hostages toward their position. Behind them, two prisoners crashed through one of the burning shelters, still grappling. "We need to get out of here while they're distracted."

The group that reached them included Ethan, the elderly couple he'd been protecting—both trembling but moving under their own power—a gray-haired man in his fifties who quickly introduced himself as Dr. Paul Chisolm, a trauma surgeon from Boston, a younger man in his twenties with his left arm hanging at an awkward angle, and a middle-aged man whose designer name golf attire was now torn and filthy, covered in dirt and what looked like dried blood.

"Where is she?" Ethan's eyes locked on Noah. "Where's my sister?"

"A man named Mark took her." Noah glanced back at the ongoing battle. Prisoners were still going at each other with savage fury, the smoke thickening. "He's armed. Dangerous."

"Mark who?" A vein pulsed in Ethan's temple. "What the hell happened?"

"Mark Thompson. He killed his wife and took Skylar hostage," Vanessa said quietly, her voice strained. She swayed slightly, and the doctor moved to steady her, his eyes immediately assessing her blood-soaked bandage. "This entire nightmare is my fault."

Ethan's nostrils flared, his face flushing red. His muscles coiled as if he wanted to run toward his sister right now, injuries and impossible odds be damned.

"Then we rescue her," Ethan said simply, his tone allowing no argument.

"We will," Noah promised, meeting his gaze. "But first we need to get out of here before they remember they have hostages to watch."

An explosion rocked the far side of the camp—probably the improvised firebombs detonating. The blast sent burning wood, shattered glass, and chunks of metal flying. Prisoners scattered, some with their clothes on fire, screaming. The heat rolled across the compound in a wave.

"My God," Dr. Chisolm breathed, his face pale.

"Time to go," Noah said urgently, already moving. "Now."

They headed south toward the overgrown tropical wilderness, supporting the injured and keeping as low as possible. Behind them, the camp continued to burn and tear itself apart. What had started as a coordinated hostage situation had devolved into complete self-destructive anarchy.

Ethan, despite his pronounced limp, took point and guided them away from the camp. The elderly couple clung to each other, moving as fast as their aged legs allowed. The young man with the injured arm and the golfer brought up the rear, glancing back to ensure they weren't being followed.

Behind them, the rest of the hostages—perhaps a dozen dazed and filthy figures who had been huddled together under a tree—stumbled into motion at the first explosion. Some bolted straight into the dense jungle, crashing through vines without looking back. Others froze for a heartbeat, eyes wide at the sight of prisoners running wild with bloody knives and other weapons in their hands, before panic sent them sprinting in every direction—toward the beach, deeper inland, anywhere that promised distance from the bedlam erupting around them.

Noah's group made it perhaps two hundred yards into the jungle when another series of explosions erupted from the camp. The ground shook beneath their feet.

"They're going to kill each other," Dr. Chisolm muttered, helping the elderly woman over a fallen log.

"Good," Ethan said. "Saves us the trouble."

Noah understood the sentiment—these men had terrorized innocent people, had held them hostage for days—but he was more focused on the immediate implications. They had to put serious distance between themselves and the camp before the fighting ended and the men in orange hunted them down.

"We need to keep moving," Noah said, pulling Diego's water-stained map from his pocket. According to the map, there was a small stream about half-a-mile southwest. "There's a stream in this direction. We can regroup there, treat the wounded, and figure out our next move."

"What about Skylar?" Ethan demanded, stopping so abruptly the golfer nearly collided with him. "You said Mark took her. Where?"

Noah quickly explained everything that had happened—the confrontation on the north beach, Mark's revelation about the stolen Cross, Skylar's capture. How Vanessa had been injured and how Diego had died in the sand. How the last time he'd seen Skylar, she was headed out on a small fishing boat with a gun pointed at her.

"You let him take her?" The words came out strangled.

"I had no choice," Noah replied, meeting the man's gaze and refusing to look away. "Mark has a gun. Vanessa was seriously wounded, Diego was already dead, and I had no way to catch a boat on foot." He paused, his throat tight. "She's smart, she's tough, and if anyone can survive this, it's her."

Ethan stared at him for a long moment. Then the tension in his shoulders gradually eased. He nodded slowly. "You did what you could, but now we find her. Whatever it takes."

"Agreed," Noah said. "But we do it smart. Otherwise, we're handing Mark another hostage."

Behind them, the sounds of battle were beginning to fade, replaced by the crackle of flames consuming wood and fabric, and occasional distant shouts—whether of triumph or agony, impossible to tell. The hostage camp was destroying itself, which solved one problem but created a host of new ones. Without the prisoners focused on guarding the hostages, they were free. But without knowing where the various factions had scattered to, the entire island had become even more dangerous.

Vanessa swayed in Noah's grip. "I need to sit down soon or I'm going to pass out."

Noah tightened his grip around her waist. "We're almost there. Just a little farther."

A lie. They still had terrain to cover, and she was fading with every step. He kept his voice steady anyway. Sometimes, lies were all you had.

His mind kept circling back to Skylar as they walked. Was she all right? What was Mark doing to her right now? And Russo—the memory of his dead eyes and cruel smile made Noah's stomach turn. Every minute that passed was another minute she spent with a man who'd murdered his own wife to protect his deal.

But something else was taking shape beneath the fear. He had Ethan now. A small group of allies. They'd made it out of the camp alive, and they knew things—the stolen Cross, the meeting with Laurent, the section of the resort where Mark planned to make the exchange. They weren't helpless anymore. They could act.

Together, they'd track down Skylar—and then make Mark answer for his actions.

He hadn't forgotten the promise he'd burned into himself as she'd looked back from that boat, eyes locked on his across the widening water. He would find her. No matter the cost, no matter how long it took.

24

The rope bit into Skylar's wrists as the prisoners bound her hands in front of her, the coarse fibers scraping skin already raw from salt water and sun. The shorter one—Jean-Claude—kept glancing toward the jungle as if expecting someone to emerge at any moment. His movements were nervous, agitated, the kind of twitchy energy that came from too much adrenaline and too many days without real sleep.

"She not goin' nowhere now," Jean-Claude said, testing the knots with a satisfied grunt. His hands were rough, and he worked the rope as if he'd restrained plenty of people before. He pulled the final knot tight enough to make her gasp.

Skylar slumped against the boulder that had betrayed her, its rough volcanic surface biting through her shirt and into her spine. The knee she'd abraded against rock that first day pulsed with dull fire. She tried to shift, hunting for even a fraction of relief, but the taller convict stepped in at once. His shadow slid over her like a heavy hand, pinning her in place.

"Stay still," he warned.

Jean-Claude held up a radio—the cheap walkie-talkie type

the Meridian employees had carried at Tesoro Bay. "Mark ask us to keep eye on dis stretch of beach. Say if you make it to shore, it probably be somewhere 'round here."

"How many of you are working with him?" Skylar kept her voice steady despite the fear coiling in her chest.

The tall, scarred prisoner shrugged, squatting down beside her. Up close, the network of old injuries crisscrossing his face. Knife scars, pale and puckered. The flattened bridge of a nose broken multiple times. With a chunk missing from one ear, the cartilage torn away by something sharp. "Not many. Most of the guys who broke out are doing their own thing—settling old scores, looking for ways off Saint Marielle. But Mark made it worth our while to stick around and help."

"We supposed to patrol anyway," Jean-Claude added, his nervous energy making him talkative. He couldn't seem to stand still, shifting his weight from foot to foot like a boxer warming up. Sweat ran down his face despite the ocean breeze. "Baptiste handpick us from de prison for de break. Was supposed to be small—six, maybe seven guys. But tings get out of hand, you know? Guards start shootin', more inmates break free. Whole ting turn into a mess." He shrugged, a sharp, jerky movement. "But Baptiste, he know who to trust from de old days. When Mark need extra hands after, Baptiste know who to call."

So Mark's operation was smaller and more desperate than she'd thought. He wasn't some criminal mastermind with an army at his disposal—he was a man improvising with whatever resources he could scrape together, relying on a handful of escaped convicts who were in it for immediate payment rather than long-term loyalty. That information might be useful. Might give her an opening.

If she survived long enough to exploit it.

"Boss said to call the minute we spot anything," the tall prisoner said, settling into a more comfortable position beside her. His proximity made her skin crawl—close enough that she could smell him, stale sweat and something sour underneath. He pulled out the radio and thumbed the transmit button. Static crackled. "Lucky for us, you practically swam right into our arms."

Skylar closed her eyes, trying to center herself the way she did before a difficult climb. Fear was the enemy. Panic would shut down her ability to think clearly, to spot opportunities, to survive. She needed to find some advantage in this situation. But the rope around her wrists was expertly tied, the knots tight and professional, and she was miles from any help. The Coast Guard Zodiac she'd seen was long gone, probably patrolling beyond the northern coastline by now.

Jean-Claude raised the radio to his lips, his thumb pressing the transmit button. "Boss, we got somethin' you gonna want to see."

Static crackled for a moment before Mark's voice came through. The strain was audible even through the cheap speaker—barely controlled stress, a man whose plans kept falling apart. "What is it? I told you to keep radio chatter to a minimum."

"Dat girl who went swimming? She alive. We got her." Jean-Claude couldn't keep the pride out of his voice—the hard-earned smirk of a street kid who'd just pulled off the score of a lifetime.

A pause stretched across the airwaves, long enough that Mark's silence became its own answer. Then his voice came again, sharper now with surprise and something that might have been relief. "Where?"

"West Beach, near de rocks. She wash up like a gift from de ocean."

Mark would be recalculating now, adjusting his strategy on

the fly. The man was many things—murderer, thief, manipulator—but he wasn't stupid. He would see this development as both an opportunity and a complication. She was valuable to him again, leverage he could use. But she was also proof that his control wasn't as absolute as he'd thought.

"Stay put," Mark's voice commanded through the speaker. "Don't move from that position. We're docking right now, and then we'll come to you."

The radio clicked off. The tall prisoner lit a cigarette, as if the world wasn't falling apart around them.

Jean-Claude grinned, revealing missing teeth and blackened gums. "Payday coming, mon ami."

The scarred prisoner nodded, his eyes never leaving Skylar's face. He took a drag of his cigarette. "Yeah. And this time, we'll make sure she doesn't go for another swim."

Skylar stared out at the ocean. Tears pricked her eyes, hot and unwelcome. She'd made it to shore alive, and now she was right back where she'd started—Mark's prisoner, with even fewer options than before.

Get up. Keep fighting. You're not done yet.

The thought surfaced unbidden, sounding almost like Noah's voice in her head. Steady. Rational. Believing in her even when she couldn't believe in herself.

But her body didn't respond. Exhaustion had seeped into her bones. She was so tired. Tired of running. Tired of fighting. Tired of surviving one crisis only to face another.

"Looks like your luck ran out, sweetheart," the scarred prisoner said. The gaps in his grin gave him a predatory appearance, like a shark that had been in too many fights.

"You don't have to do this," Skylar said, forcing her voice to stay calm and reasonable despite the terror clawing at her throat. "Whatever Mark is paying you, it's not worth spending the rest of your life in prison."

The scarred prisoner laughed, a harsh sound devoid of humor. "Lady, we're already escaped convicts. What's a little kidnapping on top of everything else?"

"The Coast Guard is here," Skylar pressed, trying to plant seeds of doubt. "Saint Marielle is probably crawling with law enforcement by now. It's only a matter of time before they reach Tesoro Bay. How do you think this ends for you?"

Jean-Claude shifted nervously. His eyes darted toward the jungle as if he could sense the net closing around them. But the tall prisoner shrugged, unmoved. "Same way it always ends for guys like us. But at least this time we get paid for the trouble."

Skylar closed her eyes, trying to summon the same mental strength that had gotten her through her climbing accident. But her throat was raw with thirst, a different kind of suffering.

The sound of approaching footsteps made her look up.

Mark appeared from around a rocky outcropping to the south, his face flushed with anger and exertion. His once neat appearance had become disheveled—his shirt soaked with sweat and clinging to his chest, his hair wild from the wind and spray, his shoes wet and covered in sand. He looked like a man whose careful plans were unraveling thread by thread.

Russo followed a few steps behind, and Skylar's stomach dropped. The big man looked exactly as he had on the boat—cold, calculating, dangerous. But something had shifted. On the boat, he'd been Mark's muscle, following orders. Now his posture suggested something different. The way he walked slightly to the side rather than behind Mark. He had the casual confidence of someone who knew the power dynamic had changed in his favor.

Mark stopped a few feet away, catching his breath. "Thought the ocean might have finished you off."

"Should have." Skylar mustered what defiance she could manage.

Russo stepped closer. "Mark said to keep looking. Said you were tough. Guess he was right."

"We don't have time for this," Mark snapped. "We need to get to the fence before Baptiste loses patience."

"Your timeline, not mine." Russo's tone was casual, but the challenge was unmistakable. "You're the one who needs that Cross. I'm already getting paid."

Mark's hands clenched into fists at his sides. Color crept up his neck. "We discussed the terms—"

"We discussed a lot of things before your plan started falling apart," Russo interrupted. His voice remained calm, almost amused. "Before you lost the girl off the boat. Before everything went to shit. Last I checked, I'm still the only one who can kill that fence without frying himself or setting off alarms. New circumstances mean new terms."

There it was. Skylar could see it clearly now—Russo was renegotiating in real time, exploiting Mark's desperation. It seemed Mark needed Russo to get through that electrified fence. Russo knew it, and he was squeezing every advantage out of that knowledge.

"Fine. We'll discuss your new terms after we have the Cross," Mark said through gritted teeth. "But right now, we need to move."

"We?" Jean-Claude spoke up, his nervous energy transforming into something more aggressive. "What about our deal? You promise us payment for helpin' wit' dis whole thing. And extra for findin' de girl like you say."

"And you'll get it," Mark said, dusting sand off his hands with sharp, agitated movements.

"When?" the scarred prisoner demanded, taking a step closer to Mark. His body language shifted from casual to threatening. "We've been doing your dirty work for days. My boys are getting restless, wondering if you're gonna skip out on us."

Mark's alliance with these escaped convicts was more fragile than it appeared. They were partners of convenience.

"You'll be paid when the job is complete," Mark said, his voice tight. "Not before. That's how this works."

"That ain't how *we* work," Jean-Claude shot back, his nervous energy transforming into aggression. "We take risks, we get paid. Simple."

Russo moved forward, positioning himself between Mark and the other two prisoners. "Back off," he said. Both men immediately stepped back. Whatever hierarchy existed among Baptiste's chosen men, Russo clearly sat at the top of it. "You two get paid after we get through the fence. After Baptiste hands over the Cross. That's the deal."

"Deal keeps changing," the scarred prisoner muttered, but he didn't press further.

Russo turned to Mark. "But he's right about one thing. We need to know you're good for it."

Mark wiped sweat from his forehead with the back of his hand. "It's handled. I have payment."

"What payment?" the scarred prisoner snapped. "You told us there was cash coming from some rich lady. How the hell are you paying now?"

"He's got the pearls," Russo said flatly.

Mark's head snapped toward him. "Shut up."

"He took the rich lady's pearls and then shot her." Russo's expression remained unreadable. "—Antique, right? Worth what, a couple mil? Maybe more?"

"Baptiste wanted cash," Jean-Claude said nervously. "He ain't gonna like this change."

"Baptiste will take what I offer him," Mark snapped, but his voice lacked conviction.

Uncertainty flickered across Mark's face. He was gambling now, hoping Baptiste would accept alternative payment.

Hoping he could talk his way through yet another complication in a plan that kept falling apart.

Jean-Claude let out a harsh laugh that held no humor. "Man, you crazy."

"Those pearls are worth more than what he's asking," Mark said.

"Don' matter what dey worth," Jean-Claude shot back. "Matters what Baptiste want. And he don' want to fence stolen jewelry. He want clean money he can use right away." He turned to Russo. "You know dis man. You know how he is about changes. He gonna be pissed."

"And our cut?" the scarred prisoner pressed, sensing the whole plan might be unraveling.

"After I verify the Cross is authentic and complete the transaction—however that happens—then you get your money," Mark said, irritation flashing across his face. "Split it however you want."

"However that happens?" Jean-Claude's voice rose. "You don' even know if he gonna take dem pearls!"

"Baptiste said no money, no Cross," said Russo. "You screw this up, we all walk away empty. And some of us—" his gaze slid to Mark with cold calculation, "—won't walk away at all."

The threat hung in the air, unmistakable.

"Mark," Skylar said, trying to keep her voice steady, "you don't have to do this. I won't say anything. I swear. Let me go, and I'll disappear. You'll never see me again."

She willed him to hear what she wasn't saying—that she could give him an escape route, that killing her or dragging her deeper into this would only make everything worse when the truth came out.

"And what?" Mark laughed harshly, bitterly. "You'll keep quiet about murder, theft, and smuggling? Forgive me if I don't trust your word, Skylar. You've proven remarkably resourceful at staying alive and causing problems."

Even though he rejected her offer, the thought gave her something to hold on to. She'd survived things that should have killed her. She'd jumped from a moving boat into the open ocean. She'd outsmarted Mark once already.

She could do it again. Somehow.

25

V anessa stumbled for the third time. Noah caught her before she went down completely. The stream marked on the map had to be close.

It had to be.

Then they could follow it straight to the resort.

"How much farther?" Vanessa asked, her voice tight with pain.

"Not much." Noah tried to sound reassuring while consulting the map. Problem was, they were in the middle of an undefined green patch, and somewhere in it there was supposed to be a stream. But as the sun sank lower in the sky, it dawned on him they'd gotten lost. The map was too vague with limited landmarks.

Danny volunteered to scout ahead, cradling his injured arm. "Lemme climb this rise—might see somethin' from up there." He scrambled up a slope with surprising agility despite his pain. At the crest, he froze, then waved frantically. "Oi! Coastline—southwest. That's the resort dead ahead."

They were approaching the resort area, stream or no stream.

After a long slog through suffocating green, a collective sigh escaped the group. Smiles flickered briefly before fear reclaimed them; those orange-uniformed convicts could be lurking anywhere, ready to drag them back to the hostage camp's watchful guards and rifles. Freedom hovered at the edge of the tangled brush, but one wrong step could mean recapture if they weren't careful.

"I have an idea." Dr. Chisolm pulled out his cruise card—a black plastic rectangle marking him as one of the premium passengers. Dirt and blood smudged its surface, but the magnetic strip appeared intact. "The Sunset Beach Club. I paid fifteen hundred dollars extra for VIP access during the shore excursion. It's supposed to be exclusive, secure, and with medical facilities."

"How far?" Noah studied the map, but there were no labeled buildings on it.

"North end." Dr. Chisolm moved closer, pointing to a section of trees near the base of the mountains. "Built into the hillside overlooking the main beach. We can skirt around from this direction." His finger slid across the map from the jungle, around the foothills, and straight to the club without ever being seen from the main tourist zone. "If the electricity is still running, my card should work. The place has a medical station —they stock it for everything from jellyfish stings to cardiac events. Rich passengers expect immediate care." He eyeballed Vanessa. "We could stabilize the wounded."

"What if prisoners took it over?" Danny asked. "Place like that would make a nice headquarters."

"It's possible," Dr. Chisolm admitted, wiping sweat from his forehead. "But the club was designed for exclusivity. Electronic locks on every entrance, security glass, cameras everywhere.

They built it to keep out anyone who hadn't paid their premium."

The club offered their best chance for medical help and temporary safety. Yet Noah hesitated, his gaze drifting toward the coastline visible through the trees. Somewhere out there, Mark had Skylar. Every minute they delayed...

"You're right. We need to get everyone medical attention first." Noah swallowed his guilt, accepting others needed help, too. "Get them secured, then—"

"Then we go after Skylar," Ethan interrupted. "You and I will check out the watersports dock while the others take shelter."

Dr. Chisolm's eyes narrowed at Ethan's knee—swollen tight against his torn khakis. "You're in no condition—"

"I'll be in worse condition if something happens to Skylar while I'm sitting around," Ethan said. "She's out there with killers. Every minute we waste arguing is another minute that creep has to disappear with her. I'm not giving up on her. Not for anything."

The finality in his voice ended the debate.

The small group pushed through the remaining jungle, undergrowth gradually giving way to manicured landscaping that marked the resort's outer boundary. Palm trees lined pathways that had been pristine three days ago now showed signs of hasty abandonment—a poolside bar with bottles overturned and glasses shattered on the tile, lounge chairs scattered like dominoes, towels fluttering in the breeze. Flies swarmed over a buffet table, where lobster and tropical fruit had begun to rot in the heat. The sweet-sick smell of decay hung heavy in the humid air, making Noah gag.

But no men in orange. No movement at all. No sound except the buzz of insects and the distant crash of waves.

Where did everyone go?

"There." Dr. Chisolm pointed through a grove of perfectly spaced coconut palms.

The Sunset Beach Club rose from the tropical foliage—a fortress of wealth disguised as paradise. High stucco walls painted brilliant white stretched in both directions, topped with hand-painted tiles depicting scenes of the Caribbean. The barrier completely concealed whatever luxury lay beyond, protecting its exclusive clientele from even having to see the common tourists. Bougainvilleas cascaded over the walls in vivid bursts of magenta and orange.

"Bloody hell," Robert muttered, taking in the opulent display. "What did you say the damage was for a day pass to this place?"

"Worth every penny if it keeps us alive," Martha replied, though her eyes widened at the sheer extravagance.

Dr. Chisolm led them toward the main entrance—an archway that belonged in a Mediterranean villa rather than a Caribbean beach club. Frosted glass panels etched with the club's logo flanked the entrance, somehow untouched by the chaos that had consumed the rest of the island. The card readers looked military-grade, more sophisticated than anything Noah had designed for his own security clients. Polished marble columns flanked mahogany doors carved with intricate patterns of sea life—dolphins, turtles, manta rays frozen in perpetual motion.

A bronze plaque near the entrance read: "Sunset Beach Club—Est. 2019—Where Paradise Meets Perfection."

"Here goes nothing," Dr. Chisolm said, sliding his black cruise card through the reader.

Silence. Then a soft beep, green light, and the satisfying click of heavy locks disengaging.

The doors swung open on whisper-quiet hinges, releasing a blast of cool air from within.

"Guess the main power's still on." Noah noted the subtle hum of climate control, the soft lighting that illuminated the entrance. "Maybe they run on solar. Place like this could have its own power grid."

They moved quickly through the interior, Dr. Chisolm navigating with the confidence of someone who'd memorized the layout during his previous visit. The corridor could have been lifted from a luxury hotel—original paintings in gilt frames, fresh orchids somehow still pristine in crystal vases, marble floors polished to mirror brightness. Classical music drifted from hidden speakers, Vivaldi continuing his performance for an audience that had fled days ago. The disconnect was surreal —wealth and refinement existing in a bubble while mayhem consumed everything beyond these walls.

"Medical station should be through here," Dr. Chisolm said, heading toward a discreet door marked with a small red cross. "Should have everything we need."

Inside, the bay was compact but impeccably equipped: bright surgical lighting, a padded exam table, locked cabinets of pharmaceuticals, an autoclave still humming faintly, even a portable X-ray unit and suture kits laid out like instruments in an operating theater. Noah and Ethan eased Vanessa onto the table while Dr. Chisholm snapped on nitrile gloves he'd found in a cupboard and began a rapid assessment—checking pulse, blood pressure, the soaked field dressing Noah had reapplied in the jungle.

"Through-and-through, no major vascular damage from what I can tell," he murmured, voice calm and clinical. "She's lost blood, but she's stable enough for now. I'll clean it thoroughly, get fluids and antibiotics started, and then suture."

He looked at Vanessa first. "You comfortable with me handling this?"

She managed a faint nod, eyes already half-closed.

Noah glanced at Ethan, then back to the doctor. "Doc, any chance there's food and water around here?"

Dr. Chisholm didn't look up from prepping a tray. "Main kitchen and pantry are down at the far end of the east corridor. Walk-in fridge should still be running, plenty of packaged food, bottled drinks. Help yourselves."

Danny, Robert, Martha, and Harold exchanged quick, relieved glances and slipped out, their footsteps fading softly down the corridor.

Dr. Chisholm addressed Noah. "When I'm finished, I'll bring her to the main lounge on this level. It has the most comfortable seating. We'll regroup there, decide next steps."

Noah lingered a moment longer, meeting Vanessa's eyes until she gave him the smallest reassuring smile. Only then did he and Ethan withdraw, pulling the door closed behind them with a quiet click.

Back on the beach, Skylar remained where Jean-Claude and his buddy had left her—sitting against a boulder, wrists bound, watching Mark unravel.

"We need to move," Mark said, snapping his fingers at Jean-Claude and the scarred prisoner. "You two continue your patrol. Report anything unusual—Coast Guard, military, other survivors."

"And our payment?" the scarred prisoner pressed.

"Like the man said, you'll get it once the deal's done," Russo said. "Now go. Keep this area locked down."

Jean-Claude's face twisted with barely suppressed anger. He opened his mouth as if to argue, then caught Russo's cold stare and shut it again. "Come on," he muttered to his companion, and they headed down the beach, their voices carrying back in low, resentful grumbles.

Once they were out of earshot, Russo turned to Mark. "I know right where the fence's junction box is. Baptiste doesn't like waiting. We should move."

"How long to make it safe to cross?" Mark asked.

"Two minutes to cut the power, maybe another minute to cut through the fence." Russo's gaze slid to Skylar. "She wasn't part of the plan. Baptiste's not gonna be happy about extra complications."

"She keeps Reed from doing anything stupid. That's all Baptiste needs to know."

Extra complications. The words settled cold in her chest. Whatever happened when they reached that fence, she needed to be forgettable—just another piece of cargo, not worth the trouble of dealing with. Draw no attention. Cause no problems. And watch for any chance to run.

Russo grabbed her chin. "But she'd better not slow us down or make noise. We get one shot at this."

She shook herself free of his sweaty grip. Then Mark took hold of Skylar's arm, and they started moving.

They scrambled up from the rocks, across the sandier parts of West Beach, to reach a paved path littered with broken beer bottles and lined by well-maintained shrubs. A golf cart lay overturned in the bushes, its contents scattered. The welcome pavilion, where cruise passengers had once checked in for shore excursions, stood with its windows smashed, colorful banners torn and twisting in the breeze. Someone had spray-painted crude messages on the walls and territorial markings from the prison gangs.

She knew this path. She'd walked it before, with Noah, when rescue seemed within reach. Somewhere out there was the Meridian Voyager, with its buffet lines and pool deck and blissfully ordinary problems. That life felt like a fever dream. This nightmare was real.

Then she caught sight of a white hull through gaps in the foliage—a Coast Guard boat, half a mile out and moving fast.

Rescue was right there—real, tangible, moving through the water with purpose. And they were completely unaware she existed. The cruelty of it nearly buckled her knees.

Mark stopped abruptly, his hand tightening on Skylar's arm. "Is that—"

"Coast Guard," Russo confirmed, barely glancing at the water. "They're expanding their search. We need to move faster."

Mark's head swiveled between the boat and the path ahead. "But if they saw us—"

"They didn't, and they won't," Russo cut him off. "Not if we move fast and finish this exchange."

After making it past the watersports dock and Seashell Beach, they turned onto an overgrown dirt path that most tourists would never have noticed, half-hidden behind a cluster of sea grape trees.

"You'd better hope he'll accept those pearls," Russo said, glancing back over his shoulder.

Mark's face went pale. Sweat ran down his temples despite the shade. "Baptiste's a businessman. He'll understand the value—"

"I said I'd get him through the fence," Russo interrupted. "What happens after that is between you and Baptiste." He shrugged and then settled his cold gaze on Mark. "But if he's not happy, and this deal goes sideways? You'd better hope you can run fast."

The tension crackled between the two men. Russo clearly didn't care if the whole thing fell apart once Baptiste crossed that fence.

While Dr. Chisholm did his work and Ethan went to join the others in the kitchen, Noah ventured toward the floor-to-ceiling windows overlooking the beach. The view stopped him cold— miles of sand stretching into the distance, the water reflecting the orange and pink hues of the setting sun. The sky was ablaze with color, deep purples bleeding into reds along the horizon. Paradise at its most beautiful, and yet all Noah could see was the approaching darkness. The sun was sinking fast, maybe thirty minutes from disappearing completely. Already, shadows were lengthening across the beach, and some of the resort's emergency lighting had begun to flicker on, preparing for nightfall. Behind them, the orange glow of fires still burned in the jungle, sending columns of smoke into the colorful sky.

Skylar was somewhere out there. Held by men who'd already proven they'd kill without hesitation. Was she hurt? Terrified? Still fighting? Or had Mark already—

No, he couldn't let himself finish that thought.

The kitchen door opened. Ethan limped down the corridor, carrying a small plate and a bottle of something. He'd left his crutch behind so he could carry it all, moving carefully with his injured knee.

"Raided the VIP pantry," Ethan said. The plate held an assortment of aged cheeses, cured meats, and fancy crackers. "Figured you hadn't eaten in a while. The beer is some imported brand I haven't heard of. Hope that's okay."

"Thanks." Noah took them, though his stomach was in knots. He forced himself to take a bite of Manchego anyway. His body needed fuel, even if his mind rebelled against the idea.

Ethan lowered himself onto a club chair near the window, wincing as he straightened his injured knee.

"The doctor should take a look at that," Noah said. "He might be able to do something for the swelling."

"I'm fine." Ethan's tone left no room for argument. He prodded the knee gently and sucked in a breath, belying his words. "One of them caught me with a golf club when they grabbed us at the pier. Went straight for the knee." He shook his head. "I should be out there looking for Skylar right now. Instead, I'm stuck here, useless."

"You're not useless—"

"I'm her big brother. I'm supposed to protect her." Ethan's voice was raw. "And when it mattered most, I wasn't there."

The guilt in Ethan's voice mirrored what Noah felt in his own chest. "I was there," he said quietly. "And I still couldn't stop them from taking her."

Ethan looked at him.

"I walked us right into it. I knew Mark had a gun." Noah set down the plate, his appetite gone. "I should have kept us hidden. Should have waited for a better moment. Instead, I dragged Skylar into a situation I couldn't control, and Mark used her against me."

"You were trying to help."

"And she's gone because of it." Noah took a drink of beer, letting the bitterness rest on his tongue for a second or two. "I keep thinking about it. Every second. Everything I could have done differently. If I'd just stayed back—"

"You couldn't have known how it would play out."

"Maybe not. But she's out there with a killer because I made the wrong call."

Ethan was quiet for a moment, staring across the hall at an oil painting of sea turtles swimming over a bed of coral. "How did you two end up together?"

"We were on the same snorkeling trip. When everything went sideways—the prison break, the gunfire—the boat left without us. We swam to shore together." Noah remembered those first chaotic hours. "We've been trying to survive ever since."

Ethan studied him. "What was she like out there? In the jungle, all alone?"

Noah thought about the dangerous hike up the mountain, running away under gunfire, almost sliding into the ravine. Every impossible moment when giving up would have been easier than going on.

"She was the reason I made it," he said finally. "There was this climb we had to do—" He stopped, reliving the vertigo in the ravine, her steady voice guiding him across. "I'm not good with heights. She talked me through every step. Kept me moving."

"That's Skylar." Ethan smiled faintly. "After the accident, she wouldn't let anyone help her. Kayla and I took turns staying with her during recovery, and she fought us all the way. Insisted she could manage on her own, even when she couldn't walk to the bathroom without passing out."

Noah could see it clearly: Skylar gritting her teeth through pain, waving off her brother's help, insisting she was fine when she clearly wasn't. He'd watched her do the same thing in the jungle—downplaying her injuries, refusing to slow down, never admitting how much she was struggling.

"The worst part wasn't the physical therapy," Ethan continued. "It was watching her shut everyone out. Friends stopped calling because she didn't return their messages. She said she didn't want to be anyone's burden." He shook his head. "She came out of it stronger, but lonelier."

The thought of Skylar alone, shutting out the world, hollowed something in Noah's chest.

Ethan pushed himself to his feet with a wince. "When we go after her, I'm coming with you."

Noah looked at Ethan's swollen knee. The man could hardly walk down a corridor, let alone face down Mark and his tattooed prisoner friend.

"We'll figure it out," Noah said. "We're going to get her back."

"Damn right we are."

He limped back toward the kitchen, pausing at the doorway. "Whatever it takes, Reed."

Then he was gone, and Noah was alone with the window and the water and the weight of a promise he intended to keep. When the time came to move, Noah wasn't sure how much help Ethan would actually be—or whether bringing him along would put them all at greater risk.

But that was a problem for later. Right now, they needed a plan.

Then, a new sound cut through the silence—the distinctive high-pitched whine of an outboard motor at full throttle.

Noah's head snapped toward the water. Out beyond the club's wide windows, a Zodiac raced toward shore. The orange and white Coast Guard markings stood out sharply in the dying light, the boat's searchlight already cutting broad arcs across the darkening sea. White foam churned from its bow as it tore in at emergency speed.

Relief slammed through him. "The Coast Guard!" he shouted down the corridor toward the open kitchen door. "They found us!"

26

Ethan was first through the kitchen door, nearly tripping over his own feet in his rush. Harold and Martha walked out next, arms linked for support, faces brightening with hope. Robert bounded after with a ragged cheer, banana in hand, and Danny emerged last with a bottle of orange juice to his lips.

Ethan broke from the group and joined Noah at the window, eyes locked on the approaching Zodiac. "They'll find Skylar," he said. "Boats, helicopters, rescue teams—they'll get her back."

The door to the medical bay clicked open. Dr. Chisholm emerged first, rolling down his sleeves, followed by Vanessa walking slowly under her own power—pale but upright, her arm now professionally bandaged and immobilized in a clean sling. Fresh gauze bulged beneath her torn blouse, no fresh blood seeping through.

She managed a thin smile when she saw the group clustered at the windows. "He does good work," she said quietly, voice steadier than before. "I'll live long enough to watch the cavalry arrive."

A faint, weary smile tugged at Dr. Chisholm's mouth—the first real one Noah had seen from him. "About time," he murmured, fatigue etched around his eyes.

But even as relief washed over the group, Noah's mind remained fixed on the woman he'd failed to protect. Waiting for the authorities to mount a search and rescue operation could take hours, maybe days. Skylar needed help now.

As their group emerged from the beach club's entrance and headed toward the beach, they crossed the abandoned tourist zone where kiosks and gift shops had been ransacked. One of the Coast Guard officers spotted them and raised his hand in greeting.

"U.S. Coast Guard. Are you folks okay?" the officer yelled from the prow of the boat. "We're conducting rescue operations for cruise passengers stranded on the island."

Dr. Chisolm waved both arms above his head. "We have injured people who need immediate medical attention."

The Zodiac's motor cut to an idle as it approached the shallows. Two officers jumped out, their boots splashing in the surf as they steadied the boat and hauled it to shore.

"Everyone stay together," called the lead officer, his voice carrying natural authority. He was young, maybe thirty, with a crisp uniform and an alert posture. "We're going to get you out of here, but we need to move fast. There's still hostile activity on other parts of the island."

"How many people are you missing?" another officer asked.

"There's at least one more," Dr. Chisolm replied, gesturing toward Noah and Ethan. "A young woman they know was taken by one of the criminals. Abducted."

"My sister," Ethan said, lurching forward on his crutch. Sand shifted beneath him, and he nearly went down before catching himself. "Skylar Harris."

"You have to find her. Skylar was kidnapped earlier today

by a man named Mark Thompson," Noah added. "He's armed. He killed his wife and has been working with escaped prisoners."

The officer's expression grew grim. He pulled out a small notebook, flipping it open. "Mark Thompson. Can you give me a description?"

"White male, about fifty, maybe five-ten," Noah said. "Dark hair. He was wearing—" What had Mark been wearing? His mind scrambled. "A Hawaiian shirt. Khakis."

"And your sister?" the officer asked Ethan.

"Twenty-six, five-seven, brown hair," Ethan replied, his voice cracking. "She's a climber—athletic build. She was wearing..." He closed his eyes, trying to remember.

Noah filled in the description. "She was wearing a Meridian employee uniform like this." He gestured at his pants. "And a polo shirt. She had her swimsuit on underneath that. Pink."

The officer wrote it down. "Sir, we'll add her to our missing persons list, but right now our orders are to evacuate confirmed survivors."

"But you'll look for her?" Ethan's chest heaved. "You'll send teams?"

"We'll do everything we can," the officer replied, his tone professional but noncommittal. "But our immediate priority is getting you folks to safety."

"She's out there with a killer." Ethan's voice rose. "Every minute—"

"I understand, sir. But we need to follow protocol. Get you to safety first, then coordinate for hostage recovery."

The evacuation happened fast. Vanessa walked aboard under her own power, leaning heavily on Dr. Chisholm's arm but conscious and alert. The doctor climbed in beside her. Harold needed help to navigate the surf, so Martha supported him on one side while an officer took the other.

Ethan accepted help despite his obvious reluctance to leave without his sister. "I should stay and help look for her," he protested, but his injured knee buckled and two officers had to catch him before he fell face-first in the sand.

"Not in your condition, sir." The lead officer's grip was firm but not unkind. "You'll be more help to your sister if you're well. Let us do our job."

As they carried Ethan to the Zodiac, Noah hung back, his feet rooted in the sand. Every instinct screamed at him to get on that boat, to escape while he could. Safety was twenty feet away. Medical attention. Food. Water. An end to this nightmare.

But Skylar was still out there.

The elderly couple made it into the boat without incident. Robert and Danny followed.

Noah found himself at the back of the evacuation line, watching as they helped lift Ethan into the Zodiac. His friend—because that's what Ethan had become in the span of a few hours—looked back at him. Their eyes met. Ethan's mouth opened as if to speak, but no words came. He nodded once, sharp and quick.

The sun hung low on the horizon, maybe ten minutes from disappearing completely. Once it did, finding anyone on this island would become infinitely harder. Anything could be hidden in those lengthening shadows. Anyone.

As the last of the survivors boarded, Noah scanned the shoreline one final time, searching for a clue that might indicate where Mark had taken her. The beach stood empty except for—

His breath caught.

Down the beach, maybe two hundred yards away, he saw a familiar silhouette—Mark's boat, tied to the watersports dock, bobbing gently in the water.

Skylar.

. . .

Noah made a decision that would have been insane a week ago, back when his biggest worry was quarterly earnings reports and software development schedules.

He stepped backward into the shadows, away from the Zodiac and rescue. As he retreated, the Coast Guard officers were focused on loading the injured. They'd never have let him go after her if they knew. They'd restrain him, call him a liability, while Skylar disappeared forever. By the time they mounted an official search, she could be dead.

To him, Skylar was the priority. The only one worth saving.

The mistake on the beach still burned in his gut—standing helpless as they dragged her away, choosing Vanessa's bleeding wound over Skylar's terrified eyes. He'd made the logical choice, the right choice by any measure. But it had been eating him alive ever since.

He'd be damned if he'd let it happen again.

The Zodiac's twin engines roared to life, churning white foam as the pilot reversed from the beach. Noah pressed himself behind a tiki bar. The structure's weathered planks provided a good hiding spot as sand flew from the boat's prop wash. The inflatable craft pivoted smoothly before turning toward open water. Then its engines opened up, and it accelerated toward the massive Coast Guard cutter, whose lights glowed in the twilight a half mile offshore. Within seconds, the rescue craft became another set of running lights against the darkening horizon, taking everyone to safety.

Everyone except him.

And Skylar.

Noah waited until the sound of the engines faded to a distant hum before emerging from his hiding spot. He moved carefully, hyper-aware that escaped prisoners could be anywhere, then circled behind the tiki bar. An abandoned grill station sat nearby, its lid propped open. He crouched low and then spied a long-handled grill fork—solid steel, two wicked tines, just enough reach to keep a knife at bay. Better than nothing. He wrapped the handle in a bar towel for grip, the improvised weapon steadying his nerves. The sun had nearly disappeared now, the last sliver of orange sinking below the horizon. Darkness would be complete in minutes.

The watersports dock lay ahead. Mark's boat sat at the far end—a small fishing vessel that had seen better days, its paint peeling, its hull scarred. The same boat that had carried Skylar away hours ago. Apparently abandoned, it bobbed gently against the dock, lines creaking with each swell.

Noah crouched behind a concrete piling at the dock's edge, with fork in hand, studying the boat for signs of life. The cabin windows were dark, and no movement was visible on deck. The boat lay quiet, offering no hint of life beyond the water slapping against its side.

But when the boat rocked on a lazy swell, the open cabin doorway shifted into view. For a moment he saw them: a pair of legs stretched out on the floor inside—unmoving, one shoe missing, blood darkening the cuffs of the khaki trousers. The captain's legs.

Noah's stomach tightened. The man was dead.

He tore his eyes away, nausea flickering low in his gut, and looked down the beach—just in time to see three figures about to enter the shadows of a path that led into the jungle. The resort's perimeter lighting caught them briefly—Mark's distinctive build, unmistakable even at this distance, and his convict partner, Russo. And between them...

A woman, stumbling slightly, her hands clearly bound in front. Braided hair. The right height, the right build.

Skylar.

Noah's breath stopped. She was alive—captive, yes, but alive. They were heading for Tesoro Bay's southern boundary. The fence.

Why the fence? The captain was dead on his boat. The water was crawling with Coast Guard.

Someone was waiting on the other side. Had to be.

If they were able to get past the electrified fence, finding her would become nearly impossible. By morning, she could be deep in the island's interior—or dead like Julia. Mark had already murdered his wife. What would stop him from disposing of another witness?

The sun dropped below the horizon, stealing the last natural light. The trio reached the jungle's edge, seconds from vanishing completely.

His old life whispered logic: wait for professionals, trust trained personnel. The old Noah Reed would have deferred to those with experience.

But that man had never met Skylar Harris and fallen in love with her.

He knew it then without question.

He loved her.

Noah cut across the sand toward them. Fear existed, but it couldn't override the single imperative driving him forward.

He would face any threat, accept any risk. Losing her was unacceptable.

The darkness ahead promised violence. Possibly death.

He advanced anyway, closing the distance between himself and the men who held the woman he loved.

Whatever came next, he was bringing her home.

27

The dirt path cut through tangled landscaping. Overgrown hibiscus and bird of paradise had been left deliberately wild to screen the service trail from the guest areas and had spilled untended across the walkway. With the sun gone, mosquitoes swarmed in thick clouds.

What Skylar wouldn't give for some bug spray.

Whenever she stumbled, Mark pushed her forward. His fingers dug into her shoulder hard enough to leave bruises. The man who'd seemed so controlled not long ago was fraying at the edges.

Russo walked ahead. He'd been quiet, scanning their surroundings constantly, as if alert for threats. The Coast Guard sighting shook him up after all.

They'd been walking for maybe ten minutes since leaving the dock, heading steadily inland and a bit uphill. The sound of the ocean had faded behind them, replaced by the constant buzz of insects and the occasional call of tropical birds settling in for the evening.

The fence lay somewhere ahead, dividing the resort from

the rest of Saint Marielle. Three days ago, it had kept the tourists in their bubble of safety. Who would've guessed the real threat would come from the ocean instead in the form of escaped convicts?

"Mark," she said, the words tumbling out before she could stop them. "Whatever happens when you meet Baptiste—I have nothing to do with any of this. I don't know anything about the Cross, about your plan—"

"Shut up." Mark didn't even glance at her, his attention fixed on the path ahead. "You know too much. You've seen too much. That's all that matters."

The flatness of his tone—no anger, no emotion—turned her blood cold. She pressed her lips together, but her mind wouldn't stop working. Mark had promised Baptiste cash. Millions in a bank transfer. Instead, he was carrying pearls.

When the man on the other side of that fence found out about the switch, things were going to get ugly. For all of them.

Eventually, the path opened into a small clearing where a fence stretched across the tangled jungle. Fifteen feet of heavy steel mesh rose from the earth, crowned with several rows of razor wire. Warning signs in multiple languages screamed "DANGER - HIGH VOLTAGE" in bright yellow letters, their universal symbols showing stick figures in the frozen moment of electrocution.

A low hum emanated from it, the kind of sound that made the hair on her arms stand up. Whatever voltage ran through that metal, it wasn't meant to deter. It was meant to kill.

Skylar peered through the mesh as darkness gathered. On the other side lay nothing but wild jungle—thick, rugged, endless. The real Saint Marielle. The kind of place where a person could disappear forever.

Then she saw him. A man perhaps twenty yards back, partially obscured by palms and undergrowth. Even from this distance, she could see he was well-dressed—white linen shirt somehow still crisp, tailored pants without a wrinkle, silver hair perfectly styled despite the humidity. Everything about him seemed wrong against the backdrop of tangled vines and wild ferns. He held a satellite phone to his ear, his posture radiating controlled tension.

"There he is," Russo said, pointing. "That's Baptiste."

As if hearing his name, the silver-haired man pocketed his phone and moved closer to the fence, careful to stay several feet back from the electrified barrier. His cold gray eyes assessed them through the mesh.

"Mark." The way Laurent Baptiste said his name made it sound like a disappointment. His accent held hints of French mixed with Caribbean inflections. "You're late."

"We had complications," Mark said. "And the Coast Guard showed up."

"I have my own complications." Laurent gestured toward the jungle behind him. "My driver's waiting with the Jeep, but we need to move fast before the authorities expand their sweep."

His steely gaze shifted to Russo. "Your prison break was supposed to be surgical. Six men, minimal attention. Instead, you created a massacre that brought the Coast Guard and half the Caribbean military to this island."

Russo's face darkened. "That wasn't on me. Your contact at the prison opened the wrong cell block. Guards started shooting, and everything went to hell. You want someone to blame, look at your own people."

"My people didn't shoot three guards and release forty inmates." Laurent's words cut like glass.

"My people didn't plan a half-assed operation," Russo shot back. "You want clean? Then don't hire prison gangs to do your dirty work."

Laurent's mouth twisted. "At least we agree on something."

The air crackled with tension. Mark shifted nervously between them, clearly aware his precarious deal depended on these two not killing each other before the Cross changed hands.

"Russo," Mark said quickly, breaking the standoff. "Can you kill the power?"

"Yeah." Russo finally dragged his glare off Laurent and headed for the junction box on the utility pole, shoulders rigid. When he opened it, a set of wire cutters and a voltage tester had been stashed inside. "Give me two minutes."

"Make it fast," Laurent called back. "Every second we stand here is a second too long."

Russo ignored the pressure, working methodically on the junction box. He tested several connections with the tester, then began cutting specific wires. "You're lucky I worked electrical for three years before I went in," he muttered, more to himself than anyone else. "Need to isolate this section without triggering the automated failsafe."

Skylar's wrists were raw from the rope, fingers numb and prickling. She stared at Russo's hands moving deftly through the junction box wiring, thoughts spinning. The moment that fence died, her value expired. Hostage on the other side? Loose end left behind? Or a quick bullet to make sure she stayed quiet?

A fence post close to where Russo worked had additional equipment installed—a control panel with blinking LED lights. Russo opened it, studied the wiring for a moment, then made several quick cuts and connections.

The constant hum of electricity died, and the warning lights on the nearest fence section went dark.

"Done," Russo said. "But the automated safety system will

detect the interruption. We got maybe five minutes before the backup power kicks on."

"Then move," Laurent said.

Russo approached the now-safe section of fence, pulling on heavy work gloves that had been tucked in a back pocket. Then he took the wire cutters and began cutting through the chain-link mesh.

Within less than a minute, he'd created an opening large enough for Laurent. The older man ducked through the gap, straightening on the resort side of the fence. Up close, he was even more imposing—six-two at least, with the bearing of someone accustomed to absolute control.

Laurent's gaze swept over the group, landing on Skylar. His eyes narrowed. "Who is this?"

"She saw too much," Mark said. "I couldn't leave her behind."

"Couldn't leave her behind." Laurent repeated the words slowly, his expression hardening. "I said no complications. No witnesses. And you bring me one?"

"She's not your concern."

"Everything that threatens this operation is my concern." Laurent studied her for a long moment, then dismissed her with a shake of his head. "We'll deal with her later. The payment—show me confirmation the money transfer went through."

Sweat beaded Mark's forehead. "There's been a complication—"

"Another complication?" Laurent's voice dropped to something lethal. "You assured me the money would be waiting."

"I have payment." Mark pulled Vanessa's necklace from his canvas bag. "Antique pearls. Worth probably more than two million, authenticated, perfectly matched—"

Laurent's face flushed with rage. "Pearls? You're offering me jewelry instead of cash?"

"They're worth more than you asked for—"

"I don't care what they're worth!" Laurent's composure shattered completely. "Do I look like a fence? Do you think I run a pawn shop? I told you I needed clean money I can move immediately. Not some trinket I'd have to risk selling on the black market!"

"It's an authenticated antique, acquired legally," Mark pressed. "Any serious collector—"

"Will require provenance I can't provide without exposing myself!" Laurent stepped closer, his voice rising. "Where did these come from? Who's looking for them? You think I want that kind of heat?"

Russo moved between them, his bulk creating a physical barrier. "Hey. Both of you calm down."

"Stay out of this," Laurent snapped.

"Can't do that." Russo crossed his arms. "You two start fighting, we all get caught. I was promised safe passage to the Dominican Republic once this deal went through. Every minute you stand here bitching about pearls is another minute closer to me going back to prison. Mark made you an offer. You want to walk away empty because you don't like his payment method, that's your call. But the clock's ticking, and I'm not spending the rest of my life in a Saint Marielle cell because you two can't make a deal."

"The pearls could be worth more than the agreed price," Mark insisted. "I'm offering you a premium—"

"I want what we agreed on." Laurent straightened his cuffs, the gesture somehow threatening despite its elegance. "Cash. That was the deal."

"You have the first half of the payment. The pearls cover the rest and then some," Mark said quickly. "That's fair."

"It's not fair, it's a liability." Laurent's face was flushed, a vein pulsing in his temple. "I have expenses. People to pay. I don't have time to offload stolen jewelry through back channels!"

"Then take something else," Russo said. His eyes found Skylar and stayed there, something ugly flickering behind them. "You're short on payment, right? She's worth that. Easy."

Skylar's blood turned to ice.

The meaning slammed into her with sickening clarity. He was talking about selling her. Trading her like livestock to cover Mark's debt.

"What?" Laurent studied her with new interest.

"American woman, young, fit," Russo continued. "I know you got contacts in that business. With one phone call, she's worth more than those pearls. Less traceable too."

"You're talking about human trafficking," Laurent said, but Skylar caught him considering the proposal. The coldness in his eyes made bile rise in her throat.

"Call it debt settlement," Mark said quickly, seizing on the idea. "I take the Cross, you take her and the pearls, and we're square."

Horror crashed through Skylar. Images flooded her mind—concrete rooms, chains, buyers who saw women as merchandise. She'd heard the stories, read the statistics, but never imagined she'd become one of them.

"Human cargo is messy," Laurent said slowly. "Too many variables. Too much attention from the authorities."

"But profitable," Russo added. "And solves your payment problem. You could be making money with her tonight."

What Russo implied made her nauseated. How had things gone so wrong that this would be her fate?

Laurent assessed her with detached professionalism. He was actually considering it. Actually calculating whether she was worth the additional risk.

"Her plus the pearls covers the missing payment," Laurent said finally. "But you owe me a favor. One call from me, anytime, and you answer—no questions."

"Done," Mark said immediately, relief flooding his face.

"No." Skylar choked on the word. "Please. You don't have to—"

Russo was already there—moving fast from the hole in the fence. His hand clamped over her mouth, palm rough and unyielding. "Shut up." She fought, twisting hard, but his grip was iron.

Then, Skylar heard something that sent hope surging through her chest.

Multiple voices rose over the crackle of radio static, while flashlight beams appeared in the trees beyond the barrier.

"What the hell—" Laurent spun toward the sound, his carefully maintained composure shattering. "That's the military. Saint Marielle's Defense Force."

"I thought you said they were still in the capital," Mark hissed. "Rounding up prisoners."

"They were supposed to be," Laurent said, his voice tight with barely controlled panic.

The lights were moving closer and advancing steadily.

"Where's the Cross?" Mark demanded.

Laurent's eyes darted toward a specific point beyond the fence—a cluster of rocks near a fallen palm tree, maybe twenty yards into the wilderness.

"You left it out there?" Mark's voice rose in disbelief.

"It was the safest location until I had confirmation of payment," Laurent snapped. "I don't carry merchandise worth millions until I know the buyer's money is real."

He pinned Mark with a stare, one eyebrow lifting a fraction —the silent equivalent of, *and we both know how that turned out.*

"Then go get it," Russo said. "We'll wait here."

"I might be seen," Laurent replied. "And that fence—" He gestured at the metal barrier. "If it reactivates while I'm on the other side, I'm trapped."

The flashlight beams grew brighter, cutting wider arcs through the trees as they closed in. Voices sharpened—shouted commands overlapping in Spanish and English. Then came the dogs. They were tracking Laurent's scent, following the trail that led directly to the fence.

Russo's head snapped toward the noise, and the palm clamped over Skylar's mouth slipped away. Laurent's calm mask cracked—he scanned the darkness beyond the barrier, jaw working silently. Mark paced in a tight circle, breath coming in short bursts, eyes darting between the approaching lights and the dark jungle behind them as if measuring how far he could still run.

Mark grabbed Laurent's arm. "Thirty seconds. That's all we have before they're on top of us."

"And go where?" Laurent demanded. "My extraction plan had the military busy on the other side of the island, not swarming nearby."

A vehicle engine roared to life somewhere deeper in the darkness beyond the fence—the Jeep, growling awake. Laurent's head snapped toward the sound.

"No—" Laurent started forward, but the engine revved higher, then faded as the vehicle sped away into the jungle. His driver had abandoned him.

"Looks like your ride just left," Mark said.

Laurent went rigid, then unleashed a stream of French curses at the retreating sound.

"Time to improvise," Russo said. He jerked the rope between Skylar's bound hands, hauling her against his side. "You stay quiet or you lose a few teeth. Understand?"

Skylar sucked in a breath.

"Our fishing boat is still docked at Tesoro Bay," he continued. "We move fast, we might slip past the Coast Guard before they lock down the coastline. Go get your Cross."

The rope snapped taut like a whip-crack through her wrists. Pain flared hot and bright, shooting up her arms.

"Run across open beach to a fishing boat with the Coast Guard patrolling the water?" Laurent's laugh was bitter. "That's suicide."

"It's better than getting caught here," Mark shot back.

The soldiers were close now. Individual silhouettes resolved in the gloom, advancing in a coordinated sweep pattern designed to catch anyone trying to slip through.

A flicker of hope sparked inside her. These were the good guys. Any second now, they'd see the compromised fence, the waiting criminals, and her, the bound hostage.

Laurent stared at the approaching lights. His face hardened as the dogs' barks sharpened. Mark's patience snapped. He drew his gun, aiming it at Laurent's chest.

"Get the Cross, and we head to the boat together. We'll figure out the Coast Guard once we're on the water," Mark said.

A slow, dismissive smile spread across Laurent's face. "You point that gun as if it means something. Kill me and the Cross stays on Saint Marielle, hidden in the jungle. My people will know who to blame, Mark. You'll never outrun them."

Mark's finger twitched on the trigger, desperation burning in his eyes. Without the man alive and cooperative, the Cross—and Mark's only way out of his own mess—was lost forever.

Mark lowered the weapon with a low curse. "Your call, Laurent. We can stand here measuring dicks while the military surrounds us, or we can both walk away rich."

Laurent's mouth curved—a cold, humorless smile. "Crude as always, Mark." His gaze lingered on Skylar for a moment. Then he approached the cut gap in the fence.

"If I'm not back in thirty seconds," Laurent said, "that fence reactivates and you lose everything." He tested the barrier before slipping through. "Don't you fucking dare leave without me."

He disappeared into the darkness beyond.

"How long does he have?" Mark asked Russo.

"Bypass should hold another few minutes. Maybe." Russo kept his eyes on the soldiers. "After that, who knows."

Laurent slipped through the gap.

"Watch the fence," Mark said. "If he comes back with anyone following him, I want to know."

Russo checked the rope binding her wrists, yanking it tighter until she gasped, then released her. "You run, I'll catch you. And I won't be gentle about it." He positioned himself where he could watch both the gap in the fence and the approaching military.

Mark stood rigid, gun trained on the darkness, counting seconds.

Then, a burst of static split the silence. A radio transmission, close enough to hear every syllable.

"*All units, fall back to checkpoint alpha. Repeat, fall back to checkpoint alpha. Suspect apprehended in sector seven.*"

The flashlight beams beyond the fence stopped their advance. Skylar watched them hover, then slowly begin to retreat.

Russo stepped closer to the gap, tracking the withdrawal. "They're pulling back."

Mark's stiff posture finally broke. He lowered his gun slightly, exhaling. "About damn time something went right."

For one precious moment, both men had their backs to her.

Her climbing accident surfaced in her mind—that terrible

moment of freefall, the impact, the hours of waiting in agony for rescue while her shattered body screamed. She'd survived by staying alert, by refusing to surrender to the pain and fear. This time, there was no rescue team coming. No one knew where she was.

She had to save herself.

She had to try.

Skylar bolted. Her bound hands made running awkward, her injured leg shrieked in protest, but she sprinted toward the darkness of the jungle anyway.

She didn't make it far. Behind her, Mark swore and abandoned his position at the fence. His footsteps pounded across the ground, closing the distance in seconds. His hand seized her shoulder, spinning her around so hard she nearly fell. The gun barrel pressed against her temple before she could draw breath to scream.

"Don't," he hissed, leaning in, his breath hot against her face. "I can't shoot you without bringing those soldiers back, but I can break your legs and drag you to that boat. Your choice."

The absolute conviction in his eyes told her he meant every word.

Skylar stopped struggling.

"Good girl." Mark lowered the gun from her temple. "Russo, come get her."

Russo crossed from the fence and grabbed her arm, yanking her upright. Her window had closed.

Then Laurent emerged through the gap, clutching a leather satchel against his chest.

The Cross.

"They're retreating." His expression held grim satisfaction. "Caught my driver trying to flee in the Jeep. Serves him right for abandoning his post." He glanced over his shoulder. "But we move now before they realize they arrested the wrong man."

Mark gestured toward the path leading to the resort. "Let's go."

Laurent led the way, clutching his prize. Russo shoved Skylar forward, keeping pace. Mark brought up the rear, gun drawn, checking over his shoulder every few steps.

Then a voice cut through the darkness from somewhere ahead—a voice that sent electricity racing down her spine.

"Let her go, Mark."

28

Noah emerged from the jungle path, blood roaring through his veins. He'd found them.

They formed a grim procession: a tall man with silver hair led the way, clutching a leather satchel against his chest. He looked as if he'd stepped out of a yacht club, radiating the kind of money and power that didn't get its hands dirty. Russo followed, one hand locked on Skylar's arm, shoving her forward, her body sagging with exhaustion. Mark followed close behind, gun drawn.

Three men. One captive woman. And Noah, stepping out of the shadows with the grill fork gripped tight in his sweating palm—two steel tines against three men. Nowhere near enough of a weapon, and nowhere near enough courage for what he was about to do.

He didn't care. He'd crawl through hell on broken glass if it meant getting her back.

"Let her go, Mark."

The group froze.

"Noah," Skylar whispered, and the relief in her voice made his chest ache.

She was alive—standing, breathing, looking at him with those eyes that had haunted every moment since the boat had pulled away. But the rope binding her wrists, the bruises forming on her arm where Russo gripped her—it ignited something primal inside him. These men had taken her, terrorized her, and now they thought they could keep her.

Not while he was breathing.

"You just don't listen, do you?" Mark aimed the gun at Noah's chest. "I gave you a chance to walk away. That offer's expired."

"Didn't want it then. Don't want it now." The words came out steady, but Noah's mind was racing. He'd spent the whole pursuit focused on finding her—not on what he'd do when he did. Now here he stood, facing a gun. Every instinct screamed at him to charge forward, fork in hand, but Mark's finger hovered too close to the trigger. "Skylar, are you hurt?"

"I'm okay."

The strain in her posture told a different story. Three days of running and surviving had pushed her body past its limits.

One wrong move from him, one aggressive action that spooked Mark into pulling that trigger, and she'd pay the price. Noah raised his hands slowly, the grill fork dangling loosely from his right grip—visible but non-threatening, a pathetic excuse for a weapon that wouldn't frighten anyone. Controlled. Surrendering. But his fingers stayed wrapped around that handle, ready to drive those tines forward if the moment came.

"This is touching." The silver-haired man turned, straightening his cuffs. The expensive clothes and aristocratic bearing made it clear this was Mark's contact. A man who had resources and the connections to use them. "But we have a boat to catch and authorities to evade. Kill him or leave him—I don't care which. Just do it quickly."

"Shut up, Laurent," Mark snapped.

The man with the silver hair narrowed his eyes. "We don't have time for this. The military could return any moment."

Military? The net was tightening. Noah could feel it. These men were going to pay for everything they'd done—Julia, Diego, all of it. But none of that mattered if Skylar was still caught in the middle when it all came apart. He had to free her first. There had to be a way out of this.

"I said shut up." Mark's gun stayed fixed on Noah, his eyes flicking briefly to the grill fork clutched in Noah's hand. "Reed, I don't know how you found us, but that pathetic barbecue tool isn't going to help you. You're going to turn around and walk away. Right now."

"Not without her."

Mark laughed—a harsh, desperate sound. "You don't get to make demands. You're about thirty seconds from getting a bullet in your chest."

"Then shoot me." Noah surprised himself by taking a step forward. "But you do that, and those soldiers hear the gunshot. They come back, and your whole escape plan falls apart."

Mark's jaw tightened. Noah had found the leverage point—the one thing keeping him alive.

Laurent checked his watch, impatience radiating off him. "This is wasting time we don't have. The Coast Guard is sealing off the coastline as we speak."

"He's right," Russo said. "We need to move."

"Nobody's moving until I say so," Mark snarled. But his confidence was fracturing, the manic edge in his voice growing sharper. Things were spinning out of his control.

Noah watched Laurent's face. The annoyance had vanished,

replaced by something colder. The look of a man recalculating an investment that had just gone bad.

"Mark." Laurent's voice dropped to something almost reasonable. "We both need that boat to get off this island. Fighting each other accomplishes nothing. Give him the girl and let's move."

"He'll bring the authorities right to us," Mark said.

"Then tie him up, too. Knock them unconscious. I don't care." Laurent clutched the satchel tighter against his chest. "But every second we stand here arguing is a second closer to prison."

Mark's eyes darted between Noah and the path leading to the dock. The gun wavered.

"The Cross," Noah said, taking a chance. "That's what this is all about, isn't it? That satchel he's carrying."

Laurent's expression flickered—the first crack in his composed facade.

"Don't go there, Reed," Mark warned.

"You killed Julia for it. Shot Diego. Kidnapped Skylar." Noah kept his voice steady, buying time, hoping someone—anyone—might be close enough to hear. "All for a stolen artifact—and you think Laurent's actually going to hand it over? Look at him, Mark. He's already planning how to cut you loose."

"I'm warning you."

"There's something else you should know, Laurent." Noah shifted his attention to the silver-haired man. "That boat you're counting on? The captain's dead."

Laurent went still. "Excuse me?"

"Ask your partners here what happened to him. I saw it for myself." Noah nodded toward Mark and Russo. "Because without someone who knows these waters, that boat's not getting you past the Coast Guard."

Laurent's eyes cut to Mark, cold and lethal. "Tell me he's lying."

"He's trying to divide us," Russo said. "Oldest trick in the book."

"Is it working?" Noah asked.

Mark's finger twitched on the trigger. The gun kept moving —from Noah to Laurent and back again. A man with too many threats and not enough bullets.

"The girl," Mark said suddenly. "You were going to take the girl as part of the payment. That was the deal."

Without warning, Mark grabbed Skylar from Russo's grip and shoved her toward the fence—away from all of them. She stumbled and fell to her knees in the dirt. "She stays with me until the deal is done."

"There is no deal anymore." Laurent brushed an invisible speck from his sleeve, utterly indifferent. "Your operation collapsed. The authorities are everywhere. I'm taking the Cross and leaving. What happens to you after that is not my concern."

"Like hell." Mark aimed the gun squarely at Laurent's chest. "Give me the Cross. Now. Or I'll put a bullet in you and take it anyway."

Laurent's eyes widened fractionally, his hand tightening on the satchel.

"You're making a serious mistake," he said carefully.

"Give. Me. The. Cross." Mark's voice shook. "I've got debts you can't imagine. People who'll kill me if I don't pay. That artifact is my only way out."

Noah's gaze swept the scene. Mark and Laurent were locked in their standoff. Russo watched from the sidelines, arms folded, waiting to see who came out on top. And Skylar was on her knees near the fence, wrists bound, head bowed.

Then she looked up. Their eyes met.

Noah didn't hesitate. He moved while Mark's attention was elsewhere, positioning himself between Skylar and the gun.

"Your financial problems aren't my concern," Laurent said coolly.

Something broke in Mark's expression. "Russo. Get the girl. Bring her here."

Russo uncrossed his arms and started forward. Noah blocked him, raising the grill fork between them, tines aimed at the convict's gut.

"Don't," he said, his voice low and dangerous.

Mark pointed the gun at Noah's chest. "Move aside, Reed. Now."

"No."

"I will shoot you." Mark was coming apart, desperation bleeding through every word. "I swear to God, I'll do it."

"Then shoot me," Noah said. "But she stays where she is."

Mark's finger twitched on the trigger.

But Skylar moved first.

29

Noah positioned himself between her and the gun, and Skylar felt something shift in her chest—a tectonic realignment of everything she'd believed about herself.

That cliff face in Colorado had stripped away every illusion about rescue, about help, about anyone coming to save her. Ethan had been there during her recovery, pushing her through physical therapy, refusing to let her quit—but he hadn't been on that ledge with her. He hadn't felt the hours drag by in white-hot agony, alone with the absolute certainty that if she survived, it would be because of her own stubborn refusal to die. She'd rebuilt herself around one truth: in the end, you're alone.

But this man was about to take a bullet for her.

Mark's finger moved. Noah stood like a stone.

Skylar launched herself off the ground, bound wrists and all, and buried her skull in Mark's ribcage with every ounce of strength she had left.

Because she loved him. God help her, she loved him.

They went down together. The gun went off on impact—a

wild shot that hit the junction box and ricocheted at a vicious angle, catching Mark in the shoulder. The force of it spun him sideways.

Mark screamed—a high, animal sound. The weapon slipped from his grip as he clutched at the ruined mess of flesh and shattered clavicle, his eyes rolling white with shock.

Noah lunged forward, still gripping the grill fork in his left hand as his right hand closed around the gun. Russo charged at the same instant, massive and fast. Noah swung the fork upward with desperate force—felt the tines punch through fabric and sink deep into Russo's forearm. The convict bellowed, staggering back, the fork jutting from his arm like a grotesque flag.

Noah brought the gun up with both hands, aiming at Russo's chest. His hands trembled, but the barrel stayed true.

Mark lay groaning, clutching his wounded shoulder where the bullet had torn through. Whatever fight he'd had left was gone, bled out along with his bravado.

"Don't move," Noah said to Russo.

Russo, with the grill fork still embedded in his bleeding forearm, went still, eyes narrowing as he weighed his options. He wrapped his free hand around the fork's handle and yanked —tines tearing free with a wet sound that made even Laurent flinch. Blood poured faster now, dripping onto the ground. His gaze traveled from Noah to the gun to Laurent to the cut section of fence.

Laurent edged backward toward it, hands raised. "This has nothing to do with me. I'm walking away."

"Nobody's going anywhere," Noah said.

Noah's attention caught on the junction box where Russo had disabled the fence.

"That's a terrible bypass job, by the way," Noah said. "Those connections are unstable. When that tape heats up from the current draw—"

A sharp crack cut him off. Sparks erupted from the junction box as the electrical tape gave way. The wires separated with a sound like a gunshot.

The fence hummed to life with lethal voltage.

Laurent took his chance anyway. While Noah's attention split between the sparking junction box and Russo, the artifact dealer bolted toward the dark section of fence where Russo had cut through.

"The fence is hot!" Noah shouted.

Laurent dove through the gap.

He nearly cleared it, but at the last second his shoulder connected with the severed fence wire.

The scream was inhuman. Laurent's body seized, muscles locking as fifty thousand volts coursed through him. The Cross tumbled from his grip as he convulsed, smoke rising from where his linen shirt had begun to burn.

Then the voltage threw him backward like a rag doll, and he hit the ground in a heap. He didn't move again.

Skylar and Noah stared at the motionless body, the acrid smell of burned fabric and worse drifting on the humid air.

"My God," Noah whispered.

For the first time, Russo looked genuinely rattled. But it lasted only a heartbeat before his gaze slid toward the resort path.

"Don't even think about it," Noah said, bringing the gun back to center on Russo's chest.

Russo stood near the fence, arms half-raised, blood still streaming from the puncture wounds in his forearm. The acrid smell of Laurent's death hung in the air. Downhill on the path behind them, Mark lay crumpled where he'd fallen, one hand pressed against his ruined shoulder.

Or so Noah thought.

From her angle, Skylar saw what he couldn't—Mark's free hand creeping toward a jagged rock near his head, his face twisted with rage despite the blood soaking through his shirt.

"Noah!" she screamed.

Mark surged up from the path, swinging the rock in a vicious arc. Noah spun, but not fast enough. The stone connected with his wrist, and the gun flew from his grip, skittering across the dirt. Mark collapsed back onto the path, spent, as if the effort had drained whatever energy he had left.

Russo didn't hesitate. He lunged for the weapon.

Noah threw himself forward, catching Russo's legs. Both men crashed to the ground near the fence, grappling in the dirt.

Skylar scrambled toward the gun, her bound hands throwing off her balance. She reached it first, fumbled to wrap her numb fingers around the grip, her wrists screaming against the rope.

Behind her, Russo threw Noah off with brute force. The big man rose, chest heaving, his eyes locking onto Skylar and the weapon she struggled to hold.

"Give it here, girl." He moved toward her with slow, deliberate steps. "You don't even know how to use that thing."

Skylar's hands shook. She couldn't get her finger to the trigger with her wrists bound like this.

Noah tried to rise, but Russo kicked him back down without breaking stride. His attention never left Skylar.

"Nowhere to run this time." He spread his arms wide, taunting her. "Go ahead. Shoot me."

The boat. The knife. His hands on her. The things he'd whispered about what he'd do once they were out to sea.

She wasn't going to be his victim, and she sure as hell wasn't going to watch him kill the man she loved.

Skylar forced her numb finger onto the trigger and aimed at the center of his chest.

She pulled.

Click.

The sound was deafening in its emptiness. The gun was out of bullets.

Russo didn't hesitate. He charged.

Noah tackled him from the side, driving them both toward the fence. Russo threw him off easily, but the momentum carried him backward, his boots sliding on the loose dirt near the junction box.

The sparks. The exposed wires. The hum of lethal voltage.

Russo's hand shot out for balance. It found the junction box instead.

The voltage hit him like a freight train.

His body went rigid, eyes wide with shock. The smell of burning flesh filled the air as electricity arced through him, his muscles locked in spasm. Smoke rose from where his palm had fused to the metal box.

Then the circuit breaker somewhere in the resort's infrastructure finally gave way. The power died with a hollow thunk.

Russo collapsed forward, his hand still touching the dead junction box, his chest no longer rising.

Silence descended over the clearing.

Skylar dropped the empty gun and ran to Noah, throwing her bound arms around his neck. He caught her, his own arms wrapping tight.

"You okay?" he managed, his voice rough.

"Am I okay?" She pulled back to look at him, her eyes burning. "You almost got electrocuted!"

"But I didn't." His hand came up to cup her face, thumb brushing her cheek. "We're alive. You're alive."

"Because you came for me," she whispered. "When you had every reason to save yourself, you came for me anyway."

"Skylar." His voice cracked on her name. "There was never a choice. From the moment I realized they had you, nothing else mattered except getting you back."

The words she'd been holding back broke free. "I love you."

His eyes widened, searching her face. "You—"

"I love you," she repeated, the truth of it settling deep in her chest. "I think I have since the cave, maybe before. I love you, Noah Reed, and I need you to know that before—"

He kissed her. His mouth found hers with desperate relief, one hand tangled in her hair, the other pulling her closer. She kissed him back with everything she had, bound hands trapped between them but not caring, not caring about anything except this man and this moment and the fact that they were both still breathing.

When they finally broke apart, both gasping, Noah rested his forehead against hers.

"I love you too," he said quietly. "I was so afraid I'd lost you."

"You didn't." She pressed her lips to his again, softer this time. "You found me."

Mark groaned nearby, reminding them he was still alive.

Noah found a knife in Russo's pocket and cut Skylar's bonds. The rope fell away, and she flexed her raw, bleeding wrists, wincing.

"We need to get Mark medical attention," Noah said, though his tone suggested he'd rather let the man bleed. "The Coast Guard was at Shell Beach earlier. They evacuated Ethan, Vanessa, and some other survivors."

Skylar's head snapped up. "Ethan's safe?"

"Safe," Noah confirmed.

Noah pulled her against him one more time, as if reassuring himself she was real. Alive. His.

"Let's get off this island," he said. "And never come back."

Skylar managed a tired smile. "Best idea I've heard all week."

The nightmare was finally over.

———

The path wound downhill toward the beach. Noah kept one arm around Skylar, taking as much of her weight as she'd let him. Ahead, Mark shuffled along in silence, hands bound with the very rope he'd used on Skylar.

On the way down, she'd told him everything—jumping from Mark's boat, the desperate swim, dragging herself onto rocks only to be grabbed by two of the escaped prisoners. That swim had emptied her reserves completely. Now her body was running on fumes. Noah's grip on her tightened. "A little further."

She didn't waste breath on a reply.

The satchel containing the Cross swung from his shoulder. He'd picked it up from the dirt near Laurent's smoking body without a word. All those lives lost over a stolen relic. At least now it could go back where it belonged.

Shell Beach had been transformed. Coast Guard lights blazed across the sand, turning night into harsh white day. What had been a single zodiac and a handful of personnel was now a full operation—uniforms everywhere, equipment in organized rows, a medical tent near the gift shop. Reinforcements had arrived.

The relief hit him so hard he almost dropped.

They'd made it.

"Thank God," he managed as they stepped onto the beach.

A stocky officer was already heading their way, radio in hand. "Lieutenant Stavros, Coast Guard." His gaze swept over them—Skylar sagging, Noah barely holding her up. He took in Mark's condition with a raised eyebrow: bleeding, hands tied behind his back. "Anyone else out there?"

"Two dead at the fence," Noah said. "Laurent Baptiste and a prisoner named Russo. Electrocuted when the power came back on."

Stavros's expression stayed neutral, but his eyes sharpened. "And him?" He nodded toward Mark.

"Mark Thompson. He's connected to the prison break—helped fund it, coordinated with someone on the inside." Noah drew Skylar in tighter. "Pushed his own wife off a cliff. Shot a resort employee named Diego. Kidnapped her."

"That's a lie," Mark rasped, but the words had no weight.

Stavros signaled to an armed crewman near the medical tent. Mark was hauled away, still mumbling denials.

"We've got a holding area for the recaptured escapees," Stavros said. "He'll be treated and held there until transport." He turned back to Noah. "You said he funded the prison break. How do you know that?"

"Because we watched the whole thing fall apart." Noah slid the satchel off his shoulder and opened it. The Cross caught the floodlights—gold filigree, rubies and emeralds clustered along each arm. Centuries of craftsmanship meant to inspire faith. Instead, it had inspired murder.

Stavros's eyes widened. "The Saint Marielle Cross. We knew it was stolen, but we assumed it was already off the island."

"Almost was." Noah held out the satchel. "Laurent Baptiste was the dealer—he's dead at the fence. Mark was the middleman. And the buyer?" He paused. "A woman named Vanessa Park. She was evacuated earlier today by a Coast Guard crew."

Stavros took the satchel carefully. "We've been operating on the assumption that this was an organized smuggling operation. You're telling me you two can tie all the pieces together?"

"Every one of them."

"Then you've just become my two most important witnesses." Stavros glanced at Skylar, frowning at her condition. "But it looks like that debrief is going to have to wait." He keyed his radio. Seconds later, two medics appeared.

"Ma'am, can you walk?" one asked.

She nodded, and Noah helped her toward the large medical tent nearby. Inside, portable lights illuminated a makeshift clinic—cots lined up in rows, supplies stacked on folding tables, monitors beeping softly. One of the medics guided her to an empty cot.

The moment Skylar lowered herself, her legs buckled, muscles that had carried her through hours of hell finally giving out. Noah caught her, easing her down gently, then he took a seat in a metal folding chair. The medic began his examination, and Noah saw the damage for the first time in proper lighting—deep rope burns on both wrists where the bindings had cut into flesh, her uniform pants torn and bloodstained.

Rage bubbled up fresh in his chest. Mark had done this to her.

Then the medic exposed her lower leg, revealing an angry red laceration from her swim to shore that first day.

Lieutenant Stavros sat in another chair next to Noah. "We'll need to recover the bodies you mentioned. Get formal written statements from both of you in the morning. We're keeping everyone on the beach overnight—too dangerous to transport in the dark, and we're still rounding up survivors from other parts of the resort."

He stood. "The medical team will finish treating your injuries, then you both can rest. There's water, food, blankets."

The medic cleaned and bandaged Skylar's leg wound and wrapped her wrists.

Noah knelt beside her with a water bottle. "Drink. You need it."

She managed a few sips before the medic checked her pulse and blood pressure. "Your pulse is rapid and thready, blood pressure's dropping. The cut on your leg is already showing signs of infection, and you're severely dehydrated—beyond what oral fluids can fix. You need IV antibiotics and proper monitoring. We'll prioritize you for first transport at dawn."

He was already reaching for an IV kit, prepping her arm for the line.

"Noah..."

"I'm right here," he said, settling onto the cot next to hers. His body ached in places he hadn't noticed before. "I'm not going anywhere." Fatigue pooled behind his eyes.

The surrounding beach was alive with activity—Coast Guard personnel conducting patrols, medical staff checking on survivors, the constant crackle of radios coordinating the operation. But inside the quiet of the medical tent, the world narrowed to the two of them.

"When Mark took you," Noah said quietly, the words finally breaking free, "when I saw that boat pull away from the beach with you on it—I've never been so afraid in my life."

"I know." She reached for his hand, her fingers threading through his. "I was terrified too. I thought I'd never see you again. But you found me."

"I'll always find you," he promised.

DAY FOUR

30

As dawn broke, the first sound Skylar heard was the distant thrum of helicopters cutting through the morning air. She opened her eyes to find her hand still clasped in Noah's. At some point during the night, he'd pushed their cots together so they could remain close.

"Do you hear that?" she whispered.

He opened his eyes.

The sound grew louder, multiplying into what seemed like an entire fleet of aircraft approaching Saint Marielle. Noah's hand tightened around hers as the helicopter sounds multiplied, grew closer. They were finally getting off this island.

It's really over.

Through the tent opening, the beach operation had shifted into high gear—both Coast Guard and Saint Marielle military personnel checked equipment, medics prepped supplies, using radios to coordinate transport. Lieutenant Stavros entered their shelter, his demeanor professional and direct.

"We need to move to the main pier," he said. "A joint operation command post is being established there."

A medic disconnected Skylar's IV line and helped her stand.

She swayed briefly, the dizziness lingering, but the fluids had steadied her enough to move.

"Easy," the medic said. "You're still lightheaded—take it slow." He directed his words at Noah. "Keep her upright and get her to the pier. We'll have more fluids waiting there."

Noah nodded, slipping an arm around her waist.

As they emerged from the tent, Skylar's legs felt wobbly beneath her. Her head was still thick, every thought requiring extra effort to form. She said nothing, gripping Noah's hand tighter. Whatever was wrong could wait until they were off this island. She wasn't going to delay their evacuation or make Noah worry when they were this close to safety.

The scope of the rescue operation was staggering. The ocean around Saint Marielle had transformed into a flotilla of Coast Guard vessels, military boats, and support craft, while overhead helicopters circled.

Noah's hand squeezed hers, his grip steady. "Look at all of this."

She nodded, not trusting her voice, focusing on putting one foot in front of the other while the world tilted slightly around the edges.

As they made their way toward the pier, Noah pointed northwest where helicopters hovered in a cluster above the jungle. Skylar could make out small figures rappelling down ropes into the dense foliage below.

"The hostage camp?" she asked.

"Has to be," Noah replied. "Hunting down the remaining prisoners."

Ethan. Her brother had been there. Safe now, Noah had told her, evacuated with the other survivors. The relief she should have been feeling was muted by the strange fog filling her head, but she clung to the knowledge anyway. They'd both made it. Once she was stateside, she'd get the complete story from him.

All of this for us.

It was humbling and overwhelming. She'd spent days feeling forgotten and abandoned on a dangerous island with killers and criminals. Now, it seemed as if half the Caribbean fleet had mobilized to ensure their safety.

"Passengers from the Meridian Voyager," called a Coast Guard officer approaching them on the pier. "We need to get you processed and evacuated immediately."

Skylar found herself separated from Noah within seconds as medical personnel descended on them with clipboards, scanners, and urgent questions about injuries and medical conditions. The efficiency was impressive but also isolating— she could see Noah twenty feet away being questioned by what looked like federal agents, but the distance might as well have been miles.

"Wait," Skylar called out, trying to step toward him. "We need to stay together."

But a medic gently guided her toward a triage station. "Ma'am, I need to clear you for transport. Standard medical check before evacuation."

Before Skylar could respond, he'd placed a digital thermometer under her tongue. The seconds ticked by while he checked the bandages on her wrists and examined how she was favoring her left leg where the wound had been bandaged. The thermometer beeped. The medic's expression shifted immediately as he read the display.

"103.4." He looked up. "That's not good."

He pulled a red sticker from his clipboard and pressed it onto her paperwork, then immediately waved over another medical officer. "Priority case. Possible sepsis. She needs the first medical evacuation."

"Wait—" Skylar started, but the second medic was already there, taking her other arm, guiding her away from Noah farther down the pier.

Noah tried to keep Skylar in sight as officials swarmed around him, but the activity of the rescue operation made it nearly impossible. Every few seconds, someone new appeared with questions or forms that demanded his attention.

"Noah Reed? I'm Petty Officer Taylor." A blonde woman in a Coast Guard uniform approached, consulting a tablet. "You're from Princeton, here on a corporate retreat with the Meridian Voyager?"

"Yes, but—" Noah craned his neck to see over the crowd. Skylar was being examined by medics near a boat marked with red medical crosses. "Can you tell me where they're taking her?"

"Standard triage process—we check everyone's condition and make sure they get appropriate medical attention. Some go out immediately; others follow once they're cleared," Taylor replied.

Nearby, Mark Thompson was being loaded onto a stretcher, his wounded shoulder properly bandaged now, but probably in need of more advanced medical treatment. Federal marshals flanked the gurney, weapons visible, their presence making it clear that Mark's legal troubles were only beginning. The man who'd killed his wife and Diego, who'd terrorized Skylar, was finally being taken into custody. The satisfaction Noah expected didn't come—only a bone-deep weariness and the singular need to stay with Skylar.

"Where are you taking Skylar Harris?" Noah asked. "We

survived this together. I'm not leaving without knowing she's safe."

"Sir, I understand your concern, but—"

"No, you don't understand." Noah's control was fraying, three days of fear and adrenaline finally catching up to him. "That woman and I made it through three days of hell together. Where is she going?"

The uniformed woman's professional demeanor faltered slightly. "Mr. Reed, I have my orders. The medical cases go first."

She'd seemed fine this morning. Maybe a little weak, but who wouldn't be after what they'd been through?

"Sir?" Petty Officer Taylor was waiting for his attention. "We need to document your statement about the events on the island. It'll help us coordinate with the investigation."

Noah forced himself to focus on her questions, providing a condensed version of the past three days—Julia's and Diego's murders, Skylar's kidnapping, the prison break, the confrontation at the fence. His answers came automatically while his eyes tracked Skylar's location. Medics were loading her onto the boat with red crosses.

She's sicker than she admitted. The realization settled in his gut like lead. Her hand had been too hot in his during the walk to the pier. She'd stumbled more than once, blaming it on fatigue. He should have noticed.

"Mr. Reed?" Another voice interrupted. A man in an expensive suit pushed through the crowd—distinctly out of place among the military and Coast Guard personnel. "FBI Special Agent Matthews. We need to discuss your witness account of the smuggling operation and the deaths of Laurent Baptiste and the prisoner known as Russo."

The questions came rapid-fire after that. Noah found himself answering queries about the Saint Marielle Cross—yes, he'd recovered it from Laurent's body; yes, Lieutenant Stavros had it secured as evidence. Questions about Mark's connections to the escaped prisoners, about the timeline of events, about Russo's role in facilitating the prison break.

He knew each answer was crucial to building the case against Mark Thompson and whatever remained of his smuggling network. But every minute spent in interrogation was another minute away from Skylar, another minute watching her be prepared for departure on the medical cutter.

Noah tried to break away from the questioning, but Agent Matthew's firm hand on his arm stopped him.

"Skylar!" Noah called out, but she was already too far away to hear over the noise of engines.

The cutter's horn sounded. Lines were being cast off.

"We're not finished here, Mr. Reed," Matthews said, his grip tightening. "There are mainland connections to this operation we need to understand. Mark Thompson didn't arrange that prison break alone. Someone on Saint Marielle provided access, coordination, and inside information. We need your account of everyone involved."

Noah's hands clenched into fists. "How long will this take?"

"As long as necessary." Morrison's expression was sympathetic but unyielding. "I know you want to be with Miss Harris. But right now, your testimony is critical to making sure the people responsible for this nightmare face justice."

The Coast Guard cutter pulled away from the pier, its engines churning white water as it headed toward the hospital ship anchored with the fleet offshore.

Skylar disappeared from view as the boat rounded a bluff.

"Let's continue," Matthews said, pulling out a recording device. "Tell me everything you know."

Noah took a breath, pushing back the ache to follow her. Skylar was getting proper medical care. Doctors, antibiotics, a hospital ship with resources the beach camp couldn't provide. She would be fine. She had to be fine.

But as he answered Matthews's questions, one thought kept circling through his mind: He'd promised to always find her. And now she was being taken away while he stood trapped on this pier, watching the gap between them grow wider with every passing second.

Skylar found herself on the deck of a Coast Guard cutter, surrounded by medical equipment and personnel who seemed determined to catalog every injury she'd accumulated over the past three days. The attention was both comforting and suffocating.

"Dizzy? Nauseous? Any confusion?" A female medic of about Skylar's age checked her pupils with a small flashlight.

"I'm okay," Skylar managed, though the words took more effort than they should have. "When will the other rescued passengers be joining us?"

"We're prioritizing based on medical need." The medic wrapped a blood pressure cuff around Skylar's arm. "Your fever and that infected wound put you at the top of the list."

The cuff tightened and then released. The medic's frown deepened as she read the display.

"Blood pressure's still low. We're going to get another IV started and push more fluids." She signaled to another crew member. "Let the hospital ship know we need to get anti-biotics on board ASAP."

The pier grew smaller as they pulled away from Tesoro Bay. Noah was still back there somewhere, lost in the swarm of officials and personnel. For a moment, Skylar thought she heard someone calling her name over the engine noise, but when she turned, she couldn't spot him through the crowd.

Relief and unexpected loss warred in her chest as Saint Marielle shrank behind them.

"The man who was with me," she said to the medic, fighting to keep her voice steady. "Noah Reed. Do you know which boat he'll be on?"

The medic consulted her tablet, scrolling through what appeared to be a passenger manifest. "Multiple evacuation vessels are departing for different facilities. I can't tell you his assignment."

Skylar's chest constricted. She'd taken for granted they would stay together after all they'd been through. The possibility of their being separated hadn't occurred to her until this moment.

He'll find me. After what happened between us, after what we went through, he'll find a way.

But as the island grew smaller, practical reality began to intrude. Noah had his life waiting—his company in New Jersey, his business empire, his carefully constructed world that had nothing to do with her. Once he was back in that world, three days on an island with a rock climber from Colorado might feel like a fever dream, a strange detour he'd eventually file away as an unusual experience.

And even if she wanted to find him—how? She knew his name. She knew he owned a tech company in New Jersey. But she had no phone number, no email address, no concrete way to reach him.

All she had were memories. His arms around her in the cave. His voice promising he'd protect her. The way he'd positioned himself between her and Mark's gun without hesitation. The look in his eyes when he'd told her he loved her.

But memories couldn't bridge the gap between Colorado and New Jersey, between her world and his.

The medic inserted a new IV line, the needle sting barely registering through Skylar's growing haze. The cool liquid entered her bloodstream, and tiredness crashed over her like a wave.

"Try to rest," the medic said quietly. "We'll have you at the hospital ship in twenty minutes."

As Saint Marielle disappeared completely behind them, a different kind of fear took hold—the first real fear since the rescue. Not that someone would hurt her, but that she'd never see Noah Reed again.

The evacuation boat Noah had been assigned to filled rapidly with other Meridian Voyager passengers—faces showing the same mixture of relief and shell-shock. He recognized a few people: a couple from his snorkeling excursion, some crew members, passengers he'd shared meals with on the ship.

As their vessel pulled away from Saint Marielle, Noah stood at the railing, watching the island grow smaller. Smoke rose from several points inland where military operations continued. With the hostage camp being secured, the remaining escapees were rounded up. The entire criminal network that had terrorized this paradise was finally being dismantled.

Victory. Survival. Justice.

The words rang hollow.

Because somewhere out there on the Caribbean Sea, Skylar was on a different boat, heading to a different destination, growing more distant with every passing minute. And he had no way to reach her beyond knowing she was a rock climber from Colorado who'd survived three days of hell at his side.

He'd promised to always find her.

But he had no idea how to keep that promise.

The wind picked up as they gained speed, salt spray misting his face. Behind them, Saint Marielle faded into the haze—the island where he'd met her, where he'd fallen in love with her.

Three days ago, the federal contract had been everything. Months of work. His company's biggest deal. Now it felt like noise from a life that belonged to someone else.

The cruelest part was that they'd made it. They'd survived. Only to watch her disappear over a different horizon.

THREE MONTHS LATER

31

S kylar stood at the floor-to-ceiling windows of the Aspen
Mountain Resort's conference center, watching snow dust
the peaks in the distance. The irony wasn't lost on her—she
was speaking about survival in a five-star resort where the
biggest danger was running out of champagne at the cocktail
reception.

But a speaking career found her, not the other way around.
After the news of the Saint Marielle crisis broke, corporate
event planners started calling. They wanted to hear about "real
leadership under pressure" from someone who'd actually lived
it, not theorized about it in business school.

Skylar adjusted the wireless microphone clipped to her
blazer—a far cry from her usual climbing gear—and turned
back to the audience of business executives filling the elegant
conference room. Soft lighting, plush chairs, and not a single
life-threatening situation in sight.

"The moment I realized we were truly alone at the resort,"
she said, clicking to the next slide, an aerial shot of Saint
Marielle's rugged coastline, "I had to make a choice. Let fear

paralyze me or use everything I'd learned from climbing to navigate an entirely different kind of dangerous terrain."

The audience was rapt—no one checking phones, no side-long conversations, every face turned toward her. These successful professionals were hungry for authentic stories of crisis leadership, something their corner offices and quarterly reviews couldn't provide. But as she spoke about trust, survival, and making impossible decisions, a strange disconnect opened between her and her own words—as if she were describing someone else's experience.

Noah would understand.

The thought ambushed her—sudden, unwelcome, and as sharp as it had been three months ago. She forced herself to keep talking, to ignore the familiar ache that accompanied every memory of him.

"When you're facing a life-or-death situation," Skylar continued, "you discover that all your assumptions about what matters get stripped away. What remains is what's truly essential."

She'd tried to contact him, of course. Multiple calls to Reed Security Systems resulted in polite but firm responses that Mr. Reed was unavailable and couldn't be reached for personal matters. His assistant was professional, borderline cold, as if Skylar were another sales contact trying to get through.

Eventually, she stopped trying. If Noah had wanted to find her, he would have. The message was clear enough.

"The question isn't whether you'll face a crisis," Skylar said, advancing to her final slide, a stock photo of a rock climber at a crux move reaching for the next hold. "The question is whether you'll have the courage to—"

Movement at the back of the room caught her eye. Someone slipped in during her presentation —a man in a dark suit standing by the doorway, partially shadowed by the room's strategic lighting. His posture—shoulders set in that particular way, head tilted slightly as he listened—made her breath catch.

No, it couldn't be.

When he stepped into the light and she saw his face clearly, the words died in her throat.

Noah.

He looked different—more polished. The swimming trunks and Meridian staff uniform she'd last seen him in were replaced by an expensive suit that fit him perfectly. But his eyes were the same. Warm. Intense. Fixed on her as if she were the only person in the room.

For a long moment, Skylar simply stared at him, their gazes locked across the space. A few audience members followed her attention, turning in their seats to see what—or who—had stolen her focus. One woman nudged her neighbor, whispering.

Skylar recovered quickly, tearing her eyes away. "I apologize," she said to the audience, her voice a little unsteady. "The past has a way of showing up when you least expect it."

Soft laughter rippled through the room. A few knowing smiles appeared on faces throughout the audience.

"Let me conclude by saying that survival isn't about making it through the crisis," Skylar continued, her eyes finding Noah's again despite herself. "It's about what you choose to do with the life you've been given afterward."

The applause was enthusiastic, but Skylar barely heard it. She was too aware of Noah in the back of the room—watching her handle questions from the audience, sign copies of a feature article that had appeared in a business leadership publication, and exchange business cards with executives who wanted to book her for their own events.

She felt his gaze like a physical weight. *Professional,* she reminded herself. *Stay professional.*

When the session ended and the audience began filing out, Noah stayed where he was, hands in his pockets, waiting. Skylar moved through the remaining attendees on autopilot—smiling, shaking hands, promising to follow up—while her whole body hummed with nervous energy.

Then the room was empty except for the two of them.

"Hello, Skylar," Noah said, his voice carrying across the space between them.

"Noah." She stayed where she was. The distance felt necessary. Safe. "I didn't expect to see you here."

"I've been looking for you," he said.

"Have you?" Skylar kept her tone polite, distant—the same professional mask she'd worn for three months. "Because I tried calling your company several times. Your assistant was very clear that you weren't available for personal matters."

Something flickered across his face. Pain, maybe. Or regret. "Skylar, I never got those messages. There were legal complications, company restructuring, a federal investigation because of Vanessa's involvement in what happened—"

"I understand." The words came out softer than she'd intended. "You had a lot going on."

She studied his face, searching for the man she'd known on the island beneath this expensive suit and corporate polish. He was still there—in the way his gaze softened when it met hers, the vulnerability he couldn't quite hide.

"Would you..." Noah gestured toward the door. "Could we talk? Privately?"

Skylar hesitated. Part of her wanted to refuse, to protect herself from whatever new hurt this conversation might bring. But a larger part—the part that had dreamed about him every night for three months—needed to hear what he had to say.

"My suite is upstairs," she said finally, gathering her materials into a leather portfolio. "We can talk there."

. . .

The suite was far more luxurious than anywhere Skylar usually stayed—the corporate events company had booked her into the resort's best accommodations. Floor-to-ceiling windows framed the snow-covered Rockies. A sitting area with elegant chairs faced a small fireplace. The bedroom door stood open, revealing a king-sized bed with crisp white linens.

Noah moved to the window, his back to her, looking out at the mountains. The late afternoon sun caught the side of his face, highlighting the new lines around his eyes. The past three months had marked him too.

"You look good," he said without turning around. "Different, but good. Strong."

"I am different." Skylar settled into one of the suite's chairs, grateful for something solid beneath her. "The island changed me. I couldn't go back to who I was before."

"Is that why you became a motivational speaker?"

"I needed something to do with it all. The speaking circuit found me, and I discovered I was good at helping people understand crisis in a way textbooks can't teach." She paused. "What about you? Still running Reed Security?"

Noah turned from the window. Something melancholy settled over his features.

"I left Reed Security," he said quietly. "A few weeks after we got back."

Skylar stared at him. Of all the things she'd expected him to say, this wasn't one of them. "You what?"

"I couldn't work there anymore." He moved away from the window, pacing toward the sitting area. "Every day, walking into that building, seeing Vanessa's empty office, dealing with the investigation into her involvement with the smuggling ring... it was all tied to the island. To you. To everything I'd lost."

"But that was your company. You built it."

"I built it with her help." Noah finally sat in the chair across from Skylar, leaning forward with his elbows on his knees. "And after everything that happened, I couldn't stay there with her shadow hanging over it. The media attention, the way our clients looked at us, the federal investigators showing up every other week... it wasn't the same company anymore. It wasn't what I wanted."

Her carefully constructed defenses began to crack. She'd spent three months convincing herself he'd moved on, that what they'd shared meant nothing once real life resumed. That she'd been foolish to believe three days could mean anything lasting.

"So what did you do?" she asked.

"Sold my shares. Used the money to start something new." He paused, his eyes never leaving hers. "And I thought about you. Every single day."

"But you didn't call." The words came out sharp. "You didn't email. You didn't try to find me."

"I knew where you were." Noah's voice was quiet. "Within weeks of getting back, I had your address in Colorado, your phone number, and eventually your speaking schedule."

Skylar turned to face him, stunned. "Then why—"

"Because I was a coward." He said it simply, without excuse. "Every time I picked up the phone, every time I started to book a flight, I convinced myself you'd moved on. That you'd realized what we had was just... circumstance. Two people clinging to each other because they had no choice." He ran a hand through his hair. "I told myself you deserved better than some guy who reminded you of the worst three days of your life."

"That's not—"

"I know." He cut her off gently. "I know that now. But back then, I was terrified. Terrified that I'd show up, and you'd look at me like a stranger. Terrified that everything I felt was one-sided. That I'd built it up in my head into something it never was."

Skylar stood, needing distance, needing to move. Her leg protested slightly as she walked to the window he'd vacated, but she ignored it. "So what changed? Why now?"

"Because being afraid of losing you was easier than actually losing you." Noah stood too, closing some of the distance between them. "I tried to move on. I threw myself into the new company, worked eighteen-hour days, dated people who weren't you. And none of it worked. I couldn't forget you, Skylar. I couldn't forget the way you made me want to be braver than I actually was."

He took another step closer. "Three months of playing it safe, and I was more miserable than I'd ever been. So I finally asked myself what scared me more—rejection or spending the rest of my life wondering what might have happened if I'd just had the courage to try."

Her vision blurred. She blinked hard, focusing on the view outside.

"I waited," she whispered. "I tried to find you. And when your assistant made it clear you didn't want to be found... I thought maybe you were right to keep your distance. Maybe what we had wasn't real. Maybe it was only the island, the danger, the circumstances."

"It was real." His voice came from right behind her now, close enough that she could feel the warmth. "It was the realest thing that's ever happened to me."

Skylar turned slowly, and when her eyes met his, she saw the same pain she'd carried for three months reflected back at her. The full weight of their separation hung between them.

"I should have been braver," Noah said. "All the reasons I

gave myself for staying away—they were excuses. Fear dressed up as logic."

"You let me think you'd forgotten me." The words came out raw, unguarded. "I left messages. I tried everything I could think of. And you knew where I was the whole time."

"I know." His voice cracked slightly. "And I'll regret that for the rest of my life. I told myself I was protecting you—giving you space to heal, to move on without some reminder of the worst days of your life showing up on your doorstep." He shook his head. "But the truth is, I was protecting myself. It was easier to imagine you'd moved on than to risk finding out for certain."

She turned away. The late afternoon sun warmed her face, but inside she felt exposed, unsteady. Everything she'd believed for the past three months was shifting beneath her feet.

"I don't know what to do with this," she admitted. Clouds drifted by as the seconds ticked. "You're standing here saying all the things I wanted to hear three months ago. But I've spent all this time convincing myself it wasn't real and learning how to live without you."

"I'm not asking you to forget that," Noah said quietly. "I'm only asking for a chance to prove I won't disappear again."

She kept her eyes on the mountains, the sky, and a hawk circling above. "I gave a presentation last month in Denver," she said, her back to him. "There was a moment during the Q&A when someone asked about the emotional aftermath of surviving something like that. I started to answer, and I realized I was talking about you. About us. About how the hardest part wasn't surviving the island—it was coming back to a world where the person who'd become the most important thing in my life had simply... vanished."

"Skylar—"

"I finished the presentation." She closed her eyes, the memory still raw. "I gave them a professional answer about healing and moving forward. But afterward, I sat in my hotel room and cried for two hours because I realized I was lying—I hadn't moved forward at all. I'd only gotten very good at pretending I had."

She felt him step closer. His fingers brushed her shoulder—tentative, questioning. When she didn't pull away, he turned her gently to face him.

"I've thought about you every single day," he said, his hands coming up to frame her face. "Every morning when I wake up, every night before I fall asleep. I've replayed every conversation we had, every moment we shared. I was so afraid I'd idealized it in my memory, but seeing you now..." He paused, searching her eyes. "Skylar, what I feel for you is stronger than it was on Saint Marielle."

Her eyes filled with tears. One escaped, trailing down her cheek.

"I was so afraid you'd moved on," she whispered. "Forgotten about us."

"Never." Noah's thumb caught the tear, then traced the line of her jaw. "Forgetting you would be like forgetting how to breathe."

Noah tilted her chin up, giving her time to pull away if she wanted. She didn't.

When his lips met hers, it was nothing like their desperate kiss on the beach three months ago. This was soft, questioning—asking rather than demanding, seeking permission after so long apart.

Skylar's answer came immediately. Her arms wound around his neck, her body fitting against his with the kind of recognition that defied the months of separation. Her fingers found the back of his neck, threading into his hair the way they had in that cave when the world had been falling apart around them.

"I missed you," she whispered against his mouth, her breath warm on his lips. "I missed you so much it hurt."

"I'm here now." Noah's arms tightened around her waist, pulling her closer. "I'm here, and I'm not going anywhere."

The kiss deepened. Three months of restraint, of pretending, of maintaining careful control—all of it crumbled between them. His hands pressed into the small of her back. The space between their bodies disappeared entirely.

Noah had spent ninety-three days trying to remember exactly how this felt. He'd failed. Memory was a pale shadow compared to the reality of holding her again.

"Noah." She pulled back just enough to look into his eyes, her lips swollen from kissing, her cheeks flushed. "I need you to know what happened between us on the island... it wasn't just two people who needed someone—anyone—to hold on to. I fell in love with you."

The words hit him like a wave, knocking something loose in his chest.

"I fell in love with you too," he said, his voice rough with emotion. "I think I fell in love with you the moment you chose to leave Ethan at that camp and trust me enough to go to the beach. I knew what that decision cost you—walking away from your brother when every instinct screamed at you to run to him. But you trusted me anyway."

"I trusted you," she agreed. "I still do."

This time when they kissed, there was no hesitation, no uncertainty. Heat bloomed between them, familiar and electric. His hands moved to the buttons of her blazer, fingers trembling slightly despite his best efforts.

"Skylar, are you sure—"

"I'm sure." She covered his hands with hers and helped him with the buttons.

They moved together toward the bedroom, leaving a trail of discarded clothes—her blazer draped over a chair, his jacket pooled on the floor, her heels kicked aside. When Noah lifted her onto the bed, Skylar pulled him down with her, refusing to let any distance remain between them.

The late afternoon sun slanted through the bedroom windows, painting stripes across the white sheets. Noah took his time relearning her—the curve of her shoulder, the hollow of her throat, the small scars that marked her skin from their ordeal. A thin line on her shoulder where she'd cut herself on volcanic rock. The fading remnants of rope burns on her wrists. Each one a reminder of what they'd survived.

"You're so beautiful," he whispered against her collarbone.

Skylar's hands ran down his back, pulling him closer. "I dreamed about this. About being with you again."

"So did I." He kissed the spot where her pulse fluttered beneath her jaw. "Every night."

When they finally came together, something settled deep in his chest—a rightness he hadn't experienced since the island. This was what he'd been searching for through months of lawyers and investigators and sleepless nights. This was what all of it had been for.

"I love you," Skylar breathed against his ear, and his throat tightened with emotion.

"I love you too. God, Skylar, I love you so much."

He wanted to memorize every detail—the way her fingers gripped his shoulders when pleasure overtook her, the way she looked at him afterward, her eyes soft and vulnerable.

For the first time in three months, the hollow ache in his chest was gone.

They lay tangled in the sheets afterward, her head on his

chest. Their breathing gradually matched rhythm. Outside the window, the sun had begun its descent toward the peaks, painting the sky in shades of orange and pink.

Noah felt Skylar relax against him. The tension that had gripped her since he'd walked into that conference room finally eased. His own muscles loosened in response, the tight knot of worry he'd carried for months finally unraveling.

"What happens now?" Skylar asked eventually—the same question she'd asked him in the cave, but with an entirely different meaning.

Noah pressed a kiss to the top of her head. "Now we figure out how to build a life together. I know it won't be simple— you're traveling for speaking engagements; I'm starting fresh with a new company. We're in different states. It's going to take work."

"What kind of company?" She shifted to look up at him, her chin resting on his chest.

"Emergency communication systems." The idea had crys- tallized watching news coverage of how badly the Saint Marielle crisis had been mishandled. "Technology that helps organizations maintain coordination during disasters—the kind of systems that might have prevented the mess we experi- enced on the island. I've been working with some former government contacts, people who understand crisis response from the inside."

"That makes sense." A smile touched her lips. "Taking what happened and turning it into something that could help people."

"We're both doing that, in different ways. You with your speaking, me with technology. Maybe that's what survival is supposed to look like—not only moving on but making some- thing meaningful out of what nearly destroyed you."

"And I still want to climb," Skylar said. "This leg—" She

shifted slightly, and he felt her wince. "It's permanent. The doctors said I'll always have the limp. But I've been training around it, finding new ways to approach routes. I'm not giving up what I love."

"I wouldn't ask you to." Noah ran his fingers through her hair. "I'm not asking you to change anything about your life. I'm only asking if there's room in it for me."

She was quiet for a moment. Then: "There's always been room for you. Even when I thought you were gone. I kept a space for you, hoping."

His arms tightened around her. "Then we figure it out as we go. Just like we did on the island."

"One problem at a time," she murmured, echoing his words from that first night.

"Exactly."

Skylar woke to find Noah still asleep beside her, his breathing slow and even. Morning light filtered through the curtains, softer than the afternoon sun had been.

She studied his face in the quiet—the slope of his nose, his parted lips, the morning stubble shadowing his jaw. He looked younger in sleep, the weight of the past three months temporarily lifted. She resisted the urge to kiss him, not wanting to wake him yet.

They were both marked by what they'd survived. Changed in ways that would never fully heal. But maybe that was the point. Maybe love wasn't about finding someone undamaged. Maybe it was about finding someone whose damage fit with yours.

Noah stirred, his eyes opening to find her watching him. A slow smile spread across his face—unguarded, genuine.

"Good morning," he murmured, his arm tightening around her waist.

"Good morning." Skylar settled back against him, her head fitting into the hollow of his shoulder. "Sleep well?"

"Best I've slept since Tesoro Bay," he admitted. "I kept having dreams about losing you—searching and never finding you, arriving too late. But this time..."

"This time you found me," Skylar finished.

They lay still for a while, watching the sun climb higher over the mountains. The room was cool from the air conditioning, but Noah's warmth beside her made Skylar reluctant to move. She'd spent so many mornings waking up alone, reaching for someone who wasn't there. Having him here, solid and real, felt like a gift she hadn't earned.

"So how do we actually make this work?" she asked eventually. "You're in New Jersey starting a new company. I'm based in Colorado when I'm not traveling, which isn't often. My speaking schedule is insane for the next six months."

Noah gently rubbed her arm. "We're honest about what we need. We communicate, even when it's hard. We don't let distance become an excuse to drift apart."

"And when it gets complicated? When we're both exhausted and there's a time zone between us and everything feels impossible?"

"Then we remember we survived three days on that island together." His voice grew quieter. "We've already faced the worst versions of ourselves and each other. We know what we're capable of—good and bad. Everything else should be easier than that."

Her throat tightened. "I'm scared," she admitted. "Scared to want this much. Scared of how much it'll hurt if it falls apart."

"Me too." Noah tilted her chin up to meet his eyes. "But the only thing that scares me more is waking up tomorrow and you're not there. I've already lived through that. I won't do it again."

Skylar kissed him then—slow and deliberate, the kind of kiss that promised tomorrow and the day after that. When they broke apart, she kept her forehead pressed to his.

"Do you remember what you said to me in the cave?" she asked. "When I thought we might not make it out?"

Noah's hand came up to cup her face. "I said I wouldn't let you face it alone. That whatever happened, we'd face it together."

"You kept that promise." Skylar's voice caught slightly. "Even when everything was falling apart, you stayed."

"I meant it then. I mean it now." His thumb brushed her cheekbone. "Whatever comes next, we face it together. No more disappearing. No more silence. We figure it out as we go."

"Together," she repeated.

"Together."

They eventually showered and dressed, moving around each other in the suite's bathroom with an ease that surprised her—Noah borrowing her toothpaste, Skylar stealing his T-shirt to wear while she dried her hair. Small intimacies that felt both new and familiar, as if they were picking up a conversation that had only been paused, not ended.

As Skylar pulled on a pair of jeans, she caught their reflection in the full-length mirror. Two people marked by survival—his scars, her limp, the shadows that would probably never fully leave them. But also two people standing side by side, choosing each other despite the complications.

No, because of them.

"Breakfast?" Noah asked, coming up behind her in the mirror's reflection. With his arms wrapped around her waist, his chin rested on her shoulder.

Skylar met his eyes in the glass. Real. Solid. Here.

She turned in his arms, rising on her toes to kiss him—brief and soft, a promise of more to come.

"Breakfast," she agreed. "And then we figure out what comes next."

They walked out of the suite together. On the island, they'd survived by moving forward even when the path ahead was unclear, even when fear said to give up. This was no different— choosing each other, choosing to keep going, choosing to believe in something beyond just survival.

Together.

THE END

ABOUT THE AUTHOR

K. J. Gillenwater worked as a Russian linguist in the U.S. Navy, spending time at the National Security Agency doing secret things. After six years of service, she ended up as a technical writer in the software industry. She has lived all over the U.S. and currently resides in Wyoming with her family, writing government proposals and crafting captivating fiction on her days off. She likes her dogs, sunrises, and car radio karaoke.

Visit K.J.'s website for more information about her writing, her books, and what's coming next. www.kjgillenwater.com.

If you enjoyed this book, K. J. Gillenwater is the author of multiple books, which are available in print and in eBook format.

Full-length Books:

- The Automated Series: System Override, Rebellion Protocol
- The Genesis Machine Trilogy: Inception, Decryption, and Revelation
- The Aurora Series: Aurora's Gold and Aurora's Winter
- Revenge Honeymoon
- Illegal
- The Ninth Curse
- The Little Black Box

- Acapulco Nights
- Blood Moon

Short Stories & Short Story Collections:

- Skyfall
- Nemesis
- The Man in 14C
- Charlie and the Zombie Factory

Audiobooks (Audible):

- The Genesis Machine Trilogy: Inception, Decryption, and Revelation